I0838735

ONCE UPON A FUTURE TIME

VOLUME 2

THE BROTHERS UBER
GROVE CITY, PA

Cover and Interior Illustrations © 2019 by Geoff Munn
Editor Cathryn Uber

Published under license by The Brothers Uber, Grove City, PA.

The Brothers Uber
www.brothersuber.com
425 Liberty Street
Grove City, PA 16127
United States of America

First Edition • Text Edition 1.0 (Print Edition)
ISBN: 978-1-943933-04-4
Printed in the United States of America

FOR THOSE WHO DREAM OF THE FUTURE
AND WORK TO MAKE IT REAL.

TABLE OF CONTENTS

BILLIE AND THE EINSTEIN-ROSEN TROLL BRIDGE
BY W.O. HEMSATH

"Blast that bogey, kid, or you'll wish I'd left you starving on the streets of Jorvura."

Heart racing with adrenaline, Billie ignored the gruff voice streaming over the comms and tried to focus. She needed to land the shot so they could finish this job, then she could break free from that voice forever.

From where she sat in the *Cerno*'s artillery bay, the view beyond her port window was nothing but dense blue plasma shield with only a streak of black at the top of her window from the shield's laser-slit.

Each hand on a control stick, she maneuvered the cameras mounted on the magnets that formed the laser-slit, as well as the hull-mounted blaster ray aimed out of it. On the display screen in front of her, wreckage of recently blasted fighter ships flew in all directions, crashing into each other with destructive momentum before changing course, creating an ever-moving minefield of debris. Swerving between it all was one last small fighter, heading for the massive blue shield of the *Icarus* beyond them.

Kabra's voice crackled in her ear again. "It's a juggernaut, Billie. It's got the thermal guard to plow through a plasma shield."

Underneath his condescending bravado was a trace of worry that hadn't been there before. And rightfully so. The *Icarus* they'd just helped Jarac steal was only a cargo ship; it had shields, but no weaponry. Hence its heavily-armed escort Jarac had hired the *Cerno* to take out and replace. But the same shield designed to incinerate small debris and protect the *Icarus* from laser attacks would also protect the attacking juggernaut from Billie's blaster if it got through.

"If you lose this payload, Billie…"

If *she* lost it? What about Nader, Pahtak, and Yaro?

The juggernaut veered through her sights, and she chanced a shot. A spot on the *Icarus*'s shield flashed a brighter blue where the imperceptible laser landed.

The juggernaut wove its way closer to the dense plasma wall.

"Billie!"

She ignored the panic rising in her throat and tracked the juggernaut's evasive pattern. Another of her unseen shots hit a piece of debris, shattering it into smaller pieces that scattered in all directions. A few bits collided with the juggernaut, but their size wasn't enough to deter it.

The traitorous safety of the *Icarus*'s plasma shield loomed seconds away. The juggernaut's flight path became less erratic as it approached. It might have the ability to crash through a plasma deflector unscathed, but only with the right angle of trajectory. It couldn't evade Billie and line up the necessary entry at the same time. The window of opportunity would be brief, but as long as she fired before they—

"BILLIE!"

She let out a slow and steady exhale. The juggernaut came to rest in her sights.

Fire.

A small blinding ball of light erupted where the juggernaut had been and vanished almost as soon as it appeared, leaving in its wake nothing but chunks of metal flying outward from the blast, some burning into oblivion as they collided with the *Icarus*'s shield in a display of bright blue flashes.

Billie called into her headset. "Keep the shields up. Incoming debris." She pivoted the cameras to scan the black vastness above, below, and around them. Nothing but distant stars and fragments of destroyed fighters ricocheting off each other, burning up on either deflector shield, or soaring out beyond the two plasma-encased ships into the void of deep space.

Radar showed nothing inbound.

"From where I'm sitting, that's the last of them," she reported.

"Nader says the same from starboard. Aft and bow are clear as well." Kabra's voice had regained its gruff, unfaltering edge as he barked orders through the headset without any praise or acknowledgment that she'd just saved their hides while the other three guns did nothing. "Retract blasters, close up your laser-slit and report to the bridge. I'll get the *Icarus* on comms while we wait for the debris to clear."

"Confirmed." Billie pulled her headset off and did a celebratory spin with her chair.

Fifty gigadorns of metallic hydrogen! It was the heist of the century, and they had pulled it off with only a crew of thirteen. Well, thirteen and this mysterious employer, Jarac.

She slowed her chair to a stop and leaned back in it, twirling one of her many dark braids around her finger with a contented sigh. All they had to do now was get to the wormhole that would dump them out in the Tybrax system, dock at the exchange station orbiting Hoggsvall, and cash out the crystals. Then she would finally have enough to break free from Kabra and buy her own ship.

Resisting the urge to daydream about what her future ship would look like, Billie touched her fingers to her lips, then laid them on the dingy and dented artillery console in front of her. The *Cerno* had been a faithful partner to her all these years working under Kabra's thumb. If her new ship was even half as reliable as this old friend had been, she'd never have to worry.

After securing the blasters inside the plasma's protection and programming the laser-slit's magnets to close up the slit in the shield, Billie set the cameras and radar detection to auto-sweep and exited the artillery bay, heading up through the vacant halls of the *Cerno* to the command bridge. She reached the main corridor just as Nader did.

"Cutting it close there," he said with his usual disdain as he fell in step next to her, reeking of stale urine and last night's rehydrated curry.

Billie squared her shoulders and walked tall, though she still fell short of him a good five inches. "Better cutting it close than not cutting it at all, like you. Did you fall asleep over there?"

"Not my fault the *Icarus* was port-side and that's where all the escorts were."

"Yeah, but all those reserve fighters from the planet came right past starboard."

"Just be grateful Kabra picked you for the job," he shot back. "Ask me, spot shoulda gone to Cobbs or Ranger. Heck, even Moze woulda been a better choice than you."

"Why? Cuz I'm a girl?" Billie glared at him defiantly.

"I was gonna say a hotheaded grunt that doesn't know her place, but sure. Girl works too."

Billie bit her tongue. It wasn't worth it. Despite working with the crew for years, she was still the new kid. No matter how often she outperformed the others on jobs, they wouldn't see it. Standing up for herself would only give him more fodder to call her a hothead.

She forced a long breath out her nose and walked the rest of the corridor in silence. He was a sexist jerk trying to get her goat, and she wouldn't give him the pleasure of knowing he had.

The doors to the command bridge opened automatically as they approached. Billie contemplated tripping Nader as they crossed the threshold but Kabra was watching with his dark eyes narrowed in on them as if they had kept him waiting for hours. His tan, leathery face was long and thin, and a disapproving scowl made it seem longer than normal. Last thing she needed was to give him a reason to dock her share of the cut. Or worse.

One more day and she'd have everything she needed to head out on her own. Finish the job. That's all that mattered.

The doors closed behind them, and the sound of metal on metal pulled Billie from Kabra's scrutinizing gaze to the two crew members behind him. Yaro sat in his weapons control seat, attempting to unscrew the bolts attaching his screens to the console. Their aft gunman, Pahtak, had arrived before them and was removing hardware and circuitry from the radar console. Around them, various pieces of the bridge were already dismantled.

"Boss?" Nader asked, apparently as taken aback by the sight as Billie was.

"Grab a tool and get to work." Kabra kicked a box of tools towards them. "Anything not needed for basic forward trajectory, strip it down and take it to the loading bay."

"Why?" Billie asked, feeling all too uneasy with this unexpected twist.

Behind Kabra, the bridge's comm screen flashed to life. A portly man with a neat goatee appeared on screen, his eyes dancing as he flashed a smile and undid the top button of the stolen captain's uniform cutting into his meaty neck.

Kabra turned his back on Billie to face the man on the screen.

"Jarac," he said, acknowledging the man.

So this was Jarac, huh? Billie hadn't been privy to any of the meetings with him until now.

"I had my doubts Kabra, but you came through," Jarac said with a dignified nod as if tipping his hat to a fellow gentleman.

The idea of Kabra being a gentleman would have been enough to make her smirk if it weren't for the strange orders Kabra had given them. Why were they dismantling the *Cerno?* She grabbed a wrench from the box of tools and took a seat at an empty navigation console, but couldn't bring herself to start unscrewing anything until she knew what was going on.

"Job's not finished yet," Kabra said to the screen without any hint of a smile in return. "My men okay?"

"The ones you insisted babysit me so I didn't abscond with all the cargo?" There was a hint of joviality to his accusation that intrigued Billie. "Yes. All six—no, eight—are alive and well." He wagged his finger at the screen. "I found the extra pair you stashed by the escape pods."

Kabra was always impossibly surly, but Jarac's good humor brought out a heightened irritability in him Billie had never seen. If Jarac's intel and inside connection hadn't provided the opportunity of a lifetime, Kabra probably would have rejected this employer strictly on the grounds of excessive mirth.

"I understand your precautions, of course," Jarac continued. "But I assure you, I am a man of my word. Once we get to Hoggsvall and exchange the hydro-crystals, you will have your thirty percent, as promised."

Thirty? Billie shot Kabra a look. They had provided all the muscle. Why did he negotiate for anything less than fifty? Nader and the others shot furtive glances between Kabra and each other. At least she wasn't the only one Kabra had kept in the dark about the smaller cut.

"Thirty percent," Kabra said, "and the *Icarus*."

"Of course." Jarac gave another gentlemanly nod. "As promised."

The *Icarus*? Again, Nader and the others seemed just as surprised as she was. Billie shifted in her seat, all her senses on high alert. Kabra might have been a gruff tyrant of a crew leader, heavy handed with the punishments when someone screwed up, but he'd never been this secretive—no, misleading—about the details of a job with her or the other crew members before.

Sure, the cargo ship was worth a fair amount, more than enough to make up for the reduced share of hydrogen payout. But that was only *if* they could sell it. Hydro-crystals were untraceable, easy to fence. Finding a buyer for a stolen ship this size could take weeks. Or longer.

"Visual scanners indicate the debris has cleared," Kabra said to the screen in front of him. "We're lowering shields and coming to you. Have five of my men meet us in the docking bay to help strip what they can while I set the autopilot."

Autopilot? None of this was part of the plan Kabra had explained before. Everything felt like she was heading into a trap, and Billie couldn't take it anymore. She cleared her throat.

"Why are we stripping the *Cerno*?"

Yaro looked at her with a trace of gratitude, as if relieved he hadn't been the one to ask. Not that it did any of them any good. Kabra only gave her a warning glare before returning his attention to the comm display in front of him, where Jarac's joviality had faded slightly as he surveyed them through the screen.

"Do you need a few minutes to talk things over with—"

"No," Kabra said. "Once the things are taken care of here, we'll board the *Icarus* and set course for the wormhole."

Jarac didn't seem comfortable with the rest of the crew not knowing what he and Kabra had clearly arranged. Billie for sure wasn't comfortable with it. She stood and spoke in a tone not to be ignored.

"Why are we abandoning the *Cerno*?"

All the men turned toward her, shocked at such a forward display. Jarac's surprise was colored with the faintest smile of respect. Billie squared her jaw, empowered by her own boldness.

"Why are we abandoning the *Cerno?*Who's buying the *Icarus*? How much are we getting for her?" She widened her stance as Kabra's eyes narrowed in on her. "You never mentioned any of this. This isn't the job I signed up for."

Kabra advanced, stopping mere inches from her face. She tightened her grip around the hard edges of the wrench as his hot, soured breath hit her cheeks. "What you signed up for was a roof over your head and someone to keep you from being picked up by alley patrols back on Jorvura.If you're not happy with how I run things, I'd be happy to sell you to Manproso. He can always use an extra mining slave."

Sell her? He was bluffing. He had to be. Still, Billie fought back the taste of bile as she resisted the urge to sit under his withering glare.

Jarac's uneasy laugh emanated from the comm screen. "Come now, Kabra. No need to keep the child in the dark or scare her out of her wits. You've picked a good crew. They deserve to know you're providing for them."

Kabra shot him a menacing look, which he ignored as he continued to address Billie, Nader, Yaro, and Pahtak.

"Your fine leader here has asked me to procure a few contacts on Hoggsvall that can outfit the ship anyway you like. The *Icarus* will be getting a weapons-grade makeover, and then she'll be your new home."

There was a moment of stunned silence before Pahtak spoke. "Boss? You know how much it'll cost to outfit a ship that size?"

Kabra stood silent, and realization sank to the bottom of Billie's stomach. Kabra knew exactly how much it would cost. She slammed her wrench onto the console in front of her.

"I'm guessing it'll cost about thirty percent of fifty gigs of hydro-crystals. Isn't that right, *boss*?"

Nader's eyebrows shot up. Pahtak and Yaro looked equally surprised. Clearly they hadn't expected to get completely stiffed on their portion of the share either.

Kabra shrugged. "She's got plasma shields, cloaking, and the framework to be retrofitted for whatever guns we want to put on her. With her size, we can house a crew twice as large, and handle jobs the *Cerno* would never have been able to do. Like this one. The *Cerno* can fight, but she doesn't have enough space to transport two gigs of crystals, let alone fifty. The universe is too big to be thinking so small. We're expanding." He pulled a panel-lifter from the tool box and tossed it at Nader. "Expansion just happens to be expensive."

Billie did her best to take slow, even breaths. Kabra had no right to trick her and the other crew members like this, but her options were limited. Even if he was joking about selling her to the mines, he wasn't joking about this expansion project. Without her cut of the crystals, there was no way she could afford to strike out on her own now. She'd have to stick with the crew a little longer, and arguing with Kabra now would only make her stay in his crew more miserable than it already was.

"If there's no other insubordination," Kabra said, "let's get to work. I want anything that might sell on Hoggsvall taken to the loading bay. No sense in giving those trolls any more than we have to."

"What trolls?" Pahtak asked. "Why aren't we just keeping both ships?"

"This is why," Jarac said from the comm screen, pulling up a file that he projected to them.

It was a Class-G destroyer, easily three times the size of the *Icarus*, with a suspicious looking dome anchored to its ventral side.

Nader gestured at the dome. "Is that a—"

"Photon net?" Jarac finished for him with a nod. "Sure is, my boy. The Phobos crew got their hands on one a few months back. My contacts say they've cloaked themselves and have been trolling the entrance to our wormhole with it."

The Phobos crew? Billie's stomach folded in on itself. Of course Kabra's secret plan involved going up against the most ruthless syndicate in the known galaxy. No wonder he had kept her and the others in the dark. They never would have agreed to come if they'd known.

"The nets have one major flaw," Kabra said. "They can reel in whole ships, but only one at a time. Which is why we're using the *Cerno* as a decoy. While they're distracted reeling in this gutted shell, we'll be gliding to the wormhole in the cloaked *Icarus* with everything we need to start over better than ever."

His confidence was astounding. And completely unfounded. She'd probably get beat for it later, but Billie couldn't help speaking up again.

"Sacrificing the *Cerno* doesn't guarantee safe passage for the *Icarus*." She folded her arms across her chest as everyone turned toward her. The others might be willing to follow Kabra blindly, but this was the Phobos crew they were talking about. Someone had to be the voice of reason.

"What if they don't take the bait?" she asked. "What if they're scanning the higher and lower frequencies for cloaking scatter and latch on to the *Icarus*? We'll have sent the *Cerno* on autopilot through the wormhole with no one on her to turn her around, and we'll all be sitting ducks on a ship with no guns and not nearly enough crew to put up a fight. We could lose both ships here." She directed her pleas to Jarac. "Why not go around? There's gotta be another way to Hoggsvall. Or another trading post where we can dump this haul."

Jarac offered a sympathetic smile. "I'm afraid the only way to reach Hoggsvall in our lifetimes is through that wormhole, and if we don't reach Hoggsvall, my buyers will be very disappointed." He leaned closer to the screen. "They aren't the kind of men who cope well with disappointment."

"But it's our ship," Billie said. "Our home. There's gotta be a better—"

A hammer whizzed past her head, smashing into the console next to her with a sickening crunch of metal that silenced everyone.

"It's *my* ship," Kabra said, another heavy tool poised menacingly in his hand. "And we're sacrificing it. End of discussion."

"Technically, it is my ship," Jarac boomed. His tone over the comms was so disapproving, the temperature on the bridge seemed to drop a few degrees. Kabra froze, not used to being addressed with such authority.

"Those were the terms of our deal when *I* hired *you*, were they not?" Jarac glowered at Kabra through the screen, who in turn only responded with a tight-lipped nod.

Jarac gave a huff of satisfaction, then looked at Billie through the screen. His demeanor changed completely as his restrained rage melted into fatherly compassion. "I hate to butt heads over this, er—what was your name?"

"Billie."

"Right. Well, Billie my dear, you're not wrong. Our plan isn't foolproof. But it is the best plan we've got, and I do believe the odds are in our favor. That said, if you can come up with a plan that saves both ships, the *Cerno* is yours once we all make it to Hoggsvall."

Kabra's eyes widened. Nader, Yaro, and Pahtak exchanged stunned glances. Yet no one dared contradict Jarac. A spark of hope ignited inside Billie; her heart beat faster as she latched onto it. She could have her own ship. She could still get away from Kabra.

"Thing is," Jarac continued, "you've only got five minutes before we have to move. Any longer, and the people whose ship we've stolen and fighters you've wiped out might have a chance to scrounge up more ships to try and track us down. And once we start moving, it's only a matter of minutes until we're in range of the Phobos scanners. Not to mention, the longer we take to fence these crystals, the more likely it is that word will get out we have them. Last thing we need is any other vultures coming after us to steal what we've already stolen."

Five minutes? Billie searched around the bridge desperately for an idea. There had to be a way to get both ships past Phobos, a way to save the *Cerno* and make it hers.

Kabra scoffed as he watched her, then dropped the tool he was holding back into the box with an indifferent thud. "Give it up, kid." He kicked a loose screw at her, which landed by her feet with a pathetic, scraping plink. "It's just a ship."

#

Captain Spira downed the last of his borthiad juice and crushed the thin polymer container in his fist while wiping the back of his hand across his mouth. From his captain's chair on the command bridge, he hurled the wadded trash at the back of his navigation officer's sleeping head, hitting his mark with forceful accuracy.

"Next time I throw *you*," he said to the man scrambling awake. "Out the trash bay."

The man gave a frightened nod of understanding before focusing on the screens in front of him.

"Look alive, people," Spira said as he stood. "We are Phobos, the gang of fear. There's nothing fearsome about a bunch of napping pirates."

Everyone on the bridge made themselves look busy as Spira took a stroll around. Not that he would let them know, but he couldn't really blame them for zoning out. The vast expanse of space outside their navigation window was empty except for the blanket of stationary stars, distant and small, that filled the right side of the window. The black, starless nothing of the wormhole filled the left, its energy pulsing in an unchanging, hypnotic loop. There was nothing coming, nothing going, nothing changing. The wormhole had never been without traffic for this long. Maybe it was time to drop anchor in a new fishing spot.

"Inbound!" shouted a crewman in front of a radar screen. "But it's small. Probably a meteor or piece of debris."

"Get me a visual," Spira commanded, heading back to his captain's chair. A comm screen appeared in front of the navigation window, displaying a similar scene of star speckled nothingness. But there, traveling with its meager thrusters at what seemed full capacity, was a tiny ship—if you could even call it that.

"Is that an escape pod?" a crew member asked.

"Looks like it," Spira said. Something that size would normally never be worth a second glance, but the men needed a little action. "That pod escaped from somewhere. Let's find out where. And why."

They all watched for a few minutes as the pod grew larger on the screen.

"Pod is within net range," a crewman announced.

"Lift cloak and launch the net," Spira said.

The small pod stopped in its tracks as the invisible net of photons locked it in place. Then it moved toward them as they reeled it in.

Interesting. The pod was close enough now for their cameras to have a clear shot through the pod's navigation window into the single chambered vessel. One occupant—a girl—manned the controls.

She wore an extravehicular mobility unit, its helmet resting on the chair next to her. She looked to be in her late teens, maybe early twenties; he couldn't tell from just her face. What intrigued Spira the most, however, was her complete lack of fear. There she sat, control of her vessel taken away from her, being reeled into a ship of intimidating size that had just uncloaked before her. And yet she showed no fear. If she had looked relieved, thinking she was being rescued, that would be one thing, but no. This young creature was a torch of passion and fury, a combination Spira found quite enticing.

"Establish a video link," he said. A crewman nodded, and moments later the zoomed in camera feed they had all been watching switched to a feed from the pod's interior camera.

"Get your grubby photons off me," the girl said with such fierceness that Spira had to smile.

"These are the cleanest photons you'll find this side of the Tybrax system, thank you very much. Now, I'm Captain Spira of the Phobos—"

"I know who you are."

"Then you know not to interrupt me." He liked her spunk, but he would not have his authority challenged in front of his men. "Now, tell me your name, where you came from, and where you were going."

"My name's Billie, I came from a ship run by a bunch of lying jerks, and I *am* going through the wormhole to get as far away from them as I can."

His crew broke into a raucous laugh around him, and he joined them.

"My dear, even if we did let you out of our net, your pod would never survive the pressures of the wormhole."

"Let me worry about the wormhole," she said, patting the EMU helmet next to her. "Now, let's negotiate the terms of my release."

The sound of his men's continued laughter was good to hear. This feisty little minnow was the perfect distraction from their monotony. Spira leaned back in his chair.

"And what could you have that I would possibly want?"

"Access codes to the *Cerno*'s shield and weaponry system."

He sat his chair back up. "You came from the *Cerno*? You're one of Kabra's crew?"

"Was," she said. "And don't let him know you've heard of him. That backstabbing slime ball already has an ego the size of a moon."

There'd been chatter the past few months of the small crew leader landing some kind of job that would make him a major player.. Spira had dismissed the idea of a new potential rival, but maybe there was truth to it.

"What exactly did Kabra lie about?"

"About how we weren't getting our fair share of the hydro-crystals we helped him nick."

At the mention of the crystals, the bridge fell silent. Spira leaned forward in his seat, his chin resting on the thumbs of his interlaced hands. "Kabra got his hands on hydro-crystals?"

"A whole gig. And they're all yours if you let me go."

There was something hiding behind all this girl's bravado. Something she wasn't telling. He searched the screen for any clue in the background. The pod consisted of just the one open chamber and nothing looked out of place. It was just the girl.

A small smile curled Spira's lips. Just the girl and the EMU helmet her hand had been protectively resting on the whole time they'd been talking.

"All the crystals?" he asked. "Even the ones you took for yourself and have hidden under that helmet there?"

The girl froze, tight-lipped, as if trying to come up with something to help bluff her way out. Her hesitation was all the confirmation he needed.

"Put together a welcoming committee," he told his men. "Have the girl and her crystals escorted to the bridge as soon as she's reeled in."

"Yes, sir," his first lieutenant said.

"Hold up," the girl said from the comm screen. "Kabra will be coming after me as soon as he figures out I've made off with my share and his pod. Yes, I've got a handful of crystals but he's the one you really want. Thing is, the *Cerno* has plasma shields and heavy blasters, and Kabra is a hardheaded beast. He won't let you bring him in without a fight." She lifted her helmet and exposed a hydrogen canister underneath it. "This is all the crystals I've got. The damage he'll do to your ship before he lets you board will cost more than this to repair. Let me go, and I'll give you the codes to remotely disable his shield and weaponry systems."

"Sir," a crew member in front of the radar screen said. "I'm picking up a larger ship. It's coming from the same direction the pod did, moving fast. They'll have a visual on us in no time."

Everyone turned to Spira, awaiting orders. Even the girl seemed to have said her piece and was waiting on him.

It might make him look weak to negotiate with her, but she was right. There was no way she had enough crystals in that pod to offset the battle damage the *Cerno* would likely inflict, and it didn't make sense to pass up the chance to score a bigger ship just to hang on to a tiny pod.

Spira stood, pulling at the hem of his jacket to straighten it. He directed his attention toward the crewmen. "Once she sends the codes, release her."

"That is," he said, directing himself back toward her, "if you still want to be released. There's always room on my crew for a smart and fearless thief. I think you'll find the pressures of Phobos life significantly less than the pressures of a wormhole."

"I'll take my chances with the wormhole." She looked down from the camera to type something, then fixed herself on the camera again. "Codes are sent."

A crewman confirmed receipt of the codes.

"Well then, Billie," Spira said with a mocking salute. "Best of luck not dying." He terminated the communication, and the comm screen vanished. He signaled to the net operator.

"Disengage the net and re-engage the cloak. We don't want them to see us before they're within disabling range."

"What about the girl?" a crewman asked, pointing out the navigation window to the tiny pod moving toward the wormhole. "Should we keep an eye on her?"

Spira shook his head. "The wormhole will take care of her." It was a shame, really, but they had bigger fish to fry. He returned to his captain's chair at the center of the bridge but remained standing. "Pull up visuals of the *Cerno*. Let's see if we can't put a face to this Kabra I've been hearing so much about."

The long-distance camera feed projected images of the approaching ship onto the comm screen, blocking the navigation window and wormhole from view. The ship was still too far away to make out anything on its bridge through its navigation window, but the crewman had been right. The ship was moving fast. That was a good sign though. Spira and his men must have gotten their cloak back up in time, otherwise the ship would be changing course or slowing to put up shields and make a stand.

A crewman typed at his keyboard, monitoring his screen carefully. "They should be in range to disable shields and weapons in three, two—" He hit a button to transmit, and after a pause, slapped his console victoriously. "We're in!"

Spira gave a satisfied nod. He hadn't dismissed the possibility that the girl's codes would be fake, but either way, there had been no use holding her in the net, their ship exposed without their cloak, when bigger prey was coming their way.

"Time to net range?" he asked his men.

"Thirty seconds if they hold their current trajectory and speed."

On the screen, the ship was discernible now as a zodiac cruiser, battle-worn but still heavily armed. Even if the girl had lied about it having any hydro-crystals, the ship itself was still a worthy catch.

"Ready the photon net, but don't launch until they're closer. I want Kabra to have as little time as possible to scramble his men or reroute his hacked systems before we've got him anchored in our docking bay." Spira sat in his chair and pressed the inter-ship comm button on his console.

"All hands report to docking bay 2, hostile protocol." He released the button and directed his attention back to the camera feed where the *Cerno* was now in full view. Everyone on the bridge watched it get closer and closer.

"Uncloak and launch," he commanded.

The invisible net of photons shot out into the black of space, and the *Cerno* came to an immediate halt.

"Reel it in and establish a video link with Kabra, now."Spira waited patiently in his seat, watching as the ship moved laterally toward them..

"Sir, I've got an audio link, but video communications have been disabled."

Something prickled at the back of his neck. Why would a captain disable their own video comms? What was on the bridge that Kabra didn't want him to see?

A full gig of crystals wouldn't fit on a bridge that size; it would take up at least half the ship's cargo space. Perhaps Kabra was keeping some of the crystals on the bridge near him for extra security.

Or maybe, Spira's mind rationalized, the video comms were simply damaged.

No. It was something else. Thirty-five years in this line of work had given him a pretty accurate instinct for when something didn't seem right. And right now, something definitely wasn't right.

He pressed the button to begin audio transmission. "This is Captain Spira of the Phobos Crew. Whose ship have I captured?"

There was a slight pause. "Name's Kabra."

"Why are you hiding, Kabra? Establish video comms. Now."

Again, another pause.

"We have business in Hoggsvall that won't wait, so get on with it," Kabra said. "Name your price."

The audacity of his replies didn't match the hesitations that came before them. Something other than nerves had to be causing those delays.

"All your business is with me, now," Spira said. "Your ship will be reeled into our docking bay, and met by my armed men. If you come without a fight, I will consider—"

"Sir!" a crewman whispered urgently, as he waved to get Spira's attention.

Spira muted the audio link with the *Cerno.* "What?""I'm picking up chatter on the back channels of a hydro-crystal heist. They say a cargo ship carrying fifty gigadorns was hijacked, and its entire security escort destroyed."

"The whole ship was hijacked?" Spira asked, dialing into every instinctual red flag he had. The crewman nodded.

Spira stood so quickly, his men all sat a little taller.

"Scan the extreme ends of the spectrum," he ordered the men monitoring the radar console. "Look for cloaking scatter."

He turned to the crewman at the communications console. "The *Cerno*'s a diversion. I bet Kabra's relaying his audio from that stolen cargo ship. That's why there's a delay and no video. Track the audio signal to its original source."

Spira turned to the rest of the men on the bridge. "I want all eyes scanning for that cargo ship. It's here. I can feel it."

There was a buzz about the bridge, a kind of electric energy in the men as they all re-tasked their cameras and sensors to find the cloaked cargo ship lurking somewhere in the black depths before them. Spira inhaled deeply. It was the kind of energy that made one feel alive.

It didn't take long before a crewman at the radar console almost jumped to his feet. "There!" he said, pointing to an area on his screen. "Heavy amounts of scatter. Enough to cloak a cargo ship."

"Is it in range of the net?" Spira asked.

"Yes, sir."

"Release the *Cerno* and relaunch at the cargo ship. We're about to land the biggest fish yet, boys."

Out the navigation window, they all watched as the released *Cerno* advanced toward the wormhole opening. On the far right side of the window, a slight distortion of the bespeckled black of space inched closer toward them. A wave of excited chatter rippled across the bridge.

"Establish video link with the cargo ship on my personal screen. And I want all non-essential bridge crew in the docking bay for hostile protocol. If that ship needed a security escort, it likely isn't armed, but that doesn't mean the men on board it won't be."

"Yes, sir."

Spira settled into his chair, unmuting his audio comms. In a moment, a smaller comm screen flashed to life before his chair. A stout man with a well-trimmed goatee smiled at him through the screen.

"So your video comms do work, I see," Spira said, trying not to show just how much the man's smile unnerved him. "I take it you're Kabra?"

"Actually, my name is Jarac. Though Kabra is here somewhere if you'd like to speak to him. He will be disappointed to learn you figured out his little autopilot-audio-relay trick, but such is the life of a thief, no?" His stubby fingers reached up and smoothed the beard around his mouth. "Now then, name your price, Spira."

Jarac's voice certainly differed from the man who had claimed to be Kabra,and his voice was almost as unnerving as his smile. There was no fear or even annoyance to be detected in it; he was nothing but calm and rational civility.

Spira didn't like it. He rolled his shoulders back.

"There is no price that will spare your ship or the crystals. Your lives, however, are still on the table."

"Very well. What must we do?"

"Come easily. No guns, no resistance. Have all your men lie face down in the docking bay, hands stretched above their heads."

"Sounds reasonable," Jarac said. "I'll give the order now."

Something was definitely off. Nobody surrendered this easily, at least not without a healthy amount of fear. Spira scanned the video feed behind Jarac, but couldn't see any other bridge crew. There didn't seem to be much background noise when he spoke either, at least not the kind that came with a fully-staffed bridge. So either all his men were already waiting at the docking bay to put up a fight, or Jarac had them loading into escape pods. Or something else. In any case, , Spira needed a better visual to get a read on the situation.

"If you're planning to come easily, there's no point in keeping your cloak up," he said. "Take it down. Now."

"Of course." Jarac signaled to someone out of frame of the video feed.

So there *was* someone else on the bridge with him.

Out the navigation window, a giant cargo ship seemed to materialize out of nowhere, closer than Spira had realized it was. No exterior guns that he could see, and no pods trying to escape. The ship just kept drifting toward them as they reeled it in.

Spira directed his attention from the navigation window back to the comm screen in front of him. "How many men do you have on board? And before you answer, know that if the number we find is not the number you tell me now, everyone we find dies."

"We have thirteen men," Jarac replied. "Though I must admit, most of them were really looking forward to making it to Hoggsvall. Perhaps we can come to an agreement. You follow us through the wormhole, we go to my buyers and sell the crystals that you've already deduced we have. We'll split the payout fifty-fifty, then go our separate ways. It's mutually beneficial. My men and I get to keep our ship and a little of the payoff we had planned on, while you make easy money without the hassle of finding a buyer or dealing with hostages. Some of my men, I hate to admit, are less than hygienic. Talented, don't get me wrong, but you really don't want them bunking next to you, if you know what I mean."

Spira didn't know what to make of this man. He seemed to possess a refined sort of intellect, yet here he was, prattling on, oblivious to the facts of his situation.

"I have you trapped, as sure as gravity on Frotma III, yet you're suggesting I just give up your ship, hostages, and fifty percent of the crystals?"

"You're right." Jarac nodded. "I was being greedy. We'll split the crystals seventy-thirty."

Spira snorted. The man wasn't clever. He was insane. "You have nothing to negotiate with."

"Oh, I'm not negotiating." The corners of Jarac's mouth turned up a little higher. "I'm waiting."

Warnings went off in Spira's mind. He narrowed his eyes on Jarac. "For what?"

"Captain. There's an escape pod," a crewman shouted. "But it's—it's moving *toward* the cargo ship."

"What?" Spira scanned the navigation window beyond his comm screen. From underneath his own ship, a small pod sped toward the massive cargo ship.

"Visual," Spira yelled. "Get me a better vis—"

A violent trembling shook the bridge. Red lights flashed on different consoles as sirens filled the air. All the crewmen began frantically reading screens, listening to their comm sets and shouting out reports.

"Explosion on the outer hull! Both thrusters reporting damage."

"Subdecks one through four have been breached. Initiating auto-seal protocols."

Another explosion shook the bridge.

"We've lost the plasma shield and the net is losing power."

Pieces of debris flew past the navigation window. Realization hit Spira as the small pod docked with the cargo ship.

Between the shouts of men and the blaring of alarms, Jarac's voice came through the comms. "Ah yes, my mistake. We have thirteen men"--he smiled triumphantly--"and one girl."

#

Docked inside the *Icarus*, Billie stood next to her pod, panting for breath inside her full EMU suit. Through the open bay doors, she admired the aftermath of her handiwork. The small bursts of fire that had erupted across the hull of the Phobos ship hadn't lingered; no flames in the vacuum of space ever did. But each explosion had been enough to blast vital pieces of the ship away infinitely.

First the thrusters. Then the plasma shield magnets.

She should have closed the bay doors immediately to protect against debris, but the sight of those chunks of metal careening freely through space, liberated from the ship that once controlled them, was too beautiful to pass up.

The audio comms in her suit crackled to life.

"Nice touch hiding the explosives in the hydrogen canister," Jarac's jovial voice said. "How many were you able to plant?"

With another burst, the weakened photon net on the underside of the Phobos hull splintered into a myriad of pieces, and the *Icarus* lurched slightly under her feet.

"That was the last of them. I wasn't able to get to their blasters before Kabra sent word that Spira was on to you."

"No worries, my dear. Our shields are still fully functional."

"Can we make our way to the wormhole with the shields up?"

"Certainly," he replied. "It's a straight shot between here and there. Reduced visibility shouldn't be an issue, especially with their thrusters down. Are you securely back? Are we good to engage shields and proceed?"

"Yes, I'm back." Billie punched the button to close the docking bay doors just as a wall of blue plasma blocked the fractured Phobos ship from view. "And now if you don't mind," she said, unlatching the helmet of her EMU suit as the bay around her re-pressurized, "I'd love it if you could take me to my ship."

CINDER ILVA
BY SAVANNAH GRACE

The walls were bleeding again.

Ilva sighed and muttered a curse under her breath, flicking the dial back on the hologram tablet. Turning the empty, rusted hull of the massive airship *Empress* into a perfect, holographic ballroom was proving...

Difficult.

"Ilva?"

Ilva's head snapped up and her hand automatically groped for the blueprints she had spread out on the dirty floor, until she spotted the person coming through the massive metal doors into the hull. "Hey Mara," Ilva said, shoving herself off the ground. The muscles in her legs twinged as she stretched. "How're the preparations coming?"

Mara, one of Ilva's two stepsisters, waved one hand airily. "You can guess. Mom's in a very sophisticated tizzy and Tabitha is nearly in tears over this or that. Yourself?"

"Feeling some of both of those," Ilva said, scuffing the sole of her massive fuzzy slipper against her scattered blueprints. "Everything's harder to holograph over walls this old and this metallic—everything wants to bleed through."

"Mm." Mara's sharp hazel gaze took in the massive belly of the *Empress*. "Persnickety walls, them."

"Don't tease."

"I'm not!" Mara protested, but her barely-suppressed smile said otherwise. "You're our best technician, Ilva. None of the other technicians hold a candle to you—I bet you'll become one of the Cinders someday."

Becoming a Cinder was every technician's dream, but it was Ilva's most of all—to work under the legendary Mr. Cinder himself, who had built the hologram technology that everyone used.

Mara kept right on talking through Ilva's glazed eyes. "—have no doubts that you'll get this job done in the next five hours."

Ilva's stomach leapt into her throat as she snapped back to reality. "Five hours? I can't even finish the prototype ballroom hologram in five hours, much less the whole shebang—what do you mean, five hours? I was supposed to get five *days*!"

"Plans," Mara said hesitantly, "change. The royal family is arriving early, so Mom says you have to get this done double-time. I was supposed to come down here and see how you were getting along." She turned and started for the stairs that led back up to the hull's double-doors. "I'll tell her you're alright."

"But I won't even have time to spruce up for the party!" Ilva stammered, brushing her hands against the faded sweatpants she was wearing.

Mara simply gave her a cheeky wave as she opened the door to the main area of the airship. "Better hurry then!"

Ilva watched in slack-jawed shock as Mara shut the heavy door, and the expansive metal hull rang with the echo of it. One of the blueprint papers rustled in its wake. Ilva looked down at the hologram tablet she was still holding and scraped a hand down the side of her face.

"Dang," she muttered, because there was nothing else to say.

And then she got back to work.

* * * * *

No one could say the commander of the airship Empress wasn't fair—but they also couldn't say that she wasn't strict.

And Ilva couldn't say that she wasn't her stepmother.

"ILVA, ARE YOU QUITE DONE YET?"

Ilva cringed as her mother's voice blared over the intercom system hooked into the ceiling of the hull. "Working on it," she replied, jabbing new buttons on the holograph tablet. The white ballroom flashed in front of her again, but a few patches seemed blurry, showing metallic walls through the fuzzy gaps.

"The royal family are arriving in five minutes. You have one hour before the party begins—please be ready in time, Ilva."

"I will, Mom," Ilva said, as the intercom system let out a pop that signaled her mother had left.

What she wanted to say was, "Couldn't you buy me some more time, Mom?"

Ilva put her head in her hands and looked at the tiled floor of the holographic room. It was nearly perfectly, nearly—but something was wrong with the coding in the holographic, and a few tiles were discolored.

The hull rang with the muted sound of Ilva sliding different pieces across the hologram, trying to make up for the gaps in the code. And then—

Thump.

Ilva's heart leapt into her throat as the *Empress* shuddered with the impact of another ship hooking up to its dock. The royal family had arrived.

"It'll be great, they said!" Ilva muttered to herself, her thing fingers shaking slightly as she frantically threw new hologram forms at the walls. "You'd make a great technician, they said! No one has a mind like yours, they said! Maybe someday you'll even be a Cinder!"

There was a loud humming sound, and then the hologram system spluttered and crashed. Ilva froze, looking at the suddenly blank screen. "You have GOT to be kidding me—"

She slammed the restart button, and there was a loud whirring as the machine slowly powered back to life. "Come on, come *on*," said Ilva, tapping the restarting screen with the heel of her hand. "Geez, what I wouldn't give for an assistant right about now—"

"Excuse me, miss?"

Ilva barely managed to suppress a yelp as an unfamiliar voice echoed through the hull. She dropped the hologram tablet and looked up to see an old man standing at the top of the stairs that led into the hull. "Um—sir, did you need ..." she started scraping her blueprints together, trying to hide them as the man made his way down the steps. "I'm rather busy, if you want something I would find Mara or Tabitha, they should be able to—"

"Oh, no, miss, I only heard someone shouting down here and thought I should see if anything's the matter...oh, are those Cinder technology blueprints? That's a wonderfully crafted hologram." He pointed with his cane at the papers Ilva was frantically shuffling. "There do seem to be a few glitches though."

Ilva froze, holding the papers close to herself. She snuck a glance at the tablet next to her, which had finished powering up. "How do you know that?"

The old man smiled, sending smile lines running along the corners of his eyes. "Why, my dear, I am the one who created Cinder technology."

For a moment, Ilva only gaped. And then she did her best to be dignified—setting her papers on the ground and scrambling to her feet. "Oh, it's an honor to meet you, Mr. Cinder—did you come along with the royal family? This hologram is pretty primitive next to yours, but it's the best I can—"

Mr. Cinder suddenly burst into a loud laugh. "Oh, not all at! I'm very impressed by what you've built here—how's about I help you run through that glitch? With the time there is before the party begins, I'll only be able to help you fix the hologram to run until midnight. It will shut off after that, but it should buy you a few hours."

"Yes, sir, thank you so much, sir," Ilva stammered, almost tripping on her own feet to fetch the tablet with the hologram codes off the ground. *Mr. Cinder was standing in the hull of her ship—*

—and looking at her glitchy designs.

Heat bloomed up her cheeks as Ilva pulled up five different images on the screen of the tablet. "Here are my codes—they're amateur, but I think they're workable."

"More than workable," Mr. Cinder said, taking the screen from her and running through the lines of coding. "This coding is well above most that of the Cinders that work under me in the royal family's ship. My, but you're an impressive technician. Here, I'll teach you how to fix these glitches to work the hologram until midnight..."

*   *   *   *   *

The walls were white. Pure, pristine white. The hologram was so realistic that Ilva couldn't feel the rust on the metallic walls they covered when she ran her hands over them.

"It's perfect," she said, rubbing her fingertips together to see if any there was any rust dust on them. There wasn't. "Thank you so much, Mr. Cinder."

Mr. Cinder inclined his head, handing the tablet back to Ilva. "It was my pleasure. But remember, it will only work until midnight. You'll have to have another hologram ready to take it's place when this one wears out."

"Oh, I will sir, thank you sir." Ilva looked down at the tablet, at the scrolls of perfect coding running up and down it. It was mesmerizing. "Mr. Cinder, I—"

But when she looked up, he was already gone.

* * * * *

Ilva prepped the party room in record time—using the hologram to produce lights and music before shoving the tablet into a hidden alcove in the back corner to keep it all running.

And then she dashed up the stairs as if running for her life, barging through the door of the hull into the bright main central of the airship and shoving her way through some very startled people—she hoped none of them belonged to the royal family—before fleeing into the more private hallways and stashing herself away into her bedroom.

"And Ilva slides into home base, safe once again," she breathed to herself, shutting her bedroom door before leaning her hands on her knees to steady herself.

Her four-poster bed had a huge dress of emerald green strewn across it, with tatters across the bodice to show the gold fabric underneath it. Ilva glared at it from across the room. Such flamboyance didn't suit her, but Mara had wanted all three sisters to match, whether Ilva was a stepsister or not. Tabitha, the second stepsister, had bet that Ilva wouldn't wear it.

Tabby, as usual, was correct.

Ilva threw open the doors to her walk-in closet and snatched a pair of deep green leggings, wiggling into them before snatching a slim gold dress off the wall. The embroidery on the back was vibrant for her tastes, but the dress had been a birthday gift from her mother, and she wanted to wear it in her honor.

The shoes she chose, however, had been a gift from her father before he passed away.

Ilva lifted the glass slippers off the shelf where she kept them, gently running her finger through the dust that had collected on them. They would be good for tonight.

She jammed her feet into them before rushing out of the closest, scraping her messy brown hair into a bun on the back of her head.

There. Not even mother would be able to pick on her for sloppiness tonight.

Ilva picked up her strewn sweatpants and t-shirt, tossing them onto her bed before looking at herself in the mirror.

"You are Ilva," she said. "Greatest technician on the airship Empress. And tonight, *you will be sociable.*"

The girl in the mirror nodded, but Ilva herself wasn't feeling quite ready. Socializing wasn't her thing. But it was Mara and Tabitha and her mother's, and tonight she would be for them.

Ilva took a deep breath and thrust her shoulders back, striding out of the room with her head held high. The party began in five minutes.

She only hoped that the hologram would hold.

*　*　*　*　*

"Ah, Ilva! Just the person I wanted to see—"

Ilva couldn't number how many times she'd heard those words, and the night was still young.

"Ah, Ilva! How lovely the room looks tonight!" "Ah, Ilva! How much you look like your stepsisters!" "Ah, Ilva!"

She was beginning to feel vaguely like punching someone in the nose. The buffet table was slowly becoming her best friend.

"How're you holding up, Ilva?"

Ilva turned away from the food to find Tabitha behind her, dressed elaborately in a dress that Mara had probably chosen. Even though she was the youngest sister, she sometimes appeared to be the oldest—though she seemed to be not all there half the time, with her zoned-out stare and dainty voice.

"I guess we'll see," Ilva replied, fiddling with a loose thread near the waistline of her dress. "Gosh, but all these royals are stuffy."

"Not all of them," Tabith murmured, sedately reaching out to move Ilva's hand away from the loose thread. "Have you met Prince Elderic yet? Oh, you must—Prince Elderic!"

Before Ilva could protest, Tabitha had linked arms with her and was dragging her through the crowd towards a young man talking to Mara on the other side of the room. "Prince Elderic, if I may introduce you to my sister, Ilva—Ilva, this is Prince Elderic."

Ilva had the sensibility to keep her mouth shut, because what would have come out was something along the lines of "Tabby, I hate you." Instead, she stuck out her hand.

Prince Elderic had the sensibility to shake it. "Ah, Ilva! It's a pleasure to meet you—just as lovely as the rest of your family, I see."

Ilva forced a smile onto her face and tried to ignore Mara's very obvious eyelash-batting at the blue-eyed prince. "Thank you, your highness. It's a pleasure to meet you as well."

"You're the one Mr. Cinder keeps going on about, aren't you? The way you two set up the holograms in this room, it's exquisite. This is a powerful ship to keep them running so well for so long."

Ilva dropped his hand and mumbled something along the lines of "oh, thank you," but inside her heart seemed to have stopped beating.

Holograms.

She'd forgotten about the holograms shutting down at midnight—

Not bothering to mutter an excuse, Ilva dashed away from Prince Elderic and her sisters, ignoring Mara and Tabitha's shrieks of protest.

"'Scuse me, move over," she snapped at the people in her path, shoving her way through the get to the corner in the far back. She tripped, losing one shoe to the crowd. She didn't bother to retrieve it—instead, she lunged forward and pressed a hidden button on the wall and stepped into the tiny alcove that appeared, shutting herself in.

The alcove promptly lit up, revealing the hologram tablet on the wall that she'd hidden away earlier. Yes, it was as Mr. Cinder said—three minutes to midnight, and the coding was slowly eating itself alive—

Breathing hard, Ilva passed shaking fingers over the screen, trying to reprogram it in record time. A ballroom with slightly blurry walls was better than a ballroom that looked like a rusted, metal belly of a ship.

One minute.

How had Mr. Cinder done it? Ilva smacked the side of the tablet. "Come on, you stupid piece of junk—"

A new line of code flashed up on the screen—Ilva tore it apart and pieced it back together properly. Thirty seconds.

Something went red in the corner of the screen—Ilva swatted codes into it until it became a light shade of green. The lights in the alcove flickered.

Five four three two—

"YOU'RE KIDDING ME," shouted Ilva, wrapping another piece of code around the holograms on the tablet when—

Wwwwfffffftttttttttt.

The awful sound of the hologram powering down shot through the alcove. Ilva wanted to curl up into a small ball and die. Already, she could hear people shouting.

"Technician Ilva! Where is Ilva the technician?"

Of course, that's what they would be saying.

Oh, her mother would have some choice words for her later.

Ilva started at the tablet, where all of the codes for the hologram had disappeared. She'd have to start from scratch.

From *scratch.*

Ilva leaned her head against the screen and took a deep breath. "Well, nothing for it," she said.

She threw her shoulders back and got to work.

*   *   *   *   *

The fastest time Ilva had built a full hologram in was five minutes.

That night, she beat it.

Four minutes later, she had a complete code for a new hologram up on the screen. It looked perfect. It *was* perfect.

Except for the fact that it was an entirely different hologram than the ballroom they had started out in. But it was that or the metal hull.

Ilva took a shaky breath and hit "ACTIVATE".

Wwwwwffffffffttttttttt.

The hologram powered up, and Ilva closed her eyes and listened to the gasps of shock.

Her mother was going to *kill* her.

Ilva put the tablet back in place and opened the door to the alcove, stepped out, and shut it again. All around her was her masterpiece.

The walls were blue, watery, strange—and the room was filled with glints of green that made it look as if they were underwater. Near the ceiling, a dolphin swam in circles, and fish darted between the startled, transfixed guests.

"Technician Ilva?"

Ilva jumped at the sound of her name, and jumped again when she saw Prince Elderic jogging towards her. In his hand, he held her glass shoe. "You lost this," he said simply.

She took it from him, looking at him warily. "Thanks," Ilva said, slipping it back on. "What did everyone think of ... the hologram?"

"They thought it was...they thought..." Elderic let out a breathy laugh, running a hand through his hair and turning full circle. "It's magnificent. Did you create this? In the span of a few minutes?"

"I...I...yeah, I did," Ilva stammered, reaching out towards one of the rainbow-glittering fish. It darted around her fingertips before swimming off. "Hope I didn't scare anyone too bad."

"You should have seen their faces!" Princed Elderic said, a grin spreading across his own. "Beyond priceless. Ilva, I would like to offer you a job."

A *what?*

... a *what?*

"A what?" Ilva said.

"A job. I would like to offer you a job aboard my family's ship—anyone this talented deserves to be one of the Cinders working with Mr. Cinder himself. Would you like to meet him? I'd be happy to introduce you."

Ilva licked her lips and tried to process proper words. *Come on, Ilva, speak.* "Um, yes, I would like that...very much, yes, thank you." She felt too self-conscious to tell him they'd met before.

"Lovely, lovely! You can start work right away, this whole hologram incident will make you famous, I do believe..."

Ilva followed Prince Elderic across the hologram room in a haze, nearly walking straight through a school of pink fish. Had that just happened?

Did she just get a job as a Cinder on the royal ship?

She was only knocked out of her daze when she realized that Prince Elderic was introducing her to Mr. Cinder, and Mr. Cinder was shaking her hand for the second time. "Told you that you weren't an amateur," he whispered with a wink. "Well done."

"Thanks," she whispered back, wings of pride unfurling in her chest as a green seahorse floated past their faces. She had a job with Mr. Cinder himself, as a technician on the royal ship. As a Cinder.

Cinder Ilva.

Ilva felt a smile lifting her lips.

It didn't sound half bad.

65

THE END

BEAST IN THE MACHINE
BY E.B. DAWSON

It was a quiet village. Isabelle knew it would be. There were only two reasons people moved to Ilford: to get away from society or to work at the world's second-best scientific research center. In Ilford, it wasn't difficult to differentiate between the two. The scientists were middle-aged men with disheveled clothes who barely saw the light of day. The locals were the ones gossiping about them in the open-air cafes. Now they peered curiously at Isabelle and her father as the pair drove by in their sedan. Isabelle stared back openly, fascinated by the open-air buildings that breathed in the fresh ocean air.

The villagers themselves had seen their share of ocean winds and salty storms. The young ones were strong with bright eyes, agile hands, and brown skin. The older ones looked like withered old trees. Though their eyes squinted at her and their mouths turned down in suspicious frowns, Isabelle smiled.

"What a quaint little place," she said to her father as they began unloading boxes into the house.

"I'm glad you like it, dear. I've heard the locals aren't so welcoming to outsiders."

"But did you see the tide pools under that sunset, Papà? I don't think I could ever be unhappy with a view like that; I don't care how nasty our neighbors are. And surely they can't be that bad."

"Well, if *you* can't win them over, love, I'll write them off as not worth knowing." Her father kissed her on the cheek, scratching her with his whiskers, then reached for his hat.

"Are you going somewhere?"

"To the lab."

"But we just arrived," Isabelle protested.

"Dr. Glass said I was to come over as soon as I arrived."

"Well, that seems like a bad precedent, doesn't it?"

"Now, now," her father chastised her gently, "I know that brain of yours. If you could postpone your final analysis of my new boss until you actually meet the man, I'd be much obliged."

"I will try to keep an open mind," Isabelle said, "but I cannot promise to keep my mouth shut."

"Fair enough. Don't do all the unpacking without me."

"I certainly will," Isabelle replied. "You always put everything in the wrong place."

"I do, don't I? Very well then. But don't work too hard. And don't—"

"Unpack your office? I wouldn't dream of it. You can make your little mess all yourself."

"I'll be back in an hour or two," he promised.

She locked the door securely behind him and turned to survey the night's work. She had learned the hard way that with him one to two hours really meant three to four. She may not like it, but there was no fighting it. The best she could do was make the house as comfortable as possible by the time he got back.

It was a small, rather crooked little cottage with a spiral staircase in the center, giving the impression that the small dwelling twisted around itself like a great oak. This was a great relief to Isabelle, who had feared the Institute would set them up in some pre-fabricated box, but she could befriend this house. She just had to earn its trust first. She'd start by giving it a little fresh air. The house must be suffocating; it smelled staler than an old sock. She wove her way through the boxes, wrestled with the latches, and pushed open both the panes and the forest-green shutters.

Crisp, salty air eddied into the room like the first fingers of high tide on a thirsty shore. It carried with it the unmistakable scent of coming rain. Isabelle took a deep breath, tied her hair back in a bandana, and set to work unpacking the kitchen.

A light rain descended on the cottage just as evening fell. Having finished the kitchen, Isabelle moved on to the living room with renewed purpose.

The steady rain on the roof kept her company. When she finished, it was nearly ten o'clock and high time to get tea and dinner ready for her father.

But she took a moment to place a gilded picture frame on the mantle. The beautiful woman stared back at her with gentle eyes, so different from the eyes that Isabelle remembered. The mother she had known as a child would have loved this house. Isabelle pushed the thought aside as her chest filled with pain and remorse, and focused on preparing dinner for her father.

Twenty minutes later he burst through the door with familiar enthusiasm, shaking off his umbrella and generally dripping water all over the entryway. His face was beaming.

"How did it go?" Isabelle asked with a grin as she helped him out of his rain boots.

"I'm sorry I'm later than expected. I just couldn't seem to tear myself away. The labs, Isabelle! I've never seen anything like it! Dr. Glass had all the best equipment. He's as eager to get started as I am. And I'm to have my own assistant."

"I'm glad."

"You've been busy," her father said as he entered the kitchen where a tray had been set out for him.

"It's a good start," Isabelle agreed. "I'll finish up tomorrow and then start looking for a job."

A cautionary look entered Dr. Richter's eyes. "Yes, I asked Dr. Glass about that. I thought maybe he could give you some recommendations. There doesn't seem to be much open, and he warned me that your association with me might blacken your resume in the village."

"I'm not sure Dr. Glass is an objective party, Papà. It's a bit too easy to reciprocate prejudice. I am determined to set out tomorrow with an open mind."

~

The rain had vanished by morning, leaving the little seaside village freshly scrubbed. But fog clung to the hills and cliff sides, and dark clouds loomed over the moody ocean, threatening another storm. Isabelle's father was off as soon as light seeped under the windowsills. She spent the first hours of the day setting the rest of the house in order before making her first foray into the village. She might as well stock the pantry and begin her job inquiries at the same time.

Tugging on her polka dot rain boots, a heavy knit charcoal gray sweater, and a slouch beanie, Isabelle descended the driveway and stepped out on the cobblestone streets with optimism. The air smelled of rich earth and a touch of salt. Gulls called back and forth above the fishing boats that bobbed up and down on the tempestuous sea. Directly in front of her, the village was waking up.

"Such a shame," the Grocer mentioned casually as he assisted the customer in front of Isabelle. "I heard a Lab Coat took up residence in the old maple house. They'll be cutting into it soon, I suspect, tearing up the hundred-year woodwork to put in their modern-day contraptions."

"Shame," the woman he was talking to scoffed. "People don't deserve a beautiful house like that if they aren't going to take care of it."

"Why didn't they just move into a townhouse, like the rest of their kind?" someone else chimed in.

Isabelle smiled. "Maybe they believe that a house shouldn't come out of a box but should have history and character."

"Ha! They call it character until the plumbing acts up a bit. Then it becomes inconvenient."

"Poor plumbing does sound a bit inconvenient." Her eyes sparkled good naturedly. "But I don't think it calls for ripping apart something as lovely as Maple House. Maybe we should give these newcomers the benefit of the doubt and see what happens."

The Grocer muttered something under his breath as he began helping her with her purchases.

"Since you've been so helpful," Isabelle continued, "I wonder if I might ask you something. I'd like to find a job. Do you know of anyone looking for help?"

The Grocer grumbled. "Nothing available for you, unless you like mopping up fish guts."

"Well, I'll never know unless I try..."

"It was a figure of speech. There's nothing open on the docks, neither," the Grocer said stubbornly.

"Well, you'll be sure to let me know if you hear of anything? I'm willing to try my hand at 'most anything."

"There may be something available." A woman stepped forward. "One of our foremost families has been looking for help around his estate for some time now."

The Grocer frowned at her. "What are you talking about?"

"They live in that great mansion on top of the cliffs. Surely you've seen it?" the woman continued.

"Sebastian Prince." The Grocer's face lit up mischievously. "She's right. If you're willing to try anything, you ought to go talk to his housekeeper."

Isabelle smiled. "I'll head up there this afternoon. Thank you." She piled up her arms with groceries and made her way back home. The dark clouds from the morning were finally moving in and an icy wind was picking up. Isabelle donned her rain jacket and snatched up a red umbrella before heading out again.

The winks and nods of the begrudging villagers had not been lost on her. She had little doubt that they meant some kind of mischief by sending her up to the Prince estate. But there could be no harm in trying. A fine, misty drizzle dropped in about halfway through the village, raising a muted symphony from the clay tile rooftops and cobblestone streets. The sound became softer, like rain falling on velvet, as she left the village behind and began climbing the hill north of the village to the great estate.

It perched above the black cliffs with solemn dignity. Isabelle had innocently assumed it was another research facility, for even though it sat a good ways apart from the clusters of labs directly east of the village, it resembled them far more than the old-fashioned fishing huts. Carved out of muted, white stone, it stood four stories tall and on closer inspection looked a great deal more like a museum than a house.

But the hike up the hill alone was worth the journey. At the foot of the cliff, the roiling black waves tossed and crashed with a graceful yet ferocious power. Farther out to sea, flocks of birds rode the swells with an elegant dignity, undisturbed by the gentle rain dimpling the water all about them. When Isabelle turned around, the sleepy village spread out before her like it had been taken straight out of a painting. After a sigh of deep contentment, she ascended the steps to the great house, feeling nearly invincible.

There was no response to her initial knock, so she tried again, putting a little more force into it. A raspy, mechanical noise caught her attention and she looked up to see a camera pointed at her.

"Hello, I'm Isabelle Richter. My father and I have just moved here and I'm looking for work. Someone in the village said you might be hiring?"

Something clicked and the door swung open.

Isabelle stepped forward, prepared to meet her host, but the ornate entryway was completely empty. She passed into the hall, which was paved with marble, and tried not to gawk at the portraits on the wall.

The door hadn't just opened by itself. Someone had let her in.

"Hello?"

There was no response. Then Isabelle heard a soft pitter-patter. She rounded the corner and stopped short in surprise. In front of her stood a tiny robot, no taller than her knee. It had two cylinder shaped legs, a round torso, two spindly little arms, and a round popsicle head with enormous turquoise eyes. An antenna protruded off the top of its head like a thick piece of hair.

"Who are you?" Isabelle asked in amazement.

The little robot tilted its head and blinked.

"I don't suppose you're the butler around here, are you?" she teased.

It turned and began walking back the way it had come, then paused and looked back at her expectantly.

"Am I supposed to follow you?" she asked.

It nodded.

"Well, all right then." This afternoon might turn out far better than she had imagined.

The little robot took her up a magnificent staircase and down a thickly carpeted hallway. On her left, a row of wall-length windows gave her a breathtaking view of the stormy sea. She wouldn't mind working in a place like this.

The door at the end of the hallway was very different than anything she'd seen so far. It was thick and metallic. The little robot raised one of its spindly little arms to a digital interface and the door popped open with a loud hiss.

"Is the interview to be in here?" Isabelle asked a little timidly.

The robot wiggled its arms enthusiastically and shuffled through the door. She followed after only a slight hesitation.

The room was nearly pitch black. There was just enough light from the open door behind her to reveal the shadowy silhouettes of antique furniture. Even the sound of the rain seemed muted behind the thick, brocade curtains.

Isabelle moved instinctively to the ten foot windows and hauled back the curtains one at a time. It took a deal of effort. Each curtain must have weighed about twenty pounds. But she was immediately rewarded with a soft flood of healthy, spring light and the soothing patter of the rain against the window panes.

"What, in the name of all things holy, do you think you're doing?" a deep voice slurred.

Isabelle whipped around.

About six feet away, a very disheveled man lay sprawled on a sofa. His posture was relaxed, his face grizzled and unkempt, but his dark brown eyes gazed at her with more menace than Isabelle had seen in her entire life. Her heart leapt in fear.

"I've come for an interview," she replied evenly, "but perhaps I've got the wrong room. I certainly didn't mean to disturb you."

He started off the sofa with more power than she could have imagined, the sparks in his eyes heating to a full-fledged fire and forever redefining intensity in her mind.

"Interview?" he snarled at her. "I thought I made it clear last time that you weren't to set foot in this house again."

Isabelle took a single step backwards, ignoring her racing heart. "I actually don't think I've ever been in this house before. Perhaps you've mistaken me for someone else."

He grabbed a side table and upended it forcefully, sending a lamp and two crystal glasses to the floor in a cacophony of shattered glass. Isabelle also noticed the rapid rise and fall of his chest and the protruding veins on his neck.

Unwanted memories flooded her mind, constricting her chest and making her palms sweaty. She shoved her emotions down with well-practiced determination, crossed her arms deliberately behind her back, and angled her body away from him. When she spoke, her voice was gentle.

"Well, that's one way to communicate, I suppose. But if you were to use words next time, I'd be much more likely to understand what you actually want." Her own words served to calm her racing heart.

The man clenched his fists and raised them to his mouth, pacing back and forth now. But he did not knock anything else over, nor did he yell at her.

A new voice spoke from the doorway. "Sebastian, what's going on? Who is this?" A small matronly woman in a crisp uniform stood in the doorway.

Sebastian turned to her like she was a lifeline. His hands were trembling now. "Get her out of here." He careened past her like a drunken man and disappeared from sight.

The housekeeper turned fierce eyes on Isabelle. "How did you get in the house?"

"I believe I was let in by your butler."

"We don't have a butler," the woman retorted.

"It was a very small robot."

The woman's eyes registered recognition. "Cog?" she called sharply.

The little robot emerged guiltily from behind the sofa, crept over to Isabelle, and took hold of her leg protectively. The housekeeper crossed her arms.

"Well, this is new for you. When did you start letting strangers into the house?" She switched her gaze to Isabelle. "Who are you, exactly?"

"My name's Isabelle Richter." Now that Sebastian had left, her heartbeat was rapidly returning to normal. "I'm looking for work. I was told in the village that you might be interested in hiring me?"

The housekeeper's eyes softened significantly. "I see. Well, I'm sorry to tell you that you were sent up here as part of a cruel joke."

Isabelle's eyes dropped to the carpet. Perhaps she shouldn't be disappointed after the reception she had received, but she was.

"But you have handled yourself surprisingly well," the housekeeper continued. "What is that you said you do?"

Isabelle's eyes returned to the woman's face. She had a sharp nose, but friendly eyes. "I can do a lot of things. But I got my degree in literature and information science."

"Well, we have a library here that is an absolute nightmare. Would you be interested in putting it to rights for us? It can be a contract job for a couple of weeks. We'll see how it works out."

"I would love that," Isabelle began hesitantly, "as long as Mr. Prince doesn't have any objections."

"I manage the household," the housekeeper replied quickly. She extended her hand suddenly. "Mrs. Kettler."

Isabelle took her hand gratefully. "I really appreciate this."

"The villagers can be cruel to newcomers," Mrs. Kettler said. She began leading Isabelle back down the hallway. "Can you start tomorrow?"

"Yes, of course. Am I to work all day?"

"I think mornings should be sufficient, don't you?"

"That's fine."

"Good. We'll see you tomorrow morning at eight o'clock. Do you need a ride home? I'm afraid the storm's still going strong."

"I'm not afraid of a little rain." Isabelle picked up her umbrella. "Goodbye Mrs. Kettler. And thank you."

~

Maple House smelled of pot roast and baked potatoes by the time Dr. Richter came home. The rain had dissipated completely by then, leaving behind a clear night with a lonely wind biting at the windows. But father and daughter were as cozy as could be after dinner, sitting with a cup of tea next to a roaring fire. Isabelle's father had talked about his work all through dinner, but now it was her turn.

"I have some news," she said as she stared into the dancing flames of the fire. "I got a job today."

"That's wonderful! I knew if anyone could win over these stubborn villagers, it'd be you. Where are you working?"

"Have you seen the great estate on the cliff?" Isabelle asked.

Dr. Richter paused with his teacup in midair. "The Prince estate?"

"Yes, that's the one. Apparently, they've got a great library that needs to be put in order," Isabelle said.

"Well, of course it's lovely you've found a job," Dr. Richter said. "How did you find the master?"

Isabelle hesitated and then smiled knowingly. "What have you heard?"

"I know he's a recluse, and people become angry when his name is mentioned, but they don't say much."

"To be fair, I only spoke with him for about three minutes."

Dr. Richter raised his eyebrows.

"I'm afraid he was quite rude and angry. I don't think he interacts with people very much."

"Do you think it wise to work for him?" Dr. Richter asked gently.

"I think it's worth a try. The villagers sent me up there expecting me to come back with my tail between my legs. Perhaps there's some value in showing them I'm tougher than I look."

Dr. Richter studied his daughter's face thoughtfully. "You have nothing to prove on that account."

"People always think I'm a pushover at first."

"They'll know different soon enough." His eyes were growing moist. He took her hand. "You're stronger than the lot of them put together."

She squeezed his hand and swallowed the lump in her throat.

"There is no need for you to work in an environment you're not comfortable with," he continued. "You've been through enough."

"Papà, when you received this job, I was happy to move here with you, because I knew what an incredible opportunity it was for you. But I want to use my degree, and until someone builds a library in this village, working at the Prince estate is my best chance. Let me at least give it a try."

Dr. Richter kissed her on the forehead as he rose to go to bed. "I hope it exceeds your expectations in every way."

~

Isabelle's walk to the Prince estate the next morning was entirely different. The presence of the sun utterly transformed the landscape. No longer a slate gray, the sea sparkled like a liquid sapphire. Every blade of grass, freshly scrubbed the day before, seemed to radiate life. Lazy clouds drifted overhead, spilling velvet shadows on the brilliant landscape below, and a soft breeze brought a gentle reminder of the last days of winter.

Isabelle was sorely tempted to skip part way up the path, but she knew there were eyes in the village watching her even now. Her own reputation mattered little, but her actions also reflected on her father.

The little robot Cog met her at the door again, but this time he was accompanied by Mrs. Kettler. The housekeeper seemed a bit flustered today. She was wearing an apron dusted in flour. Several unruly wisps of hair had broken free from her tidy bun and there were traces of flour on her chin, blouse, and hands. But she seemed cheerful enough.

"Thank heavens the sun has come out," Mrs. Kettler said as she showed Isabelle to the library. "One can only stomach so much gloomy weather. Between you and me, it doesn't help the Master any. He pulls all the curtains and sulks in the dark like a bear in hibernation."

Isabelle smiled at the woman's affectionate description.

"Sometimes, when the sun is shining, I can get away with opening the windows and it does him a world of good, though he'd never admit it."

Mrs. Kettler swung open two heavy wooden doors and led Isabelle into the library. It was so dark that at first they couldn't see anything. The housekeeper flipped the switch for the lights, but nothing happened. She made a noise of disapproval with her tongue.

"It's been so long since anyone's been in here, the lightbulbs must have blown. I'll see that Luis replaces them by tomorrow." Mrs. Kettler navigated across the floor and pulled the drawstring just beside the vaulted windows. Both curtains slid into motion at once, letting in a flood of sunlight and sending the dust motes swirling.

"Luis?" Isabelle asked as she surveyed the grand room absentmindedly.

"Our footman, of sorts." Mrs. Kettler returned to her side. "I suppose you might call him a handyman. Now, do you need anything else, dear? I really ought to get back to the kitchen."

"No. Thank you! I have what I need."

After another smile, Mrs. Kettler bustled away, leaving Isabelle to thoroughly examine the library in peace.

Great empty shelves stretched from the floor to the vaulted ceiling, twenty feet overhead, broken up by an elegant catwalk that ran the length of the wall in between the two sets of floor-to-ceiling windows at either end. Behind her and to her left an ornate carpet had been stretched before a great fireplace, furnished with a settee and two comfortable sofas. The rest of the floor was completely covered in unopened boxes.

Only the far right wall had been partially shelved, and a quick inspection of the occupants proved them to be old textbooks and outdated scientific journals. Isabelle felt a sudden twinge of alarm and threatening disappointment. Was that all these boxes were filled with? Stodgy academic work? She pried open the lid on one of the boxes. The friendly faces of Dickens, Melville, and Tolstoy sent a familiar thrill down her spine.

"Right then." She turned to Cog, who blinked his large turquoise eyes at her in eager anticipation. "We need to see what we're working with. You are a very fetching robot, but they don't keep you around just for your looks, do they?"

Cog shook his head.

"Do you have a Bluetooth connection in that little head of yours?"

The robot nodded.

Isabelle pulled a tablet out of her satchel and held it out to him. He took it reverently, then virtually connected the device to his CPU with a series of nimble keystrokes. He handed it back to Isabelle and swung his arms gleefully.

Isabelle smiled at him. "Shall we begin the inventory?"

Cog scurried to the farthest box, deftly broke the seal, and began scanning barcodes. Isabelle organized the information as it came in.

For being so small, Cog was remarkably fast. The new books were the easiest, but the pair soon found that this library collection boasted books from every century, in multiple languages, and in varying conditions. The older ones did not have barcodes and some didn't have a cover at all.

By eleven, they had made a thorough mess of the room, but Isabelle had begun to form a solid plan for documentation, categorization, restoration, and further research. Then a message came through from Cog, calling for her evaluation on an entire box. She waded carefully through boxes and piles of books to investigate.

The first thing that caught her eye was a diploma awarded to Sebastian Prince for a PhD in Neuro-Technology. She frowned in surprised confusion before continuing her investigation. Besides the diploma there were also two dissertations in Sebastian's name, an assortment of papers, and an external hard drive.

She pulled them out and set them on a side table, making a mental note to ask Mrs. Kettler about them. But when Isabelle packed up to go, the housekeeper was nowhere to be found.

Isabelle looked down at the stack in her hands and then at Cog. "I don't suppose Mr. Prince has an office?"

Cog wiggled excitedly and took off down the hall. Isabelle followed with a smile. By the time she caught up to him, the door was open for her. What she found when she stepped inside wasn't an office but a laboratory.

Cables hung from the ceiling, giving power to the clusters of equipment that dotted the room like mechanical bushes. In the far left corner she spotted a reclining chair surrounded by monitors. Right beside it sat the closest thing to a desk. It was a workbench covered by an assortment of papers and tablets.

"Excuse me, Mr. Prince?" There was no reply. Isabelle crossed the room and laid her finds on the workbench. Her eyes caught sight of the top of a piece of paper. She picked it up curiously. It appeared to be a contract, dated three years ago. Her eyes skimmed over thick blocks of text that she couldn't understand and landed on a formidable seal at the bottom: Department of Defense.

"Who let you in here?" a powerful voice spoke from just behind her, making her jump.

"I'm sorry, I didn't mean to intrude. I found something in the library—"

Sebastian spotted the paper in her hand and snatched it from her. Isabelle, feeling a bit guilty, struggled to find words. Rage began to kindle in his face when he recognized what she had been holding. The veins in his neck began to bulge again and his hands trembled.

"You have no business reading this." The words came out forcefully, as if he could barely breathe.

Her cheeks turned scarlet. "I'm sure you're right. Please forgive me."

"Forgive you?" he scoffed. His disdain gave her courage.

"My father always said I was too curious for my own good. I didn't mean any harm."

"Who's your father?" he asked sharply.

Her heart faltered for a moment, warning her somehow that he wouldn't like the answer. "Dr. Maurice Richter."

His hand clenched suddenly, crushing the paper in his hand. "You've come to spy on me," he hissed. His chest rose and fell rapidly and his eyes were glazing over.

"No," Isabelle said gently, confused by his anger.

"You've come to sabotage my work—to make me a laughing stock!" He stepped toward her threateningly, his eyes wild and bloodshot.

She took a step backwards and lifted her hands, but her voice remained calm and low. "Mr. Prince, it was wrong for me to enter your lab without permission, and I had no business touching your papers." She gestured decidedly toward the workbench, knowing it would help separate her from the source of his anger. "But I assure you that I meant no harm."

Sebastian looked like he was about to explode. She drew a line in her mind: if he took one more step toward her, she would run. Instead, he reached for the nearest shelving unit and gave it a forceful shove, sending the equipment hurtling to the floor in a cacophony of shrieking metal and splintering glass.

Isabelle stood her ground. It was not lost on her that he had deliberately chosen to take his anger out on an inanimate object instead of her. He may not look in control of his anger, but he was making choices, just as he had the first day she had met him.

"Can you tell me what is making you so angry?" she asked, fighting back tears. "I want to make this right, but I can't read your mind."

He did not seem to hear her. He turned away with a desperate destructive energy that Isabelle had seen once before: throwing monitors, ripping cables free, and shoving scaffolds to the floor.

Isabelle was not afraid anymore. Compassion stirred in her heart for this man who was clearly a victim of his own emotions. By the time his rampage had ended, his shoulders were shaking with emotion and his hands and forearms were cut and bruised. He seemed surprised to find that Isabelle was still there.

"Have you had your share of amusement?" he asked bitterly.

"Why would you think I'd find this amusing?" Isabelle thought her heart might break.

"Why else did you come here?"

"I was looking for work. The villagers sent me up here. I'm pretty sure they expected you to scare me off."

"They think I'm a wild animal," he said.

"I'm sure nobody thinks that."

"No, they do." His voice trembled. "I've heard them say it."

She cleared her throat. "Well, they don't have very nice things to say about me, either. I don't suppose you have a first aid kit around here?"

He gestured to the wall. She crossed the room, opened it, and began pulling out an assortment of items. When she returned, he looked hesitant.

"I can clean myself up." A hint of hardness returned to his eyes.

"I'm sure you can comb your hair, too, but it's clearly not on your list of priorities. Now sit down. If I don't do it, I imagine it will fall to Mrs. Kettler, and she has enough to worry about. Unless you've taught Cog how to administer first aid." Isabelle took a seat on the floor.

At the mention of his name, Cog emerged from the far end of the room and came to stand beside Isabelle, one of his little hands resting on her shoulder. Sebastian conceded and sat across from them. Isabelle donned her gloves and looked at him expectantly. He held out his arm.

"I suppose that explains how you got into the lab." His voice was thick, gravelly, and tired. His eyes were on Cog.

Isabelle touched an alcohol swab to his arm. He tensed up, but didn't withdraw. "I really should stop following him," she said. "He keeps taking me places I'm not supposed to be."

The corner of Sebastian's mouth turned up. "He seems to have developed a liking for you."

"Isn't that how you programmed him? To be generally adorable?" She spread a bandage over a network of small lacerations.

"He has a personality matrix, yes. But his imprinting programming was experimental. He doesn't attach himself to many people." Sebastian's eyes were fixated on her face.

Isabelle felt heat creeping up her neck. "Well, then. I shall consider myself privileged."

Mrs. Kettler stepped through the door. "Oh dear. Not a good day, then, Mr. Prince?"

Sebastian stood quickly.

"Shall I begin ordering new equipment?" the housekeeper asked.

"Get it here quickly. I don't care what it costs." His voice had become tight again.

Mrs. Kettler appeared surprised when her eyes fell on Isabelle. "Miss Richter, I did not know you were still here."

"Just heading out now." Isabelle scrambled to her feet. "I will see you tomorrow morning."

Sebastian kept his eyes averted as she left the lab.

The spring day was at its full glory as Isabelle walked home, but this time it failed to draw a smile from her. Her brows were drawn and her eyes limited themselves to the path in front of her feet as her mind replayed the scenes from the morning.

As she approached the village, her reverie was broken by the chatter of friendly voices. She took a deep breath and returned to the present, trying to remember if she had tomatoes to use for dinner.

"Good afternoon, there!" an old man called.

Isabelle smiled. "Afternoon!"

"You lost me a ten-er."

"I beg your pardon?"

"I bet me neighbor the beast would chew ya up and spit ya out!" The man laughed.

Isabelle crossed her arms. "That's a strange way to talk about one of your foremost families."

"Is that what our Grocer told you?" The man chuckled again. "He was just trying to pull one over on you."

"Why do the people in this village seem to take great amusement in being cruel?" Her temper was growing short.

"I suppose it was a little unjust to send you up there with no warning," the man admitted.

"Sebastian Prince is not a monster," Isabelle said firmly. A fire had lit in her and the heat was creeping up her face.

"You know that for sure, do ya? After being here a few days? There's something sure not right with him."

"Should that not evoke compassion instead of disdain?" It took a great deal to keep from yelling.

"Oh, you won't find compassion for that man in this village."

"Why not?"

"I don't pretend to understand what draws these scientists to come here, something to do with magnets."

"Magnetic anomalies," Isabelle corrected automatically. She had heard her father speak about it often enough.

"Well, we didn't ask for it," the man said petulantly. "When he came five years ago, he was like all the others: promising that his scientific advancements would be good for the village, but all they brought was harm."

"What harm?"

"It ain't right to mess with the mind."

"Surely, he didn't experiment on the villagers." She held her breath for a moment.

"Not with our permission. But people started having strange dreams. And then one day Mrs. Lewis' boy didn't wake up. He slept for two days straight then started screaming bloody murder, but still he wouldn't wake up. He died two weeks later!"

Isabelle's anger dissipated slightly and her voice dropped. "That's terrible. But why would you think Mr. Prince had anything to do with it?"

"Cause he owned up to it! He came down when he heard the boy was in a coma and he told the mother that he was gonna make it right. But nothing was made right! That's when they say he lost his mind. Most folk say it was justice long overdue."

Isabelle's eyes wandered up the hill. "If that's justice," she whispered, "I don't particularly like it."

"Well, that sentence don't come from no earthly judge. Excuse me, the missus is calling." The man scurried back to his house, leaving Isabelle to her thoughts. She hardly saw the cobblestones beneath her feet as she walked the rest of the way to her house. Her mind was tossing like a stormy sea.

~

She did not find tomatoes at home, but she made do without them, dreading a trip to the Grocer's. Her mind was heavy as she set the house in order and washed the laundry. She put together a simple casserole and popped it into the oven, then sat down with a book to wait for her father. There was no wind or rain that night, and the silence that descended on the cottage with the dark made her feel incredibly lonely.

She started when the doorknob turned, but was relieved to set about the final preparations for dinner. Dr. Richter noticed the care in his daughter's face, but he did not ask about it until after the meal was eaten, the dishes were washed, and he had exhausted conversation on his own work.

"How was your day with the mysterious Sebastian Prince?" he asked.

"Not what I expected," she said, weighing her words carefully. "He has a doctorate in Neuro-Technology."

Dr. Richter's eyebrows shot up in surprise. "Well, that explains why the villagers don't like him. But why is he anathema to the scientific community?"

"I'm not sure I have all the details, but it sounded like he took responsibility for a tragic death in the village."

Dr. Richter exhaled deeply in understanding. "Thus, he became the pariah of both communities."

"It's a bit more than I reckoned for in a day job," she admitted, struggling to keep the emotion out of her voice. She told herself angrily that she had no reason to cry.

Her father was casually swinging his reading glasses between his fingers, but his sharp eyes were on her face. "You plan to continue, then?"

Isabelle did not look at him. Even so, it took her a moment before she could get the words out. "I think I would regret it later if I backed out now. Mr. Prince's struggles really have little to do with the job Mrs. Kettler hired me for."

Her father's silence told her he was unconvinced. Despite her best efforts, a tear slipped down her face. She tried to hide it before he could see, but it was too late. He knelt by her chair and tilted her chin up until her eyes met his.

"There's no need for you to feel unsafe."

"I don't feel unsafe. Maybe I'm a fool, but I don't think he would hurt me."

"I have never thought you a fool," he said. "But I have heard enough to know that being there is bound to bring up painful memories for you."

She wiped away another tear. "I want to help him. The villagers talk about him like he's an animal, and I'm sure that's how they've treated him. They don't understand how much pain he's in. I don't understand it either, but I see it. And I'm in a better position than most people to handle it."

"Isabelle, if this is about you feeling guilty—"

"This is about me turning those years into something good," she said meaningfully. "I think it's what Mother would have wanted."

Pain flickered across his face. "I so wanted us to make a fresh start here."

"We will." She smiled at him reassuringly, wiping her watery eyes. "We are going to build a good life here. This is something that I need to do."

~

A northern wind picked up that night, driving in a fine rain. The morning in Maple House did not begin smoothly. Isabelle dropped her father's favorite mug and then burnt her hand pulling scones from the oven. She left the house a few minutes later than she had intended and attempted to make up for it with a quicker pace.

The soggy earth squelched beneath her rain boots as she marched up the lonely path to the great house on the cliff. Her brave words to her father the night before seemed a bit hollow this morning as she considered facing another emotional tempest today. It must be the gloomy weather that had her thinking this way.

She was rather glad when Cog was the only one to meet her at the door. They made their way to the library together and Isabelle's heart was soothed by the familiar routine of the work.

The storm outside grew worse, sending rain pelting against the large, paned windows, but all was peaceful within. The only other sounds besides the driving rain were the opening and closing of books, the rustling of pages, and the pitter patter of Cog's little feet as he scurried about. Today they were to start shelving, and she was eager to see the end result. Cog had already begun on the lower levels. After testing the reliability of the dusty old ladder, Isabelle began working on the higher shelves.

Around mid-morning, she heard the door open and carefully descended the ladder, fully expecting to meet with Mrs. Kettler. But the master of the house himself appeared, balancing a tea tray precariously in his hands. Noticing his bloodshot eyes and how uncomfortable he looked with it, she helped guide it to the coffee table in front of the fireplace.

"Mrs. Kettler thought you might like a cup of tea...and I thought it might be a good opportunity to apologize." He swallowed.

It was strange to see him so unsure of himself.

"How do you like your tea?" she asked.

He hesitated.

"You're not going to make me take my tea alone, are you?" There was a slight reproach in her voice.

"I wasn't sure you'd want me for company," he said.

"Well, we had better do something while we wait for you to apologize." Her eyes twinkled a bit mischievously.

"Cream, no sugar," he replied, taking a seat.

She busied herself with the tea service, occasionally stealing glances at the subdued face of her companion. "I'm naturally curious, Mr. Prince, but I know how to restrain myself if I'm given limits. I think it would be worthwhile for both of us if I were to learn yours."

"Call me Sebastian. I don't deserve any other title. And as for my limits," he smiled ruefully, "I don't even know those." Pain contorted his face and his teacup began to rattle so forcefully that he had to set it on the table. He put his head in his hands and breathed heavily. "I'm sorry."

"What are you apologizing for?" She asked.

"For not even being able to have a decent conversation," he gasped. Frustration was creeping into his voice and body language.

"Keep breathing and let it pass." Isabelle held her teacup steady. "There's no hurry on a stormy day like this."

He did not lift his face from his hands, but after a few moments, his shoulders stopped heaving.

Isabelle sipped her tea calmly. "Have you ever tried to train Cog to carry tea for you? He's just about the perfect height for a walking tea table. I imagine it'd be awfully useful at parties, too."

"How do you do that?" he asked in a husky voice.

"Do what?" she asked.

"Take whatever is thrown at you and reflect something better?"

She set her teacup in her lap and stared at it for a long moment, wrestling with the sudden anxious fluttering in her chest.

"My mother was in a car accident when I was sixteen. She was thrown from the vehicle, and though she didn't die, she suffered a traumatic brain injury." Isabelle took a moment to breathe. "She became a different person—forgetful, stubborn, irritable. Not just irritable," she corrected. "Enraged. I used to think it was my fault."

Isabelle pursed her lips and struggled to continue. "All I wanted was my mother back. I resented her and I felt so guilty for it." She looked up at Sebastian with wet eyes. For the first time since she had met him, his seemed completely clear.

"My father and I did everything we could to learn more about her condition, how to read her moods and calm her down when she was upset."

"What happened?" he asked.

"She died, three years ago. There was a blood clot in her brain."

"I'm sorry," he said.

"I've always wondered, if she had had more time, if she would have eventually come back to us," she said.

"You still had hope for her after all of that?"

"I did," she said. "I think the human brain has a remarkable ability to heal when it's given the right care."

He was staring at the teapot.

Isabelle took a deep breath and gently changed the subject. "Sebastian, I heard about what happened a few years ago with the boy in the village. But what you're struggling with is more than just guilt. Has anyone ever asked what happened to you?"

The flames rekindled behind his eyes. He stood to his feet and spoke through clenched teeth. "It doesn't matter what happened to me."

"It does to me," she protested. "I understand better than you know, and I want to help."

She watched him struggle with himself for a few long moments and was afraid he might leave the room. For once, his rational side seemed to win out.

"I was working on a project for the Department of Defense." He stood facing the window, his back half-turned to her.

"They were interested in my research involving the amygdala and the brain's connection to technology. They wanted me to explore the possibilities of weaponization—neural warfare. Weapons that could cripple the enemy's mind."

He paused. "You have to understand, I was using their funding to advance medical technology and turn the clock back on cognitive disease. My projects for the DOD was just a fraction of my work, and I never thought..."

Isabelle stood beside him, placing a hand on his shoulder. He tensed at first, but then relaxed.

"I was experimenting with shared dreaming through specific frequencies. I was tired. That night there was a surge in this region's electromagnetic energy and I didn't catch it. It amplified the frequency field and caught the outermost house in the village."

Sebastian spoke a bit more easily now that he'd reached the technical part, as if he had just crested a hill. "It wasn't ready for human testing yet. His brain waves were restricted from their natural cycles. He was caught in the shared dream space, with figments of his own imagination. After dreaming constantly for two days, his cortisol levels rose and flooded his amygdala. In the end, his brain just couldn't take the strain."

He stepped away from her touch and began pacing, clenching and unclenching his hands. "Perhaps it wasn't a good idea to have this conversation." He tried to laugh, but it came out as more of a strangled cry.

Outside the window, lightning flashed over the ocean, soon followed by a rippling crack of thunder.

Isabelle took a deep breath to steady herself. "You went in after him, didn't you?"

Sebastian picked up a book and began thumping it against the wall as he walked.

"I'd rather you didn't damage the books," she said as casually as she could.

"I have to do something," he snapped. His face was completely red now, his movements becoming desperate. "I can't...there's too much...and it's going to come out some way or another!"

He dropped the book and turned to the wall, but she read his intentions and intercepted him before he could throw his first punch.

"No, no, no!" she cried, taking his hands. "You're liable to break a bone or damage my library walls that way. I don't do woodwork, and I don't much like cleaning up blood."

He was gasping for air, every muscle in his body trembling with adrenaline. "I'm not sure you should touch me. I don't want to hurt you," he panted.

Isabelle drew one of his hands to her chest so he could feel her even breathing and placed her other hand on the side of his face. "You're not going to hurt me. Deep breaths. Close your eyes and listen to the sound of the rain. There we go. Just breathe in and out. In a second here, we can have another cup of tea and watch the waves roll in."

Sebastian's breathing calmed significantly and she knew he was past the crisis moment. He pulled away from her and crossed to stand in front of one of the tall windows. She watched his breathing return to normal and the muscles in his shoulders relax, then came and stood beside him.

"There's nothing to be ashamed of."

"I'm a grown man," he hissed angrily, "but I'm trapped in my own mind and body."

"Sebastian, your brain has been wounded. You just need a little more help."

"A little more help?" he spat the words out. "It's been three years. Three years of feeling out of control, like a wild animal."

"The brain has a remarkable ability to heal," she repeated.

"Then wouldn't it have done it by now?" he asked. "Did your mother's brain heal?"

Isabelle put a hand to her mouth.

"I'm sorry, I shouldn't have said that." He hurried out of the room, closing the door forcefully behind him.

~

Isabelle headed home early that day, leaving a note with Cog for Mrs. Kettler. She stumbled down the hill and through the village, fighting back tears with every step. They broke free as soon as she closed the door behind her.

She curled up on the couch with a thick blanket and allowed herself a good cry, fully intending to set the house in order afterwards. Sleep claimed her first, and it didn't release her until the light was beginning to fade. She woke to the high-pitched shriek of an angry wind and the electronic sound of her phone vibrating.

It was a text message from her father. He would not be home tonight. It seemed to confirm to her that the day was irredeemable. She wearily made herself ready for bed with the hope that tomorrow would be better. But it was a fitful sleep with little rest, and it ended abruptly in another vibration from her phone. But it wasn't her father calling, as she had expected. She frowned as she answered the phone.

"Hello?"

"Isabelle? It's Dr. Glass. I think you'd better come down to the lab."

~

Isabelle flew out the door with wild hair and her coat on backwards. The village was enshrouded in an icy cloud, preventing her from seeing anything beyond three feet. The half-frozen drops of water pricked at her face and neck like tiny swords. Her boots pounded on the cobbled streets with dull, lifeless thuds. The village seemed uncharacteristically quiet, but Isabelle was glad of it. She didn't want to be seen.

The lab rose up cold and forbidding in front of her, like a ghost out of the fog. Isabelle's cold fingers fumbled on the handle, but it opened from the inside and a kindly old man who must be Dr. Glass took Isabelle's arm. He held her still for a moment and looked intently in her eyes.

"What's happened?" she asked breathlessly. "Was there an accident?"

"I'm afraid this may be difficult to explain...but he won't wake up."

A pit settled in Isabelle's stomach. "Let me see him. Now, please."

He led her down a hall into a small room, where she found her father stretched out on a cot. His skin was pale and his breathing shallow, but other than that he appeared to be simply sleeping. She stroked the side of his face gently. "Papà?"

There was no response. She shook him gently, knowing how foolish she must look to Dr.

Glass. He handed her a cup of water, as if understanding that she needed to see for herself. She poured it on her father's face, hoping desperately to see him suck in a startled breath and glare at her. He did not move.

"I have tried multiple stimuli," Dr. Glass said. "Nothing works. I know this may seem very strange to you, but I have seen this before—"

Isabelle stood suddenly and faced him. "You will watch over him?"

"Where are you going?" Dr. Glass asked in surprise.

She left him without an answer and re-emerged into the gray morning with fiery resolve. The Prince estate was only about a quarter-mile from the lab, and Isabelle's feet nearly kept pace with her pounding heart.

Fear, frustration, anger, and sorrow ebbed and flowed like a fickle storm within her. As she neared her destination, a surprising sound met her ears: angry voices. Up here on the cliff, the relentless sea breeze had cleared the fog a little and Isabelle spotted a crowd gathered at the foot of the great stairs. It almost looked like the whole village had turned out, and more were coming up the path. Many of them held torches, and their eyes were fixed on two men pounding on the front door of the mansion.

"What's happened?" Isabelle slipped into the crowd.

"That monster's up to his old tricks! Preying on the innocent!" a woman answered.

"This time, there's three that won't wake up!" someone else added.

"This time he's not going to get away with it!"

Isabelle's stomach clenched and she pushed her way through the crowd and up the steps.

A man stepped in front of her. "Where do you think you're going?"

"Please, I've been working at the Prince estate the last few days. Let me find out what's going on."

"We know well enough what's going on." A man came up beside them, holding a rifle. "Let's end this now."

"Are you going to shoot someone?" Isabelle asked in disgust.

"If that's what it takes."

"Is that what passes for justice around here?" She turned to address the whole crowd. "You all take pride in hard work and tradition, and I respect that. But there is no honor in confronting an unarmed man like this. My father won't wake up either. And although Dr. Prince may be responsible, he also may be the only one who can help. Please, let me go in and speak to him!"

"He hates us! What makes you think you can change his mind?"

"Give me fifteen minutes. It can't do any harm."

The crowd appeared hesitant, but the man who had been holding Isabelle back escorted her up the rest of the stairs.

"Fifteen minutes," he said gruffly. "Then we'll do what needs doing."

Isabelle swallowed, then pounded on the door with trembling hands. "Mrs. Kettler, please let me in! It's Isabelle!" She hoped she didn't sound as desperate as she felt.

The door cracked open, and Isabelle slipped through as fast as she could before slamming it shut behind her and bolting it. The pressure in her heart eased up a bit until she saw the faithful housekeeper's face. Mrs. Kettler appeared to have aged ten years. Her chin was set firmly, but there was fear in her eyes.

"You shouldn't have come," she said to Isabelle. "They're liable to kill you along with the rest of us."

"Where's Dr. Prince?"

"He can't give them what they want."

"Please let me speak with him."

"He can't speak with anyone," Mrs. Kettler said wearily. "He's hooked up to that cursed machine again, and I fear this time it'll kill him."

"He's in the shared dream space?" Isabelle asked.

"He did not tell you everything." Mrs. Kettler beckoned for Isabelle to walk beside her. "He told you he went in to try and save that boy?"

"Yes."

"Did he tell you how he woke up?"

Isabelle hesitated. Why had she never thought of that before?

"The concept of the shared dream space had been around for years, but nobody could get it to work. It was Master Prince who postulated that it needed to source from a human amygdala, not just a machine. He was not approved to use test subjects, so he tested it on himself."

"Is that when the boy got pulled in?" Isabelle asked.

"Yes, but you are not listening to me. His brain is linked to that machine. The nightmares and terrors in that dream space are his, and they grow every day in strength. The machine is attached to his mind. He cannot be free of it, not even while he is awake."

"Why did he not just destroy it?"

"We feared the damage it would do. And he has somehow maintained hope that he could make things right."

"But what happened today?"

"He went back in sometime in the night. I found him several hours ago. But this time I cannot wake him."

They had arrived at the lab. Sebastian was lying in the reclining chair that Isabelle had spotted two days before. The monitors around him were singing a cacophonous chorus of bad news: brain waves erratic, pulse too high, blood pressure too high, cortisol levels rising. Even his skin looked unnaturally grey.

Isabelle swallowed. How much time had passed since she'd entered the house?

A small hand touched her leg. Cog looked up at her with those large turquoise eyes. She stooped down in front of him.

"Cog, have you been helping Dr. Prince with this machine?"

Cog nodded.

"How do we shut it down once and for all?"

Cog pattered over to a shelving unit, removed a tablet, and handed it to Isabelle. He pointed to his antenna as words appeared on the screen: *Dr. Prince must shut it down from inside.*

"Can I help him?"

Cog nodded. One of his tiny metallic hands touched her face and then a scanner activated in his eyes. A second later a brain scan appeared on the tablet. Cog pointed to it eagerly.

Isabelle looked at him in amazement. "Is this why you let me in that day?"

Cog nodded again.

Isabelle stood suddenly and addressed Mrs. Kettler. "Can you get out the back without them seeing you?"

"Do you expect me to leave you and Master Prince?"

"There's no point in you staying." Isabelle put a hand on the housekeeper's arm. "Please get somewhere safe. Maybe you can do some good outside."

Fighting back tears, Mrs. Kettler embraced Isabelle roughly and then retreated out the door. Cog sealed the lab behind her and returned to Isabelle's side.

"Tell me what to do, Cog."

Cog pressed a series of buttons, and a low bench slid out from the wall. Discarding her jacket, Isabelle rolled up her sleeve and held it out for Cog who applied an IV and hooked her up to the rest of the medical monitors. She laid back and took deep breaths.

Cog inserted something into her IV and the two metal wires attached to her temples began to vibrate. She felt a sudden shock and then the scene around her changed.

~

She was standing in a dark cavern. A faint light source glinted off damp walls. The sound of dripping water echoed eerily, changing octaves unexpectedly like the notes of a ghostly tune. The tiny feet of invisible insects skittered through the sand and up the cavern walls. Isabelle tried to steady her heartbeat. She couldn't shake the feeling that, whichever direction she moved, she'd run into a web containing a giant spider. And yet, she had not entered this dream space to do nothing. She had to move.

She forced herself forward, shuffling her feet one step at a time. The ground began to slope. Isabelle reached for the left wall instinctively. Her fingers met with a gooey substance. She gasped, but did not withdraw her hand. She pressed forward foot by foot, reminding herself that none of this was real. Then the ground dropped out from beneath her, and she plummeted into a cesspool of putrid liquid.

Something brushed her leg in the water, and she surfaced with a strangled cry, reaching out desperately for any way out of the water. A distant shriek echoed about the cavern. Isabelle's groping fingers found a rock ledge just as something wrapped around her left leg.

She heaved herself up, kicking furiously and trying not to wretch. Her leg came free, and she scrambled farther up the bank before allowing herself to collapse in a trembling heap. The water continued to slosh and churn behind her. She needed to get out of this cave and find Sebastian.

Her heart was pounding so hard it hurt. Every muscle in her body was trembling with adrenaline, and she could taste bile at the back of her mouth, but now she was angry. She got to her feet and forced herself forward, stumbling over gaping shadows, through spider webs, and past chambers with bone-chilling sounds coming out of them. None of it would deter her. After what seemed like an eternity, she burst out into the open night air and gasped in relief. The mouth of the cave grew larger behind her, as if trying to suck her back inside. She stumbled forward into the woods.

The forest would hold its own dangers, but Isabelle allowed a false sense of relief to wash over her. Her body needed a break. She pressed forward blindly for a few minutes, breathing slowly and not dwelling on the shadows around her. But seeking out safety was not her priority. She had to find Sebastian. How was she supposed to do that in this wild place? Her eyes caught sight of a series of ghostly spires rising above the forest. A fearsome red light pulsed from one of the highest rooms, and Isabelle knew immediately that this was her destination.

Almost as soon as she altered her course, she heard the first wild howl. She pressed forward, scrambling over fallen logs that teemed with hissing insects. Large sets of orange eyes glared at her from the underbrush. Her hands were covered with dirt and moss. The wolf cries seemed to be getting closer.

Large white flakes began to drift down from the canopy of trees, and within a few minutes, a steady snow had begun to fall. She started to slip more frequently, catching herself on raw palms which had turned red from cold. She was nearly to the outer wall of the castle when she heard the sound of padded steps in the undergrowth around her. She caught sight of shadows darting on her left and right, sometimes high in the trees.

She came up against a tangle of thorns and briars too thick for her to pass through and turned to her right. A dark shadow hunched ten feet away from her, dark as night with gleaming yellow eyes, and a square jaw the size of her head. Its shoulders twitched as if preparing to pounce.

Isabelle turned and fled, knowing it was hopeless. That monster would be upon her in seconds, tearing her to pieces with its sharp teeth. Even now it seemed to have its claws in her heart, squeezing so tight she thought it would explode from the pressure. She caught sight of it in the tree to her right just before it pounced.

The giant panther knocked her to the ground and they both tumbled down a slight incline. Its breath on her face and the heat of its body seemed to be the very embrace of death itself. A claw sliced her left arm. She struggled to hold back its mighty head with her small hands.

Suddenly, the panther was ripped off her by a great and terrible force. She struggled to sit up, leaves and twigs pulling at her hair. Two large shadows wrestled in the darkness, yelping and growling as they tumbled back and forth.

Isabelle did not stay to watch. She scrambled away on her hands and knees, ignoring the thorns and rocks that tore at her skin. After about twenty feet she made it to her feet and resumed her headlong plunge into the foliage. Her chest ached and her heart burned with fear.

Something tried to surface in her mind—something she needed to remember. This wasn't real; it was a dream. She needed to find Sebastian. A great shadow, the size of a boulder leapt in front of her, then stretched to its full height, nearly twelve feet tall. The massive bear opened its maw and gave a roar that shook the ground, reducing Isabelle's heart to a puddle.

But something else, nearly as large leapt between her and the bear, releasing its own earth-shuddering howl. The bear took a step backwards. The creature in front of her stood its ground and howled again, its voice echoing across the treetops. The bear dropped on all fours and retreated slowly into the shadows.

Isabelle stood frozen in shock. The dark shadow turned towards her. "What are you doing here?"

She gasped when she recognized Sebastian's voice. He took a step closer to her and threw his cloak about her just as the moon pierced through the clouds, allowing her to see him for the first time.

He towered over her, at least eight feet tall, with arms and legs like tree branches. His eyes were familiar, but the rest of his face was warped and disfigured.

"You shouldn't be in here," he said.

"My father…" She couldn't seem to finish the sentence, but his eyes registered understanding. They filled with regret, and he turned away in shame.

"Sebastian," she said. "There are three this time, and the villagers are terrified. I'm afraid they'll do something rash; they may have already. We need to shut this thing down."

"Don't you think I've tried?" he growled. "The failsafe won't work."

"Show me," she said.

He did not move.

"I did not come in here to let my father die. Show me!"

He led her around the corner of the wall and through a massive gate. As they crossed the courtyard, a wolf chorus rose from the south and was met by an answering chorus from the north. A shiver ran down Isabelle's spine. Sebastian marched confidently up the stairs and through the main doorway. He snatched up a torch from the wall and proceeded down a series of corridors until they came to a set of stairs.

They wound up and up for several stories until they entered a small room. In the center, above a pedestal, stood the source of the red light that Isabelle had seen earlier. A very ordinary vase held a single red rose. Red light pulsed from the rose every two seconds. Isabelle looked at Sebastian in amazement.

"Roses were my mother's favorite flower," he said. "I put this one in as a failsafe emergency shut down. Only, I can never seem to touch it."

"How did you wake up last time?" She asked.

"Waking up's not the problem—not for me anyway. I can wake up when I want, but the dream space continues for all of those trapped in it. And somehow...it stays connected to my mind.

Sometimes I think I can hear the wolves howling when I am wide awake."

Isabelle approached the rose.

"Be careful," he said.

She reached a hand out gingerly, but an invisible barrier stopped her hand. She turned back to him. There was defeat in his eyes.

"I am so sorry, Isabelle. I never meant for this to happen."

"Of course, you didn't," she said.

"No, you don't understand. I shouldn't have gone back in. I knew what the risks were. I knew others could get trapped in here again."

"Then why did you come back in?" she asked.

"Because I want to live a normal life," he said. "It has been a long time since anyone has seen me the way that you do. And I would give anything for you to see me as the man I used to be."

Tears were forming in Isabelle's eyes.

"And now I've sentenced you and your father to die because of my own selfishness."

The wild howls grew closer and more numerous. A gust blew through the castle, carrying with it a rotten stench. Stories below them, scraping footsteps sounded on the staircase. A wild fear lit in Sebastian's eyes.

"There is one solution that I have not yet tried," he said. "If this dream scape is irrevocably linked to me, then if I cease to exist, it should dissolve."

Isabelle frowned at him. "What are you talking about?"

"I have never died in here." He strode to one of the windows and peered out.

Isabelle came up beside him and took his arm. "Don't be ridiculous. You are not going to kill yourself."

Far below them, the scraping steps grew closer.

"There are things in here far worse than wild animals," he whispered. "I will not let you die because of me. Perhaps this was meant to be all along."

She took hold of his collar firmly. "I have not given up. Whatever is coming, we will face it together."

"It will kill you. Don't do this to me," he pleaded. "Don't make me watch you die."

It struck her as odd that even in this formidable form he was so very vulnerable. He might look like a great big beast in here, but it did not keep him safe from his fears.

"Sebastian," she asked, "have you always taken this form in the dream scape?"

"Not at the beginning, when I was alone," he said. "But as soon as that boy got trapped here, everything became ten times worse and I had to adapt to protect him."

"Do you trust me?" she asked.

"There is nothing we can do," he said hopelessly.

"That is a lie. I know what we have to do. You have to trust me."

His frightened eyes studied her face as the sound of the scraping footsteps drew ever nearer. Then he nodded. "I trust you."

"I know you feel like this is all your fault and that you have to be this big, strong creature to make things right. But you can't hide from your fear, you have to face it. And you have to confront it out of a place of vulnerability."

He looked at her in confusion.

"Drop the mask. I think there is one thing you fear more than that creature coming up the stairs, and it is your own weakness and frailty. The Sebastian that I know is weak, but he is also enough. Stop trying to cover up your weakness. Embrace it."

As she spoke, he began to shrink back to his normal stature. The scars and deformities vanished until he stood before her as a man again. The footsteps on the stairs were growing very loud now, and Isabelle tried not to imagine what it could be that terrified this man so much. He did not turn toward it but approached the rose on the pedestal.

A wave of fear shot out from the rose, sending Isabelle into a trembling heap against the wall. But Sebastian stood strong. He approached the pedestal one foot at a time, fighting against a tide of powerful emotions. Just as Isabelle was certain that whatever horror was on the steps would emerge into the room, Sebastian's hand reached the rose and everything went black.

~

Nothing made sense as Isabelle regained consciousness. She was lying on something soft. There was a bright light overhead and the murmuring of soft voices. The white ceiling above her was such a sharp contrast to the darkness of the dream scape that she lay in shock for a few moments. She stirred under the clean sheets and a figure rushed to her side.

"Isabelle!"

Papà's strong arms encircled her and pulled her close. His whiskers tickled her cheek and she breathed in the scent of sweat and aftershave, a scent she had thought she would never smell again. He kissed her hair, and when she drew back, there were tears on his cheeks.

"Are you all right?" She took his face in her hands. "When did you wake up?"

"Hours ago. I've been so worried about you."

"What happened?" she asked.

"I don't know how you did it, but you managed to shut that thing off."

"Sebastian!" Isabelle gasped.

Her father's eyes flickered.

"Where's Sebastian? Is he all right?"

"The mob—" he stuttered, "when they did not hear from you after fifteen minutes…they stormed the house."

"What happened?"

"They tossed the furniture through the windows and set the place on fire. You must have stumbled out on your own. We found you unconscious on the grass. I'm afraid Dr. Prince didn't make it out."

"What do you mean?" She clutched the quilt in her fist and tried to keep her voice from trembling. "He's the one who got me out of the dream scape."

"They found his watch and other evidence that he died in the fire."

Isabelle pushed back the blue and white quilt, stood, and made her way to the window. They were very close to the beach, here in the village clinic. Fifty feet away, she could see the surf pounding up on the shore, as predictable as a metronome. Gulls called back and forth as they surfed the heavy wind gusts.

"Mrs. Kettler?" Isabelle asked.

"She's safe."

"Cog?"

"Who?" her father asked.

A great emptiness welled up inside her. "A little robot with the sweetest eyes you've ever seen," she whispered.

"You must mean this little guy," her father replied unexpectedly.

Isabelle whipped around just as her father stooped out the door and picked something up. He returned with Cog in his arms. Isabelle's tears flowed freely as she scooped him up.

"He wouldn't leave your side. He kicked me in the shin when the doctor ordered me to put him out," her father laughed.

"Can we go home now?" Isabelle asked quietly.

~

There wasn't a great deal of talk at Maple House over the next week. Dr. Richter took time off work. Isabelle nearly protested it the first night, not wanting him to worry about her, but all objections left the next day, and she never thought of it again.

They settled into a comfortable routine, taking a long tea in the morning, then reading in companionable silence by the fire. They often went out walking in the afternoons, between rain showers, and Isabelle found her soul soothed by the beauty of the coast. The first afternoon, she insisted on walking up to see the ruins of the Prince estate and say her farewells. Her father offered to come with her, but she insisted she go alone. Despite his fears for her, she returned with a new peace in her eyes.

Cog settled into their home with such efficiency that they soon couldn't remember how they had lived without him. He rose early with Dr. Richter to build the fires, and every night he would retire to his little basket in the living room with a blanket and a book. He would spread his little blanket out and then begin turning pages fastidiously, as he had seen Isabelle do countless times.

Whether or not he understood what he was reading was a subject of great amusement to Isabelle and Dr. Richter. And when Dr. Richter went back to work, it was with the assurance that Isabelle was not alone at home.

Life in the village went on much the same. Most of the villagers didn't want to remember what had happened, and so they acted as if it hadn't. But the one thing everyone seemed able to agree on was that Isabelle was a compassionate, gentle soul, and they began to treat her with kindness.

It was some weeks after the fire that Isabelle was taking tea with Marjorie Williams, a captain's wife.

"You wouldn't mind walking out to the docks with me, would ya dearie?" the woman asked. "Robert's not had anything to eat since before sunrise."

"Of course. What can I carry?"

They packed up their tea and set out for the docks. Marjorie chatted the whole way, and Isabelle, who had often found she did not have much to say these days, was content to listen.

The docks were bustling with friendly activity. A boat had foundered on the rocks two days ago in a nasty storm and now the other fishermen were lending a hand whenever they could to repair it. Marjorie pressed into the noisy throng in bold pursuit of her husband, and Isabelle climbed on a rock to watch, letting the salty breeze toy with her hair.

Her eyes took in the whole scene: the ghostly remains of the Prince estate up on the cliff side to her right, the graceful dance of the birds, the rhythm of the waves, and the frenzied but cheerful activity of the men in front of her. She had learned their names over the last couple of weeks and had even exchanged courteous words with most of them. But as Marjorie returned to her side, Isabelle's eyes fell on the figure of a man who seemed both foreign and familiar.

"Marjorie," Isabelle asked, "who is that man talking to your husband just now?"

"Oh, that's the new one, named Adam."

"He's new?"

"Aye. He came into town a few weeks ago. Not much experience, or conversation, but he's willing enough."

Just then, two of Marjorie's children came running up to show Isabelle the seashell necklaces they had made.

"Where's your brother?" Marjorie asked.

"Up on the rocks." The little girl pointed. "He said he was gonna get a gull's egg for Miss Isabelle."

"He knows he's not allowed up there!" Marjorie exclaimed.

"I'll fetch him," Isabelle offered. "Lucas, come down from there! It isn't safe!" Isabelle picked her way over the tide pools with care. The wind whipped her hair, and spray from the nearby breakers touched her lips.

"Miss Isabelle, I think I could be a bird today!" Lucas extended his arms and looked at the sky wistfully.

"Not today," Isabelle insisted from down below his perch. "You'll frighten your mother. Come have tea with me. I'll give you one of my scones."

The little boy began climbing down obediently, scaling down the rock face directly over the ocean.

"Why don't you come over this way?" Isabelle asked anxiously.

"This way's easier," Lucas insisted. "There's better handholds." But just then, his boots slipped and he plummeted into the surf. Isabelle heard a scream from the beach behind her and jumped in without a second thought.

The surf slammed them up against the rock face, but Isabelle managed to wrap her arms around Lucas and absorb the blow with her body. Salty water sloshed into her mouth and eyes. If they didn't get out of here fast they could get ripped to shreds by the rocks. Lucas wrapped his arms around her, his little body trembling. Isabelle said nothing but held him tight with one arm, trying to gauge the timing of the swells.

They were thrust up against the rocks again and she felt pain shoot through her knee. She shoved off the rocks and began swimming. Her soggy clothes weighed her down, and salt water stung her throat, but she would not give up yet.

They were slammed up against the rocks several more times but managed to stay free from the undertow. Isabelle had never swum so hard in her life. For several long minutes, she felt certain they were going to drown, but then they rounded the rock outcroppings of the tide pools into open sea.

A crowd had gathered on the shore and two men were wading furiously through the water towards them. Isabelle suddenly found solid ground beneath her feet and dug into it gratefully, holding Lucas tight in her arms. Her waterlogged sweater dragged down on her like an anchor. The water was about waist deep when the two men met them. Lucas' father pried the boy from her arms and began scolding him while checking for injury.

Isabelle waved the other man off and kept walking determinedly toward the shore. "I'm fine."

The man stuck close by her side as if he didn't believe her. And when Isabelle stumbled coming up on shore, he caught her arm and lowered her down to the sand.

Her eyes stung, and she began coughing up sea foam that she didn't even know she had swallowed. She vaguely heard him call for water, and her eyes finally settled on his face.

The beard was gone, but she would have recognized those eyes anywhere. The rush of the waves, the cries of the birds, and the hum of the bystanders all faded to the background as Isabelle took a long swig of cool, fresh water, and looked into those eyes she thought she'd never see again. There was something different about them now. They weren't filled with pain and fire, only quietness and peace. She put down the water flask and held out her hand.

"I don't believe we've met."

A genuine smile crossed his face. "I go by Adam."

"Thank you, Adam, for saving my life," she said meaningfully.

His eyes misted over. "Thank you for saving mine."

THE ELF AND THE COBBLER BROTHERS
BY M.R. DELUCA

Julius and Ward Cobbler were the sons of a well-to-do shoemaker known for his shoes and even better known for his kindness. The twin boys grew up without ever being denied anything their little hearts desired, and experienced little hardship in their lives. They took over the family business as adults without knowing a stitch about shoemaking; they mostly supervised the current workers and balanced the books.

When the boys were still young men, their mother passed away; their father passed soon after.

Upon their parents' death, Julius and Ward received the inheritances they were expecting: an equal partnership in the company and a not insignificant sum of money for each brother. After careful discussion with financial experts and tax professionals and each other, the brothers agreed the best course of action was to pool their resources and overhaul the company to make it even more viable; i.e., increase profit margins.

In truth the plan came from Ward, who took his role as the older twin (by two hours) seriously, and sought to use his resulting wisdom to steer the sometimes naïve Julius through life. Julius, for his part, eagerly accepted this guidance on a regular basis.

They renamed the shop "If the Space Boot Fits" and rented big, bright billboards all over town that screamed: *You'll be over the the moon for our new antigravity boots!* Their new target market would no longer be the average worker of family, but the jet-setting crowd clamoring for luxury goods to wear on intergalactic space vacations.

They fired all non-mechanical employees—eight local workers in all, though Julius gave them generous severance packages from his share of the inheritance—and reinvested in an expensive automaton called the AutoShoeTron. This technologically advanced machine could scan the foot of the prospective buyer and then construct any and all kinds of shoes, sizes, and styles, with just the push of a button.

They spared no expense when it came to purchasing the latest, greatest technology for their business. They were not their father, using simpler but relatively inefficient methods. The brothers were never luddites in any sense of the word. Their father had always used relatively modern machines, but only those that required a human at the helm. He had stayed away from the newest, trendiest, priciest androids that cut people out of the equation all together.

It was a decision probably based on sentimentality, not good business practice. That had to change. It was the future, and the Cobbler brothers were going to use whatever was available at their disposal to get ahead.

The new machines churned out antigravity boots—popular with space travelers who worried about flying off the atmosphere-less moon—faster than all their old workers did combined. Without worrying about payroll cutting into their profits or even making a single shoe, the brothers were reaping all the rewards without doing any substantial amount of work. Life was good.

It was after closing hours one day when Julius was placing more leather into the atom arranger box. Ward called from the back office, "You know what I was just thinking about, Jul?"

"About how you can finally afford your fancy vacation to Mars?"

"No. Well, yes. It's already booked for next spring. It's supposed to be a deep, beautiful red then, perfect for touring. What I meant was, I was just thinking about how Mama and Papa used to tell us about the elves."

Julius laughed heartily as he fed another strip of leather to the machine and pushed a button to make a women's size 8 antigravity boot. They never could keep enough of those in stock. Light emitted from the machine, which whirred with activity. "Those two could spin a yarn, I could tell you that. I just loved how Papa's face lit up when he told the story. He always looked so earnest, too, like he actually believed it."

"I know. Papa gave shoes to a man who needed them, and little elves secretly came in at night to make shoes from raw leather. Then Mama stitched little clothes, in that checkered pattern she always loved, for the elves who then blessed them with a lifetime of comfort and prosperity." He chuckled. "It makes me glad that we have the AutoShoeTron. I don't want little elves running around at night and wrecking the place."

The next day, during the hustle and bustle of customers squeezing in some shopping on their lunch breaks, an old, small, feeble man hobbled into the store. He looked sickly and poor, and wore ill-fitting, decrepit old clothes and an even more decrepit-looking scarf across the lower half of his face.

He stood off to the side, away from the merchandise and by the window, rubbing his bare hands together. Though it was not quite winter, it was still too chilly not to have gloves. The man was obviously cold, and did his best to cover his coughs.

"Can I help you, sir?" Ward asked, and not kindly.

"I will be leaving soon, sir. I just wanted to breathe warmer air. It is so cold out there, and my lungs are so weak." He pulled the holey knit hat further down on his head, almost until his gentle, weary eyes.

"I'm going to have to ask you to leave. Immediately. Security!" Ward called. Customers were already beginning to stare at the man, who they could tell did not belong. "Remove this man from the premises."

Two large robotic security guards lumbered over and each grabbed one of the man's frail arms.

"I don't think you should do that," said the man not in a threatening way, but a sad one. He shook his head and allowed the robot guards to lead him outside.

"The nerve of some people," Ward scoffed.

Julius emerged from the back office, saw the giant robots, and asked, "Why did you need security? Was there a fight?"

"See that guy walking away? He decided to come in and loiter. Maybe even planned on stealing something if I turned by back."

Julius was incredulous. The ailing older gentleman shuffling away? Ward was no pushover, but this seemed harsh, even for him. "You tossed an old man out on his ear?"

"Our footwear says clean, modern, upscale—not poorhouse. People who see through the window a ragged old man probably riddled with pneumonia will just keep on walking. It's good business sense. He's not exactly our ideal customer. He even admitted that he was just staying for the heat, that he wasn't going to buy anything."

"Oh. Okay, I guess."

"Don't sweat it, Jules. Just forget him and get back to work. You'll never have to think about him again."

That night, the store burglary alarm went off. The brothers were notified in their respective homes and went to the shop immediately.

Ward, who arrived before Julius, had just finished talking with the police.

"Sorry," Julius said to his brother, "my hover-car wouldn't start right way. What happened? What did the police find?"

Ward crossed his arms, frustrated. "Nothing."

"Nothing? What do you mean, nothing?"

"The alarm tripped for some reason, but the footage shows nothing. Which is weird—you know those high-tech cameras. Any microscopic beam of light, they'll pick it up and magnify it.

"And there's more.

"Since the footage showed nothing, the police used their electromagnetic scanners to detect if any radiation from a person or object was detected in the store in the past hour. If anyone or anything entered the store, they would know."

"And?"

"Nothing and no one walked, floated, or flew in there since we left. The only radiation detected came from the machine itself. Which is damaged, by the way."

"Damaged? But I thought you said no one went in there."

"That we could see." Ward started pacing. "If some evil genius designed a way to make matter invisible, he could break in and ruin us."

"Do you think it was a competitor?" Julius wracked his brain trying to think of another luxury space boot retailer in their relatively small town. He couldn't think of even one.

Ward stopped and snapped his fingers. "I think it was that beggar who had to be thrown out earlier. He was probably casing the place! I'm not sure how he got in tonight, past both the camera and the robot guards, but I'm sure it was him. I just know it."

"That's not fair, Ward. No evidence points to this being his fault. It's probably just coincidence. You can't even give his description to the police because nothing ties him to this."

"I would gladly give them a description if I could have seen more than his eyes. He was wrapped up tighter than a skier in winter on Neptune, I'll tell you that. Probably to avoid being identified." He sighed. "We'll have to get the aeronautical repair guy in tomorrow morning—well, this morning. Only specialist in 50 miles. This is going to cost us a fortune. Good night."

As Ward walked back to his hover utility vehicle, Julius mockingly muttered under his breath, "No, Julius, don't be paranoid. We don't need to waste any of our profit on insurance. It's a small town and we have a camera and guards. Don't worry, nothing's going to happen. Ha."

The next day, the repairman came in to fix the AutoShoeTron. He replaced the giant magnets and electromagnetic pulse readers and the very expensive bottled gravity. He left behind a working machine and hefty bill.

That night, the alarm sounded again. The machine was wrecked again. The Cobblers had to call the repairman—again.

This cycle continued for days and days on end.

Before long they could not afford to pay to have the machine fixed on a daily basis, and had to leave the machine dormant and damaged, a temperamental beast that would occasionally spit out a pair of boots if someone kicked it hard enough. Their business was being ruined by an invisible force which they could neither see nor fight against. They tried to keep their shop running smoothly, but it was an uphill struggle they were definitely losing.

Julius groaned as he looked over the latest bill they couldn't cover. "Even after the guy fixed the machine, its output dwindles by the day. Mark my words, it's just going to quit one day. At this rate we'll need to make these shoes by hand. But I'd never bothered to watch Dad when he worked." He was always either too busy or found the work too tedious to learn. Growing up in a financially comfortable household, he never thought that any of the myriad of machines or robots surrounding him would ever let him down—or be unaffordable.

"Me neither. I never felt the need to learn to actually cobble shoes. We'll just have to keep these engines alive," Ward said. "If this machine blows for good, so are our chances at keeping this company afloat."

Finally, the machine just died. And so did the brothers' hopes.

Everything went downhill from there. There was practically no luxury footwear left in the store, only a handful of less expensive styles that people didn't care for anyway. They had to sell their robot security guards and cancel Ward's Mars trip to pay for the store rent and other mounting bills. The steady stream of customers had fallen to a trickle and then disappeared entirely.

After a few days of moping, Julius announced, "I've been thinking, and I've come to a decision. We need to raise money for new equipment, so let's go old school and make shoes the way dad used to make them. You know, cutting leather pieces and sewing them together by hand."

"By hand? Are you kidding me?"

"It can't be that hard. People have been doing it that way for hundreds of years, and isn't every generation supposed to be smarter than the next? I found some great holographic, interactive how-to videos on my computer. I can make the image bigger if you want to watch, too. How about it?"

"No thanks. We have advanced technology so we don't have to do menial labor like that. That we don't have said technology at the moment is irrelevant; I'll wait until a better opportunity arises, thanks. It will one day. It must."

"Suit yourself."

Day by day, Julius watched holograms, allowed said interactive holograms to manipulate his hands to the proper positions, and improved his shoemaking skills. After a while he was okay at making penny loafers and fairly decent at assembling steel-tipped work boots. He felt confident enough to put some of his better wares in the window. People walking past occasionally admired his handiwork, but nobody bought a pair.

Meanwhile, the bank's financial automatons denied their failing business any amount of seed money. Ward was combing through his old contacts, hoping to secure a personal loan. It was to no avail. It was growing all the more likely that their business, the one their father had started decades ago, would permanently close in a matter of weeks.

One snowy winter day, Ward, whose brother had finally convinced him to try making a pair of shoes, was in the backroom struggling to thread a pair of laces when he heard the door sensor chime.

"I'll get it," Julius called from the lobby. He unlocked the door and welcomed the customer. It was earlier than their normal opening time, but they were not in any position to turn down a potential customer.

Ward heard Julius' having a muffled conversation with an older man, but didn't hear the register open. A while passed. Quite a while. Was the man buying a lot? Was Julius trying to convince him to buy a more expensive pair? Could somebody, in this day and age, actually want a pair of shoes without a computer chip or circuitry? Boots meant for walking, not floating or keeping its wearers from floating away? The idea was novel, if not a little unbelievable.

Soon, the smell of freshly made cocoa wafted into the room. It was a special blend, an expensive blend, meant to entice the affluent, who had once frequented their establishment. This man with his deep pockets might be their saving grace. Hopeful, Ward stood up and entered the lobby to see their prospective   angel.

That's when he saw the potential customer. The bottom half of the face was still covered with a ratted old scarf, but there was no mistaking him— it was the beggar man with the holey shoes.

Unlike the shoes he struggled to make, Ward was fit to be tied. "You? You! How dare you show your face around here! We might not be able to prove it, but we know you were the one sabotaging our machines. I want you to leave before I call the police."

"Don't be rude, Ward." Julius' voice had an edge to it. "Nobody showed up on the cameras. It was plain old bad luck, and you can't go blaming other people like some lunatic."

"Fine. But I don't want him here. Just look at him! What will people think when they pass by? They'll say 'oh look, the Cobbler brothers have turned their once successful business into a homeless shelter. How nice. I guess we'll have to go somewhere else to buy our über expensive footwear.' We'll never get our old customers back if you let this place look a de facto soup kitchen."

"I cannot believe you, Ward." Ward was speechless. His brother had never snapped at him like that before, but he didn't want to retort. He was kind of curious as to what he would say next. "No, he doesn't dress like our previous clientele, but it doesn't hurt us to let him in for a few minutes and give him some cocoa. People fall on hard times, and in case you forgot, we're only one step away from the poorhouse ourselves through almost no fault of our own. So stop acting like you're so much better than him and, for once, act like a decent man!

"Let the man drink in peace. You can give him the third degree later, though I hope you'll change your mind."

The little man nodded his thanks and set the cocoa on the table in front of him. He unwrapped his scarf and let it hang at his side. Julius gasped as Ward gaped.

The man's ears were more pointed, and his stature smaller, but the man was indeed their father. An elfish version, of course, and an older one of the man they once knew, but the ways his eyes crinkled when he smiled confirmed it.

"Papa?" Ward, dumbfounded and unsure if he would faint from shock, sank into the nearest chair, next to his brother. "What are you— what— what is going on?"

"I thought your voice sounded familiar," Julius practically whispered. "Without the scarf, it definitely sounds like you, Papa."

"I have a story to tell you boys," Papa Cobbler said. "An important one. I want you to listen and not interrupt. Understood?"

They nodded simultaneously, still stunned.

Their father crossed his hands in front of him, as he always had when he was to make a serious speech. "I cannot explain much, as those in the earthly dimension should not know truths from the more ethereal realms. I will do my best to not reveal too much but still make sense—if that's possible. You will know one day, soon enough. Too soon, in my opinion, but that is a conversation for another time.

"In my current realm, a being previously human can biologically convert into a creature of another form. It involves a lot of study, preparation, and a slightly ticklish visit to a machine that deconstructs organic matter to permanently rearrange molecules. Anyway, after careful consideration, your mother and I decided that I would undergo the necessary training to become an elf and cross over.

"The stories I told you boys were mistaken. Elves are not mythical creatures; they are ordinary people who can cross back and forth between worlds to do good deeds for those who have proven themselves worthy. Yes, it involved some teleportation mischief with your machine, but what is an elf without mischief?" He chuckled wryly. "That's why your cameras and guards could never detect my breaking the machines"

"I applied and was approved for a project to help you, by putting you through a series of trials designed to elicit the goodness I know you possess. Julius, you faltered at first, but you pulled yourself up by your bootstraps" –he chuckled at his accidental pun- "and corrected your behavior. You showed me kindness and consideration by the end of the experiment. In short, you passed.

"If you had both passed my test, I could have given you a guarantee of a successful business, one that will amass you a fortune so vast it will last a lifetime. I would have loved to ensure you two of a life without financial hardship. But Ward failed. He let his greed and self-importance overcome his decency. He never treated me as a human being, but as a pest to be shooed away. As per my agreement in becoming an elf, I cannot allow bad behavior to be rewarded. So Julius, for you to receive this gift of wealth, you cannot ever work with your brother again, or give him a penny from your prosperity."

"Papa," Julius said as he leaned forward and caressed his father's cold fingers. "The offer is kind, and I appreciate it very much. But I will not leave Ward, or make him leave the business. He is flawed, but he is blood. I cannot and will not abandon him for riches."

"You were always my good son," he said, as he cupped Julius' cheek. He turned to his other son. "And I know you have goodness in you, Ward, even if it's buried further down than I'd like. Maybe not today, but one day, time and maturity will set it free."

Ward squirmed in both discomfort and embarrassment. He was too ashamed to admit aloud that if the situation were reversed, he would have taken the deal in a heartbeat. "Papa, how can we contact you if we need to speak with you? About the business, or anything else?"

"Your mother and I will be in touch, with the both of you. Since you now know me in my elf form, you cannot ever interact with me again in this dimension. Security issues; you understand. Though you won't be able to see or hear me in this dimension, I will transport back every so often with messages from your mother and me to let you know we're still here and watching."

He stood up, wrapped his scarf around his face, and left without as much as a glance back.

The brothers had to rebuild their shoe business from the ground up, never enjoying a comfortable living like they had as younger men. They invested in cheaper equipment, hired local workers to oversee operations, and rebranded as "On a Shoestring," a shoe store that did sell some luxury boots but mostly specialized in work boots for those who needed affordable, quality shoes. The brothers spent much of their days honoring their new lifetime warranty, fixing their old or broken shoes, for no additional charge.

Julius and Ward outgrew their youth, worked hard at their business, and settled down to marry and start families.

Julius was happy, and considered himself blessed to have a full life and a full heart.

It took time but, slowly, his love for his wife and children and customers melted the frozen sheath encapsulating Ward's heart. Though he still acted tough, he began helping people quietly and often.

He could tell his parents were proud. Once, he was wearing his favorite gift, a special hi-tech hat that regulated body temperature in weather both hot and cold, and saw a shivering young boy walking the streets. He gave his hat to the youngster, and when he returned home, he found on his nightstand a knit hat with his mother's distinct checkered pattern. He made sure to keep an eye out for signs of his parents' presence; and found the more he looked, the more he saw, and the more he understood.

For every day of their lives, both brothers taught their children to believe in things they couldn't see quite see, but were always there: elves, kindness, and love for their fellow man.

GRUFF

BY ART LASKY

"Time for bed, kids."

"Five more minutes, please?"

"Sorry, that was your third five more minutes... come on Mason, come on Princess Peanut."

"I'm not Princess Peanut!"

"Sorry, come on Madeleine."

"Not Madeleine!"

"No? Who are you then?

"I'm Maddie the Space Pirate."

"Well, it's still bedtime. I'll tuck you both in and tell you an extra special story."

"Yay..."

"Let's see now... Once upon a time..."

"Oh Papa, all your stories start with *once upon a time.*"

"How about, once upon a future time?"

"No Papa, all the rest of your stories start with *once upon a future time.*"

"You're a tough audience. Okay, let me think... here we go, this is a really really true story. It happened many, many years ago. Back when the only way to get to the Denab 3 settlement was by flying in ships. The transporter hadn't been invented yet; and spaceports were busy places. In those days it was a long dangerous journey, that's for sure. Anyway, there were three brothers and...

- Littlest One –

"Hey Liam, cut it out. I'm a fully qualified pilot, I have my own ship, and a thriving business."

"Thriving?"

"I get by, and in a couple of hours I'll be running the channel; I'm hauling a very important shipment."

"Come on Billy, you've successfully 'run the channel' fifteen times. Why don't you go the long way around this time?"

The channel was the Carniad Channel, a narrow twisting safe corridor thru the Great Carniad Hyper-radiation Barrier. It bridges the Terran trading outpost of Delancy and the Kragen colony at Denab 3, cutting two months of travel and expense off the journey. For traders with narrow margins or tight schedules, it's a shortcut worth considering, despite the threat of pirates, known locally as Trolls because they trolled the lawless length of it.

"Can't afford to, time is money, but don't you worry Liam you're my big brother, not my old nanny besides, remember the plan, our biggest brother, Starr, looks out for both of us. This run should make me enough money to upgrade my drive, then I can do the really lucrative long range hauls."

"I suppose I can't stop you. Just please remember, if your luck runs out there is a plan, follow it."

"It's lucky number sixteen, what can go wrong?"

"For one thing, sixteen's not a lucky number," said Liam.

"Whaddya mean, not lucky? Sixteen is a one and a six. One plus six is seven: lucky!"

"Lucky or not, watch your tail little brother.

***

Billy Gruff, was just into his fourth game of solitaire when the comm-link signaled an incoming message.

"This is the free ranger Reaper. Heave to and prepare to be boarded."

The pirate's voice came coldly through the speaker. Free rangers were what the pirates called themselves; it almost made them sound legitimate.

Billy reacted with an explosion of activity, throwing his ship into a full power dash for freedom, while firing his single torpedo, and sending out a distress signal. The *Reaper* easily avoided the antique war surplus weapon, and matched Billy move for move. He was contemplating additional evasive action when the computer pinged informing him that the *Reaper* had a weapons lock on him; he opened a comm-link.

"Hey there *Reaper*. This is Billy Gruff, Owner, crew, and sole passenger of the small freighter *William's Hope*. We're a leaky little tub hauling a cargo of Jovian Sweet Potatoes, hardly worth your effort."

'I'll decide what's worth my effort. Heave to and prepare to be boarded right now; behave and maybe, just maybe I won't make you do a spacewalk without your survival suit.'

"Let's not do anything hasty, my friend. How's about, for my freedom, I trade you the transponder code of the guild freighter *Bountiful*? She's due through here sometime tomorrow, with a shipment of rare Zorgan Singing Orchids. If you know her code there's no way she'll be able to sneak by."

The pirate knew of the *Bountiful* and did a quick little risk/reward assessment, sending Billy on his way, with a warning,

'Don't forget our deal, if you're lying, I will track you down, and gut you with a rusty baling hook."

- Middle One –

'This is the free ranger Reaper. Heave to and prepare to be boarded.'

The pirate's voice came coldly through the comm-unit of the merchant ship *Bountiful*. Liam Gruff sounded the all hands on deck alarm and prepared for evasive maneuvering.

"Tactical officer, arm the phaser cannons, advise when you've acquired the target."

Liam led the *Reaper* on a corkscrewing chase for nearly half an hour, to no avail.

The computer pinged informing him that it was too late, the *Reaper* had a weapons lock on them. He briefly considered firing on the Troll, but opened a comm-link instead.

"*Reaper*, this is Liam Gruff, commander of the *Bountiful*. A fight will be costly to both of us, and we are not such great a prize. Perhaps you and

I can negotiate a suitable ... shall we say toll, for safe passage."

'You are outgunned and outmanned. You can turn over your entire cargo or we will disable your engines, forcibly board you, and slaughter your entire crew.'

"*Reaper*, suppose we provide you with the transponder code of the super-freighter *Empress*, instead? She's due through here sometime tomorrow, with a cargo of rare animals for the Kragen Imperial zoo and a large shipment of Spadangran Living Diamonds."

The pirate had heard stories of the riches that the *Empress* was known to carry. He did another quick little risk/reward assessment, sending Liam on his way, after making appropriate threats.

- Biggest One –

'This is the free ranger Reaper. Heave to and prepare to be boarded.'

The pirate's voice came coldly through the comm-unit of the *Empress*. Commander Starr Gruff checked the tactical readout. The *Reaper* was a Nova Class Frigate, impressively armed by pirate standards. He did not bother responding to the troll, but issued a series of commands to his crew,

"Nav, hold steady on your course... Infirmary, and Arms yellow alert... Everyone else, action stations.

The computer pinged, informing the commander that the *Reaper* had a weapons lock on them.

'I repeat, *this is the free ranger Reaper, and this is your final warning, heave to and prepare to be boarded.'*

Starr sounded the 'all hands to battle stations' alarm and opened a comm-link.

"*Reaper*, this is merchant commander Starr Gruff. Disengage. I warn you, disengage and allow us to proceed."

'*You are outgunned and outmanned. You can turn over your entire cargo or we will disable your engines, forcibly board you, and slaughter your entire crew.'*

"*Reaper*, I am not in the mood for threats. Believe me, for your sake, this is **your final warning**, disengage."

'Commander Gruff, we've taken better than the likes of your big old cow of a ship, you have one last chance to surrender.'

In a little less than 2 minutes the *Empress* continued on her way, leaving the slowly cooling wreckage of the *Reaper* in her wake. The three brothers Gruff had all failed to mention that the *Empress* had been re-built, in the Sirian Ship Yards, from a retired Naval Dreadnaught. She retained the heavy armor, 12 batteries of Phaser canons, 20 anti-matter torpedo tubes, and a crew chief that was a retired gunnery sergeant.

JUST LIKE THAT
BY SUSAN W. LYONS

What pleases the shareholders at Grimm, Grimmer & Grimmest is that asteroid mining operations make so much money yet are so cheap to operate: cheap to set up a prefab bubble dome that surrounds the entire rock and contains its own pseudograv, stabilizer, and biosphere; cheap to swing a cargo ship around Mars to pick up precious cargo and drop off supplies; and the labor force is cheaper still because this rock also houses GrimmGulag®, the penal colony operated by a GG&G subsidiary and funded by a Corporate Homeland that wants divergents like me out of sight and out of mind. Way out of mind.

Down a mine, in fact. A narrow shaft, to be accurate.

Some might even say I was given that shaft during my check up at HappyHealthyHumans®, another GG&G subsidiary. You see, the last words that I heard on the Homeland came from my Medtek, an elf named Merry, who said in lovely bell-like tones, "You ain't ever going to pass the 'You-Must-Be-This-Tall-to-Stay-Here' test." I remember opening my mouth to respectfully disagree, but then everything went black, just like that, until I woke up on this rock. And here I've been ever since.

It's okay, though. There are six others like me, all serving life sentences for being too short for the Homeland but just the right height, as it happens, to mine the jewels that adorn the Homeland fairy princesses and the gallium and selenium that let the tech-wizards work their magic.

We usually get along pretty well as long as the bio-stabilizer keeps exchanging monometh for Oxyglobin®, but there was this one time when the supply ship was slow to come, and the Oxyglobin® ran so low that Natasha started screaming because she was getting nightmare visions from all the fumes. In fact, she mistook Walther for a vampire and chased him with a pickaxe all the way up the shaft. Afterward, Natasha felt bad until Walther told her it could have happened to any of us; the fumes probably hit her first because she is the youngest and smallest, like the canary in the coal mine.

"Huh?" said Natasha. "What's a canary?"

"A tiny yellow singer with feathers," said Molly, Natasha's mother, as she sighed and wiped something from her eye.

"What are 'feathers'?" asked Natasha.

##

But of course nightmares are not what the manufacturers of Oxyglobin® intend. They want to make sure we see happy visions that keep us whistling while we work: rainbows, leprechauns, unicorns, and even the occasional fairy princess. Maybe that's why, when for the first time we saw Ms White disembarking from The Jacob II, we thought that's just what she was: a vision of a fairy princess. She was wearing a fine blue silk dress with an immaculate lace collar, little princess heels, and lots of rings and other sparklers, some of which might have even come from our mine. I thought I recognized the amethyst set in a gold chain that showed off her skin white as snow. And was that one of our moonstones glowing in a barrette that was keeping her hair—black as night—out of her face?

For sure, she was a vision.

Morty, overcome, gaped at her splendor.

"Close your mouth before you choke on pixie dust," warned Molly. Pixie dust, of course, is what the asteroid exhales on dry days: clay particles, silicas, carbonates, limestone, cyanates, and urethanes. Sometimes the silicas make it sparkle. On wet days when the dehumidifier gives out, the asteroid coughs out pixie smog. Today was a dry day.

Morty closed his mouth and resumed breathing through his nasafilters.

The pilot, an irritated harpy by the looks of her, tossed out cartons and suitcases from the hold onto the ground before slamming the hatch.

The Jacob II chugged up through the bubbledome port, belching exhaust that sent more whirlpools of pixie dust swirling around the baggage and Ms White, who glanced our way and then opened her mouth in a big round O as if she'd just sighted a troop of orcs. She gasped. She choked, doubled over, and gagged.

And just like that I knew. "She's no fairy princess," I said. "She's for real." I ran over to her and started pounding her on her back.

"Stop!" she said, when the dust settled and she could catch her breath. "Don't touch me. You're filthy."

I stepped away. Sure enough, I had left little sooty handprints on the back of her now-dusty dress. I decided right then and there not to tell her about her first contact with pixie dust. She could figure it out on her own. Instead I said, "I'm sorry, Ma'am. I just thought you could use some help."

"From a dirty little criminal?" she asked.

I said nothing, but took another step back. Some of the others joined me.

"I'm sorry," she said. "That was rude."

"And redundant."

"What?"

"'What' that I agree it was rude or 'what' that I know the word 'redundant'?"

She looked confused.

"I'm a criminal because I'm little," I said. "So 'little criminal' is redundant. And I'm dirty because I work in a mine all day and most of the night."

"Ah," she said. "And your name is . . . ?"

"You can call me Doc," I said.

"Doc?"

"On account of I used to be an engineer before I became a criminal, and now I doctor the mine when it needs fixing. And sometimes I fix up these folks, too." I pointed to Morty, Walther, Natasha, and Molly. "When I can," and I pointed to Sleepy and Baldy, who were hanging back.

"Well, pleased to meet you, Doc, and I'm sorry about the bad beginning. I'm Ms White, your supervisor."

"We never had no supervisor," said Morty. "Excepting maybe for Doc, here."

"Well, all that's going to change now," Ms White said. "GG&G is unhappy with the downturn in your recent production rates in gallium and selenium, and so they've sent you a supervisor."

"Ah," I said. "Just like that, have they? Do you suppose they know Sleepy and Baldy have metal poisoning? They've taken pretty sick."

"I see," said Ms White, glancing at Baldy and Sleepy and then averting her eyes. She pasted on a corporate smile. "Then I bet they haven't been taking their VitaE®, have they?"

"VitaE®?"

"New GG&G product. I brought some samples. You can try them free for thirty days."

"Hmmmph," said Walther. "And then I suppose if they work you'll charge us to keep taking them. But I already 'owe my soul to the company store.'"

"'Company store'?" asked Ms White. "Do you mean GG&G?"

"Miner's term," I said. "Say, Ms White, no offense meant, but you don't seem to know much about us or about asteroid mining, do you?"

The smile faded. Her face clouded up and then rained tears. "I've been exiled here," Ms White sobbed. "Sent like a common criminal myself, just because my stepmother the CEO is jealous of my HR skills and can't stand to have me around. She took away my credentials and put me on that wreck of an AstroOrbiter and said I can't go home until production on this mine goes back up."

"HR skills, huh?" said Molly. "Not off to a great start, are you?"

Ms White sniffed. "Well, you must not know that HR stands for Human Resources, not Dwarf Resources."

"Is there a difference?" Molly narrowed her eyes, and I could see she was thinking about pitching Ms White and her silk dress and princess heels down the shaft: no nasofilters, no Oxyglobin®, and no VitaE®. Molly fisted her hands and stepped toward Ms White.

"Now, now," I said, inserting myself between Ms White and Molly and spreading my hands out in front of me. "What's in a name, anyway?"

"I'm sorry if I offended anyone," said Ms Snow, now more puzzled than upset. She reached down toward the cartons. "Look, I'm here to get you back in shape so you will raise your productivity, and I've brought along some fabulous GG&G products to help. See!" She held them up one by one for our inspection: "Munchiekins®, Little Reds®, WeenyBabies®, TweeterTots@, even some Dwarf Oranges."

"Whoa!" I said, restraining Molly. "Let's all take a few deep breaths here. Using our nasafilters, of course."

"What? Did I say something?" asked Ms White. "You're a little sensitive for an asteroid convict."

"If she says 'little' again I swear I'll kill her," hissed Molly, so I held her some more until her breathing slowed to normal.

Morty shifted from one foot to another.

Baldy scratched at his bleeding scalp.

Finally, I said, "I believe that we can all agree that it's in all our best interests to get Ms. White off the asteroid and back to the Homeland."

Everyone nodded, even Molly.

"Now, Ms White, what do you mean when you said your stepmother took away your credentials?"

"During my last Rejuvalift, she ordered the Medtek to remove my fingerprints while I was under the influence of SweetDreams®. See?" She held her soft little hands up for inspection. Indeed, the tips of her fingers gleamed blank as pearls. "Without them I can't gain entry to the offices, my palace, my accounts, or my nectar-powered unicorn."

"The guardware won't recognize your face?"

"No."

"Nor your voice? Not your retinal-scan?"

"No, and no. Only my prints."

"So without your fingerprints, you're no one? Kind of like us?"

Ms White shuddered.

"What a shame," I said. "Isn't that a shame, everyone? All that stands between any of us and personhood is a set of fingerprints."

Molly looked at me like I'd lost my mind.

I winked at her.

She frowned.

I winked again.

Then Molly started to nod. "It is indeed a shame, Ms White. Fine lady like you locked out of her own Homeland."

"Uh huh," said Morty, who poked Natasha until she started nodding her head, too. Pretty soon we were all nodding away—even Sleepy and Baldy— like those old bobblehead dolls that used to stand on the kitchen shelf in my grandfather's cabin on the Homeland. He collected what were called Presidents back then. He lined them up in a long row. When the air currents from Grandpa's drafty window shifted, all the presidents would nod their heads together. Nowadays instead of presidents we have CEO's and Boards, and, of course, tech-wizards and corporate witches, but I bet GG&G has manufactured bobbleheads for them, too.

I smiled reassuringly at Ms White. "Don't give it another thought, Ma'am. We'll raise our productivity and prove to your wicked stepmother of a CEO that you deserve to go Home. Then she'll have to give you back your identity. Don't worry, Ms White." I paused. "Someday your prints will come."

##

So we took our VitaE® and went to work as hard as we could, because that was what we thought it would take to get Ms White off the asteroid. Even Baldy and Sleepy pitched in where they could.

We'd heard the usual stories about Esmeralda, the CEO of GG&G: she was something of a corporate-witch, but she was also vain, selfish, and obsessed about her looks. Above all else, Esmeralda valued deals and profits, so she must have thought Ms White was still an asset. Otherwise she would have simply dumped Ms White on some meteor instead of our asteroid.

Whatever potential Esmeralda saw in Ms White eluded us. Our new supervisor spent the first week looking for a manicurist, masseuse, and honeydew melons. During the second week, she wandered over to the mine site for the first time and tapped Walther's shoulder as he was running the steam hose. Startled, Walther whipped around and scalded Ms White, ruining her princess heels and burning her feet. We carried her back to the barracks and fed her VitaE®. The third week she stopped washing. When the Dwarf Oranges ran out she complained about the processed food and picked the raisins out of her Miniwheats. Her hair black as night grew greasy, and pimples red as roses blossomed on her skin white as snow.

For our part, we worked hard, because we were as anxious to get Ms White off the asteroid as she was to leave. The VitaE® made a difference, and we were eating regular for the first time in a while. Maybe we still weren't whistling while we worked, but we were productive.

"Don't you want to visit the mine again?" Natasha asked Ms White one day. "We're extracting some lovely gemstones. Just don't sneak up on us like you did the last time."

"No, I don't want to go anywhere near that mine. It's nasty and filthy. And dangerous.

Besides, I'm a supervisor, not a miner," said Ms White. "That means I'm in HR, not production."

"But you supervise miners," Walther said.

Ms White shrugged.

"Well, then, how about inventorying our ores and gems so you don't get bored?" suggested Molly. "We'll bring them to you. You could tell us how we're doing and keep us on track."

"Very well," said Ms White and sighed. "Oh me, oh my. Whatever will become of me?" Just like that.

##

"Molly, you're a genius," I said one evening three weeks later. We'd just left another sack of rubies and emeralds with Ms White, who turned out to have a real knack for assaying ores, grading gemstones, and generating reports to GG&G that made us look, on paper at least, fully productive. Yes, you heard me right. I said 'paper.' You see, lacking identification in the form of fingerprints, Ms White was locked out of media access, which meant she had to write up the reports by hand and wait for the next supply ship to take them back to the Homeland. It was slow, of course. We were used to it, but Ms White wasn't, and so more tears and handwringing ensued. Truth to tell, by now the fairy princess looked a real mess, and nothing any of us said about the basic benefits of soap and decontaminated water had any effect. That's probably why, when Esmeralda herself arrived in The Grimm Queen, which was her own personal, titanium-shelled Astrocruiser that she could call from her very own fingertips, Ms White fell so easily for the old poisoned-comb trick.

##

Walther was the first to spot the ship, which he mistook for the regular transport until he noticed its sleek silhouette. He yelled to the rest of us at the mine and then ran over to the barracks and roused Ms White from her morning nap.

We all arrived at the landing site just in time to see Esmeralda prance down the air stairs in antigravity heels, a green satin parachute overall with epaulettes, and white Sanigloves®, looking every inch the CEO touring the hinterlands. Esmeralda floated straight over to Ms White, who slumped in her ragged dress and tangled, greasy hair.

"Oh dear," said Esmeralda. "I see you've gone native."

##

Esmeralda sifted heaps of emeralds and rubies through her fingers. Even uncut, the rubies glowed with their own secret, magic life. "I couldn't believe your report. I had to come see for myself. "I must say you've done well with your raw material, Dearie," she said.

"Ma'am," I said. "We couldn't have done it without Ms White. We'll miss her, but we understand why you'd want her back on the Homeland as soon as possible."

"And you would be . . . ?" Esmeralda asked, turning her gaze on me.

"You can call me Doc," I said.

Ms White said, "I want to come Home. When can I come Home?"

Esmeralda turned back to Ms White. "Well, I think we'd need at least one more report from you, dear. Just to show that this isn't a fluke. And next time, let's see more pure gallium. It's time to recoat my computer screen and nothing makes it shine like freshly-processed gallium."

Esmeralda gathered all our hard-won treasure into five Securiboxes®, turned, and floated them and herself to the top of the air stairs. There she stopped, paused, and looked down at Ms White once more. "And Sweetie, do something about that dreadful hair." Reaching into one of her pants pockets with her still-immaculate gloves, she tossed a comb down to Ms White, who caught it and stared at it uncertainly. Then Esmeralda entered the Grimm Queen, the hatch whooshed closed, and the Astrocruiser rose soundlessly through the port hole.

Ms White stared at the comb some more before raising it and absentmindedly running it through her hair. But then, just like that, she collapsed and lay as if dead.

We stood stunned. Then I remembered Esmeralda's Sanigloves® "It's the comb!" I said. "Get the comb out of her hair, but don't touch it with your hands.

Pulling her sleeve over her hand, Natasha ran over to Ms White, carefully removed the comb from Ms White's hair and placed it on the ground.

Sure enough, Ms White moaned, sat up slowly, and put her head in her hands. "What a fool I've been," she said.

I knelt beside her, took her pulse, and felt her forehead. "You'll be okay, Ms White," I said. "But I think Esmeralda tried to poison you with the comb. It's good that Natasha took it away when she did. She probably saved your life. You sure you want to go back to the Homeland? Sounds like a pretty dangerous place to me." I carefully wrapped the comb in my neckerchief and placed it in my pocket. "What was Esmeralda saying about wanting gallium for her computer?"

"New gallium coats her screen like a brilliant mirror. She stares into it endlessly, spies on her Board, strokes the panel like it was alive. Myself, I think Esmeralda is obsessed with it."

"You say she spies on others. Did she spy on you?"

"Maybe. Probably. She's jealous and she thinks the Board likes me better than her. She's probably right."

"You don't think she'd use spyware, do you?"

Ms White shrugged.

"Did she ever give you any gifts?"

"Just this amethyst necklace," she said, pointing at her neck. She narrowed her eyes. "I always wondered why she'd give me something pretty like this when she obviously doesn't like me. She awarded it to me at the last GG&GCon for 'Most Improved Corporate Face.'" Now she pursed her lips. "Say . . . !" She jerked the necklace away from her skin.

"Wait!" I said. "May I see?" I turned the necklace over and studied the setting. Then I pointed at the inset and held my fingers to my lips.

"Huh," I said. "Isn't that interesting? Walther, don't you think that's interesting?"

"If you say so, Doc," said Walther dubiously and took a closer look. "Well, yes, Doc. I think that's very interesting."

"Interesting," echoed Ms White, after a moment.

I nodded and spoke right into the amethyst: "Ms White, we need to get any poison residue out of your hair. Let's get you back to the barracks for a good old-fashioned scrub. You should probably take that pretty necklace off for safekeeping. We wouldn't want to get it scratched now, would we? We'll get you some overalls, too. Save your corporation clothes and sparklers for the next visit from The Grimm Queen." I rubbed my hands together. "Natasha and Walther, you come with me. We've got some serious planning to do and then, Hi Ho, Hi Ho, it's off to work we go! We're going to process us some gallium for Esmeralda's favorite computer."

##

Gallium on its own is not particularly dangerous, but processing it is tricky. Once you've got enough you can squeeze a chunk of gallium and the warmth from your hand will melt it. It coats surfaces and makes them bright and shiny. Witches and wizards love gallium.

Once Ms White understood what we were trying to do, she joined right in the plan. In fact, she added a few embellishments of her own. The spyware in the amethyst recorded what we wanted Esmeralda to know: that Ms White had recovered from the effects of the poison comb and was supervising a promising yield of gallium; if only Ms White could get her identity back she could access for us a new purification process that would double our yield; we were preparing the handwritten report to tell her so, but, of course, we'd have to wait for the next scheduled arrival of that slow old rust bucket of a supply ship.

##

Within a month The Grimm Queen was back. Once again, Esmeralda floated down the air steps, this time wearing eel-skin leggings under a golden dragon-scale tunic with matching antigravity boots, gloves, and handbag. She positively glittered.

"Darling," she said to Ms White, who wore a plain decon suit and waited quietly at the foot of the stairs, her hair black as night neatly braided into a single plait. "Obviously you weren't expecting me."

"What a pleasant surprise, Esmeralda. If I'd known you were coming I would have dressed up in my corporate casual. And thank you, by the way, for the use of your comb. Would you like it back?"

"No, Dear. Keep it. You look like you could still use it." Esmeralda touched her own gold-leafed hair.

"I have some good news for you, Esmeralda," said Ms White.

"And I for you, Dearie. The Board has voted to bring you Home, at least for the duration of the next Stockholder's meeting. I've even brought you your prints so that you can properly oversee the gallium processing."

"How coincidental, Esmeralda. I happen to have some fine gallium with me, more than enough to resurface your screen as well as that of every Board member. Would you like to see?" Ms White gestured grandly at Natasha, who stepped forward with a linen bag and held it out toward Esmeralda.

Esmeralda's eyes glittered as green as her namesake.

"You can touch it, Ma'am." said Natasha. "It's wonderful soft, and if you take off your gloves, you can feel it melt in the warmth of your hands." Natasha opened the bag inside which the gallium shimmered.

"Yes-s-s," said Esmeralda. Just like that.

Into Esmeralda's outstretched hands Natasha poured the gallium, which quickly took on the consistency of pudding. Esmeralda smooshed her hands together and rubbed them gently. Then she trickled the gallium from one palm to the other, admiring its silky sheen and flow. Her eyes glazed over with pleasure.

I let her go on for another moment. "Ma'am, you don't want to let it fall to the ground," I warned. "Then it'll have to be reprocessed. Give it to me now and we'll get it ready for the trip." Reluctantly, she let it drip into the bag I held out to her. I closed it and handed back to Natasha. "Make this ready for its trip to the Homeland." "Ma'am," I started to say, and then I looked dismayed. "Oh, look," I said.

"Ma'am, your pretty hands are stained. Gallium does that sometimes. Hold them out, and I'll blot them with our special cleaner."

Esmeralda frowned but obeyed. I placed the damp cloth over her outstretched hands, patted them respectfully, and lifted the cloth, which I placed carefully in another bag. "I'll bring the gallium right out," I promised. "Ms White, come with us and we'll help you pack up your gear for the trip back to the Homeland."

We were barely out of Esmeralda's sight when Ms White turned to me and clapped her hands together. "I knew someday my prints would come. I just knew it! Now I can return and take my rightful place at GG&G and enjoy everything I missed while I was gone: corporation gossip, AmazinConsumer®, the adoration of my people, vacations at Wallyworld®, foot massages, ice cream, gilded quail, lobster, and baby peas right out of the hydroponic gardens. And more than anything else, fresh fruit! Esmeralda always travels with her own food, and I bet The Grimm Queen carries juicy grapes, or ripe bananas, or, or . . . oh, what I'd give for a taste of a crisp red apple right now!"

I frowned. "I'd go slow on all that for a while. Hasn't Esmeralda tried to poison you once already?"

"You're a distrustful little woman, aren't you, Doc?"

"If you say so, Ms White."

##

The Securiboxes® were stowed. Esmeralda floated up the air stairs with Ms White right behind her. Morty led our miners in a hearty cheer: "Hi Ho, Hi Ho, it's off this world you go!" Neither Esmeralda nor Ms White paid us any mind. As The Grimm Queen left, we waved anyway.

And now we were alone again. Just like that.

"Now what?" asked Molly.

"Did you see the cloth?" I asked.

"Yes," said Walther. "And I peeled off of it a perfect impression of Esmeralda's fingerprints."

"Good. And Ms White left her little necklace behind, didn't she?"

"She sure did," said Natasha. "Of course I made sure it was tucked away out of sight. She was in a real hurry to leave."

"And the spyware?"

"Nifty little gizmo," said Walther. "A tweak here and a little coding there, and it'll do just what we want it to."

"And no one told Ms White we lifted Esmeralda's fingerprints?" All shook their heads. "So she'll never suspect that now we can recall The Grimm Queen ourselves whenever we want?

"Well then, we[ll wait until the Board meeting when everyone's busy, call up Esmeralda's ship, and fly ourselves off this miserable asteroid."

"Where to?" asked Sleepy.

Walther said, "After I convert the software in Ms White's necklace, we can figure out where to."

"Someplace with feathers, please," said Natasha.

And that's exactly what we did. We studied our options until we found a system at the end of GG&G's domain. It's called "Happily Ever After."

We're packing our bags and leaving for it next week. Just like that.

MIRABELLA'S BEAST
BY DEANNA YOUNG

Chapter 1

Once upon a time, in the not-too-distant future, the day scientists forewarned and doomsayers predicted finally came to pass. Whole countries disappeared under rising ocean tides and the seven great continents were reduced to large islands. Humanity survived by constructing massive floating cities and the world's entire population resided on these gigantic ships. Although this preserved the human race, space was limited. Everyone had be valuable, and uplift the integrity of the species if they wished to partake of the limited resources left on Earth and aboard their ships.

Mira's cheeks warmed in the afternoon sun as she stepped onto her favorite secluded deck. From here she could watch the bustling crowds several levels below, or stare out over the endless ocean, letting the salty sea air tousle her long, dark curls. She rested her back against the faux oak railing and took out her digi-reader for the hundredth time to review questions for the nursing test.

After an hour or so, she pocketed her devise, rubbed her fuzzy eyes and turned to look over the edge of the massive man-made island, losing herself in the rhythmic waves splashing twenty stories below. It was no grassy cliff overlooking the ocean, but she could pretend, for just a moment.

In an open bay below, men shouted to each other, pulling on thick ropes and leaning into their work. She couldn't make out their words, but their voices were excited. Giant, angular shaped tuna dropped from the net into an open hold.

Movement caught her eye as rows and rows of solar panels folded inward, pulling back into storage slots, disappearing from view. The sun still hovered over the horizon, hours from setting. Perhaps a storm was coming?

"Don't lean too far, you might fall in."

Mira turned, locking eyes with Brad, her ex-fiancé. "What are you doing here?"

"I'm sorry, is this deck yours." He looked around with feigned embarrassment.

She narrowed her eyes and started to turn away.

Brad laughed and waved his hands, "I'm kidding. It's good to see you, Mirabella. It's been a while." A deep dimple accompanied his broad, wolfish smile.

"Sorry, you just startled me. I thought I was alone up here."

"I saw you when I was leaving my father's office, and thought I'd come say hello."

She looked at the Governor's office window, high above her.

"I'm surprised you recognized me from that far."

"I'd recognize you miles away. You kind of stand out," he said, looking her over.

Mira's face grew hot, and her stomach twisted tight. Old, familiar feelings threatened to surface. She had to get out of here. "Um, I have some place to be, if you'll excuse me." She moved around him, heading to the stairs.

"Mirabella," he called after her. "Have you thought about how the new protocol might affect you and your father?"

She turned back to him, unable to stop herself. "What new protocol?"

He cleared his throat. "It's for citizens who are unable to work. They will no longer receive government support. If their family cannot help them, they can be transferred to a job they *can* do, or..." He looked down, picking invisible lint off his jacket sleeve, "they will be let go, to preserve precious resources."

"Let go?" Mira stared incredulously. Surely he didn't mean what she thought he did.

He shrugged. "Everything possible will be done to find them a job, but too many citizens are mooching off the system, and we have limited resources. Families will simply have to plan for retirement now, rather than depend on government retirement. That's all."

"What about the hundreds of citizens expected to retire in the next few years that haven't had a chance to save up?" Mira rubbed the goose bumps forming on her arms. "There's still plenty of room in the city. There're two empty apartments on my block alone. Why now? When was this voted on? How have I not heard of this before?" Her head reeled with questions.

Brad brushed the hair out of his eyes as a gust of wind blew from behind. "It was just made public today. But senior officials voted on it months ago, per the advisement of a city-wide growth assessment committee."

Mira scoffed. "And how many of these committee members will be affected by this order?" She shook her head, "I'm guessing none." This was so typical. She turned to leave, not wanting to hear any more.

Brad spun her back to face him, "You needn't worry. Your father has several years left to save, and you live in one of the smallest, most affordable complexes. So long as you have a solid income, you'll be fine. And if for some reason you're not," his eyes rested on her ring-less hand, "I'd be willing to help."

Mira shoved her hand in her pocket. Not this again.

He rested a hand on her shoulder, "I didn't mean to upset you. Let me take you to dinner. We can talk things over while we catch up."

She shrugged away, "I'm sorry. I have plans tonight, and I'm already late."

The metal stairs clanged with her heavy footfalls, drowning out his attempt to call her back.

Once her feet hit the main deck, she raced to the transportation platform, boarded the next tram, and collapsed onto a seat, her shaking legs no longer able to hold her up.

Chapter 2

An hour had passed, and Mira still felt shaken. She pulled a tiny cake from the oven and set it on the table where the rest of her father's birthday dinner waited. She hadn't wanted to believe him, but her research had confirmed that the proposal—with its manipulative language and supposed scientific predictions—was real. If the governor could get something like this approved, what else was he capable of? Maybe people would finally start listening to the Free Citizens Committee. They had been trying to depose Governor Wilhelm for over a decade.

Gloria, her chicken, clucked from her perch on the balcony, breaking Mira's train of thought.

"Calm down. You'll get the leftovers, I promise."

The chicken tilted her head in jerky motions, as if truly considering that.

Mira laughed and leaned out the window, passing some stale bread and fish tales to her.

Gloria clucked excitedly, pecking at the old food.

Out of nowhere, gray clouds darkened the balcony and fat drops of rain plunked onto the wooden slats. A gust of wind rattled the blinds and blew a pile of napkins off the table. Mira shooed Gloria into the little weatherproof coop she had built with scraps her father had brought home from work and closed the window.

She sighed and gathered the scattered napkins, setting them next to the pizza that was growing colder by the minute. Papa should have been home thirty minutes ago. She tapped her wrist device to contact him. He didn't answer.

His umbrella leaned against the wall, forgotten. He'd be drenched by the time he got home. And what if he slipped on the wet boardwalk? He could really get hurt.

No. He was just running a bit late. She pulled out her digi-reader to study, but couldn't concentrate. Every sound from the hallway outside brought her head up.

Five more minutes dragged by, and Mira couldn't stand it any longer. She grabbed her jacket and umbrella and headed to the tram station, following her father's daily route.

Before she knew it, she was standing in front of a tram, ready to depart. If she left now, she could get to his work before the next tram left. She hopped aboard, without a second thought, just before the doors closed.

Rain fell harder now, covering the windows in sheets of water. Mira's feet bounced with nervous energy as they passed station after station until finally arriving. She flew out the door, opening her umbrella. A thick fog had rolled in, reducing visibility to only a few feet.

"Papa, are you here?" Mira scanned the platform, checking the tram a couple of times to make sure he hadn't boarded it behind her. His blue jacket with red patches would be easily recognizable, even through the fog. He wasn't there. Maybe he was just working overtime? She tapped her wrist device, checking. No new messages. Her heart thumped harder. Something wasn't right.

She pushed through the double doors, running for the office at the end of the hall. The man at reception dropped his feet off his desk when she entered and stowed whatever he had been fiddling with.

"Really coming down out there, eh?" he said, eying her dripping umbrella and the puddle forming underneath. "What can we do you for?"

"I'm looking for my father, Sebastian Ricci. He hasn't come home yet."

The man tapped a button on his desk, and a holographic display floated above it. With a few taps and slides he pulled up a file, "Ah, yes. He's been assigned to sub-sector twenty three, and it looks like his shift has ended." He looked up at her, smiling as if the problem was solved.

"I know his shift ended, but he didn't come home."

"Well, you can talk to his Super and see if he's seen him. Mr. Griffith should still be down in sub-level twenty three. He's always there. Here—"

He scooped a ball of light from his holographic display and dropped it onto her wrist, "—that's a temporary access pass. It'll open the elevator, down the hall to the left."

She nodded. "Thank you."

"If you can't find him, I'm off in another hour. I can help search." His smile broadened, and he seemed genuine.

"Great, thanks," she said, rushing out the office and down the hall to the elevator.

It wasn't the smooth, clean type of lift she was used to. The doors opened with a cluck. Lights flickered to life as she passed some sort of sensor and stepped inside. There were large push buttons instead of touchscreen displays. Mira held in a deep breath and pressed s23, leaning against the wall as the elevator started its long descent.

Finally, the elevator ground to a halt and the doors slid open. Mira stepped out onto the landing and the variegated metal flooring moved beneath her feet. A suspended catwalk extended out as far as she could see, crisscrossed by more platforms and catwalks periodically. Above, massive gears and engines groaned and roared. Pipes ranging from the size of a small apartment to the size of a chair leg ran in all directions.

The walkway swayed and she had to grab onto a handrail for support as she acclimated to the subtle rhythm. The elevator doors closed behind her with a clank, and the rat-a-tat-tat of it returning to the upper levels echoed in her ears. With the light from the elevator gone, the room—if you could call the entire underside of the city a room—disappeared into darkness. Her eyes adjusted to the soft orange glow from a nearby furnace. Electric lanterns hung farther along the main catwalk in front of her, dimly illuminating their immediate surroundings.

"Hello? Anybody here? Papa? Supervisor person?" she called, rushing past several roaring furnaces. The dry heat in the room made it feel like she had stepped into a sauna. As if on cue, a trickle of sweat ran down her back.

How was she supposed to find anyone down here? It was so immense.

Mira rounded a corner, and the shadow of a man became visible. His form took shape the closer he came, and so did the confusion on his face.

"Who are you?" he barked, "What are you doing down here?"

He was wearing a trench coat—of all things—with the collar turned up hiding most of his unkempt bearded face. His eyes narrowed into slits and she instinctively backed up to give herself some distance as he stepped closer.

"Hello," she said nervously, "You must be Mr. Griffith. My father hasn't made it home yet, and I thought that maybe he was still down here and—"

"And you thought you'd come down to a place *you* don't belong and fetch him?" Mr. Griffith said, crossing his arms across his chest. "Bad enough I have to babysit this whole crew, but now one of my crew has an actual babysitter."

"Excuse me?" Mira said drawing back, "I am not his babysitter. I am his daughter. I happen to be looking for him because it's raining outside, and he's new to this job, and...and I was worried! I'm allowed to be worried about him." She bit her cheek to keep from saying more. How could he be so rude?

He grunted, not impressed. "Well, he's not here. Everyone's gone home. Call next time instead of just wandering around down here. It's not safe."

Mira mimicked him, folding her arms across her chest. "Fine, I'll call next time. Sorry to have bothered you." She spun around and headed back to the elevator. She was almost there when she stopped mid-stride. A blue jacket with red patches hung on a hook by the doors. She ran to it, grabbed it off the hook, and turned, chasing down the supervisor, "Wait! He's still here!"

Chapter 3

Mira held the jacket to her chest, "He's here. Somewhere."

"His shift ended over an hour ago. And I haven't seen anyone since," Mr. Griffith said, looking down at her with pitiless irritation.

"Can I just look?" Mira asked, swallowing as she realized how hard it would be to search for father on her own, but knowing she had to try, "Just tell me where he was working. I'll go look and then be on my way. Please..." She said, clasping her hands together, pleadingly.

He let out an exasperated sigh. "Fine. This way."

Mira had to jog every few steps to keep up. They passed several intersections before he turned to the right, picking up his already fast pace, racing toward a hammering sound.

Up ahead, a figure was crouching next to the hull of the ship. The figure raised its arm and began pounding on something, over and over.

"Papa?"

"What are you doing?" Mr. Griffith roared, rushing forward and seizing the old man by the back of his neck, lifting him off the ground a few inches.

"Stop!" Mira threw her weight against the beastly man, without any affect.

Mr. Griffith dropped her father, and took a step backwards, then bent, picking up a wrench, along with several pieces of a broken lever.

"What is this?" He asked through gritted teeth. The low light cast shadows across his face at odd angles, making him look inhuman.

Mira's father stood to face his supervisor, rubbing his neck, "I was performing a valve test, and this one got stuck. It was starting to leak, and I was just hitting it back into place before the pressure burst the pipe." Sure enough, water was leaking out of a joint nearby and the needle on the pressure gage above it was climbing into the red.

Mr. Griffith reached over and lifted a different lever, then used the wrench to turn what was left of the first lever, closing it off. "This is a two-step process. You must turn this lever first, then the other. Check your manual, or ask." The needle dropped as the pressure regulated. "On second thought, I don't have time for people who don't think things through on my crew. You can find yourself a different job. Now, leave."

Mira froze, her heart stopping, "He's fired?"

Mr. Griffith held up the pieces of broken lever and the wrench, giving her a dumbfounded look, "Yes, he's fired."

"Can't you give him a second chance?" She asked. The words from her earlier conversation with Brad echoed in her head.

Her father grabbed her arm and whispered, "Mirabella...this *was* my second chance."

"Humph. Try fourth," Mr. Griffith said, turning away from them to check the gauges.

"This is just a sign, that..." He sighed, "...I'm getting too old for this line of work." He glued on a fake smile and headed toward the exit. "It'll be fine. We'll figure it out. Let's go home. I've been looking forward that special dinner you promised all day."

After he got a few steps away Mira turned to Mr. Griffith and whispered, "Sir, please. My father has only ever worked as a mechanic. This is all he knows."

"I think saying he 'knows' mechanics is a little bit of a laugh right now."

"He was just flustered."

"Well, his flustering cost our crew hundreds of credits and valuable time. There could have been a serious accident. Just look at this." He waved his hands over the hull, and Mira noticed for the first time that dozens of pipes had been dented and bent out of place. "Our maintenance budget doesn't account for acts of idiocy."

Her jaw dropped, "You have no idea what he's done in his life. He's brilliant. This *isn't* like him."

He rolled his eyes, "I'm done discussing this. I've got work to do before I can go eat *my* special dinner." He turned away from her and started unscrewing broken pipes at their joints.

"Mira?" Her father called from somewhere farther up the catwalk.

"Coming!" she called back, running away before she gave into the urge to punch the supervisor in the back of the head.

***

"Mira, this looks wonderful. Real cheese too? How did you pull this off with all the extra rationing going on?" Her father said, tucking a cloth napkin into his collar.

"That's my little secret," She said, winking at him as she handed him a slice of pizza. She put a piece on her plate and forced herself to eat a few bites, despite her lack of appetite.

"You shouldn't have had to come find me..." Her father said, reaching over to pat her hand, "I'm sorry."

"Don't be. They shouldn't have transferred you down there in the first place. It never made sense. Besides, we'll figure it out. We always do." Mira took one last bite of pizza and moved to the window, letting in the freshly washed air. "I was thinking; I could get a job."

He shook his head, crumbs falling out of his mouth as he spoke, "You won't have time for school and a job."

"I've been pouring over those books for months. If I'm not ready by now, I never will be. Plus, they gave us two weeks off to study," she said, talking over her shoulder as she unlatched Gloria's cage.

"I'm sure you'll pass, and at the head of the class, whether you studied more or not. You got all the brains in this family. Even mine. Don't know how I'm functioning without it." He pulled a silly face, like he used to when she was a child, and he was trying to cheer her up.

It had the opposite effect today, reminding her how much he'd aged in the last few years. He looked worn out, like he was in his mid-seventies, not his early sixties. He should be retiring soon anyway. It was past time for her to step in and help out more. It'd be harder with the new protocol, but they could make it work.

She forced a laugh, the gesture itself making her feel better, "Do the brainless still like cake?"

"I'm not sure. I think we better find out," her father suggested, stuffing the last of his crust in his mouth, to make room on his plate.

Mira smiled, grabbed the pot of warm chocolate sitting on the stove and carried it to the table.

"You're pulling out all the stops tonight," papa said.

"Only the best for you. Look, I even found one of these." She produced a thin wax candle, lit it and stuck it in the middle of the cake, "Go on- make a wish!"

He looked at his daughter, raising one eyebrow, "Are you sure you can handle my wish?"

"Bring it on," she said, with a grin.

"Let's see. I already have you and this decadent cake..." His eyes grew distant, "Do you remember making chocolate cake with momma every year?"

"Of course, papa," Mira thought back on the last time she had made a cake with her mother. Momma had accidentally pulled the beaters out of the mixture before turning them off and cake batter had peppered the room. Mira still found hidden, dried drops of batter now and then when she was cleaning, like tiny reminders that she had been there.

"If I knew it'd come true, I'd wish for one more day with your mother. She'd be so proud of you. I'd give anything for just one more day."

Just one more day. That was something he wished for often, and it wasn't surprising that he said it now.

A pool of yellow candle wax gathered on the cake. Her father shook himself, smiled and clapped his hands together, "I've got it..." He closed his eyes, and blew so hard the candle fell over onto the cake, going out with a hiss.

Chapter 4

"Mr. Wilhelm will see you now," a willowy woman said, waving Mira into the office behind her.

Mira nodded, got up and headed through the tall office doors.

A plump man with a graying beard and thinning black hair was sitting behind a large antique-looking desk. He motioned for her to take a seat.

"Hello, Mira. It's been a while." He waved his hands, making a floating display of lights appear above his desk, "I have here your request for a work voucher while in school?" He said.

Mira squeezed her hands together, "Yes."

"I think we can make that happen." Wilhelm said.

Mira relaxed, she thought that getting him to agree to a work voucher at all would be a challenge.

"Your father was here earlier…"

"And?"

"...And, he applied for several jobs," Wilhelm rubbed his temples and sighed, "But at his age, it'll be a while before an employer picks up his application. A lot of people have been in here applying for second, and even third jobs. New jobs are going to be hard to come by."

"Because of the new protocol?" She said, forcing herself to sound curious rather than angry.

Wilhelm sat up straighter, "Yes, and I don't like it either. It's better than letting us get to the point where *everyone* starves. We've got to take care of the problem before it comes to that. Rationing isn't enough anymore."

She couldn't help noting that the top button on his shirt was undone to allow room for his swollen neck. He could stand to ration a bit tighter. She bit her tongue. Now was not the time for a fight. "I'm sorry. I didn't come here to debate."

"Right," he said, clucking his tongue, "Let's see what we have." He tapped on the floating icons, flipping through folders and finally expanding one. His eyes scanned back and forth, reading lines of text that Mira couldn't see.

"I do have two jobs. One is a cleaning job at the port-side elementary school, or we also have a busboy job at the college cafeteria. Both are part-time. Which would you prefer? Perhaps both? I could arrange that."

Mira looked at the displayed hours and wages, "Do you have anything that pays more?"

She grimaced inwardly as he looked at her in an exasperated way.

"Let me check." He flipped through some screens, "One other job just opened up, and at twice the pay of the others…" he paused looking her up and down.

"Great. What is it?"

He cleared his throat. "It's a machinist position on the lower levels—your father's old job. They've specifically emphasized that they need someone who is skilled in this area. I'm sure you don't qualify."

She gave him her most offended look, "I do."

He smiled, in a patronizing way, "Do you, now?"

She smiled back, "Yes. I am fully-educated on the inner workings of all the mechanics on this ship."

"Young lady, you will be asked to pass a test before you even meet your supervisor."

A picture of the hulking man in the trench coat and beard came to mind. She swallowed, and sat up straight. "I *can* do it."

He tapped his finger on his lip, thinking.

The door creaked opened, and Brad peeked inside, "sorry to interrupt."

He didn't look sorry as he strolled up to his father's desk and leaned in close, "The Free Citizen committee has filed a petition and they wish to meet with you later today." There wasn't a hair out of place on Brad's head, and his crisp outfit looked like it was straight off a mannequin at some upscale boutique. It probably was.

His father shook his head and leaned back in his chair, "it's fine. I've been expecting this. Their petition has no grounds. Best to get the *discussion* out of the way," Wilhelm said, not even attempting to hide anything from Mira.

Brad turned to Mira, changing his tone immediately, "Hello, Mirabella. Looking lovely, as usual. Father's not giving you any trouble, is he?"

Her stomach tightened at the familiar attention. "No. We're just wrapping up, actually." She stood to leave, "go ahead and put me down for that job."

Wilhelm held up his hand to stop her, "Not so fast. Brad, perhaps you can settle this. You know Mira quite well. Do you recall if she has any experience as a mechanic or machinist?"

Mira stared at Brad and held her breath.

He studied her for what felt like hours.

"A machinist? No. She's not a machinist that I know of."

Her stomach dropped.

"But," he continued, "She's an amazing mechanic. She can take anything apart and put it back together seamlessly. What's the job?"

"Mechanic work for the under-city," Wilhelm said.

Brad whistled, "A lot of responsibility. Sounds physically taxing as well..."

Somehow getting this job now depended on getting Brad to agree that she was up to the task. Mira looked him in the eyes, silently pleading.

He nodded and gave her a wink, "Yes. I'm sure she could handle it."

"Alright. I'm trusting the two of you," Wilhelm said, tapping the icons. "Report to this address tomorrow morning to take the test." He flung a set of glowing numbers at her. They hovered for a few seconds before sinking into her wrist. "That also has your hiring transcripts, verifying that you were in fact the one I sent. They may have a hard time believing you otherwise."

She held out her hand to shake his, overwhelmed with relief.

"Good luck then," he said, dismissing her without shaking her proffered hand as he went back to studying the images floating above his desk.

She left, and Brad followed her out, closing the door behind him, "Wait, Mirabella."

She turned, "Yes?"

"I kind of stuck my neck out for you in there, and you didn't even say thank you."

She cringed at the accusation, though he didn't seem to be saying it with any malice. "I'm sorry. You're right. I just didn't want it to appear as though you were lying for me, or anything." Although, she had a feeling Wilhelm was about to give her the work assignment before he came in anyway. "I am grateful. Thank you," she said, with complete sincerity. After all, he could have ruined it for her, and didn't.

"How about repaying me by coming to dinner with me tonight? It's been far too long since we've spent any time together."

Mira looked into his sky blue eyes that contrasted so completely with his wavy black hair. He was just trying to be nice to her, and she kept brushing him off. But the alarm bells in her head were hard to ignore.

"Brad, I'm sorry. I can't. I've got to prepare for this new job. Plus, I'm taking my nursing exam in less than two weeks. I just don't have any extra time."

He nodded. "Well, maybe I can help you study?"

She held back a sigh. He wasn't giving in. This was a generous offer. Why was she still pushing him away? He'd never been supportive before. Maybe he'd matured.

"Yeah, okay." She smiled at him, surprised that her palms were sweaty. "I'll have to figure out my schedule first."

"Great, you do that," he said, leaning over and pushing the elevator call button for her.

"Okay," she agreed. He smelled so good. The scent took her back in time and she almost leaned in to kiss him goodbye.

Just then, the elevator doors opened and a young woman with bouncy blond curls and tight jeans stepped off, "Excuse me? Can you tell me where Mr. Wilhelm's office is?"

"Yes, it's the one on the end," Brad said, pointing.

"Thank you," she said, moving past them.

Brad turned to watch her as she left. His eyes roamed up and down her body before settling on her backside. He smiled and raised an eyebrow in approval.

"Really?" Mira asked stepping onto the elevator, the pain of their break-up coming back in full force.

Two years ago, he had swept her off her feet. Anything she could want, he gave her. After a few short months, she was completely smitten, but his attention and interest diminished once she was fully his. Brad had never cheated on her that she knew of, not physically, but his eyes never ceased to wander. He reveled in the attention he got from other women, even when she was around, flirting with them and making inappropriate jokes with his friends. It had always made her feel small, and insignificant. She deserved more respect than that; she was more than just another accessory. She wouldn't put herself through that again.

"What?" he asked, confused.

She sighed, he hadn't changed. "Thank you again for vouching for me back there. I *am* grateful." She pointed between herself and him, "I just can't do this again."

The doors closed, leaving him standing there looking stunned. She blinked back tears, hating that she let herself be pulled into his spell again. She shook herself, there wasn't time for this. She pulled out her digi-reader and typed: *books on mechanism mechanics and city-ship schematics.*

Chapter 5

"Can I help you?" a man said, holding his wrist up to the door of the City Maintenance Office, unlocking it.

This man was older than the one who had offered to help her search for her father two days ago. He was dressed like belonged behind a desk, not fixing machines.

"Yes. I'm the new machinist for the sub-levels." She said following him into the office.

"Hmmm.You're a bit, um...smaller than I expected. We need someone who is experienced. You look to be what, nineteen or so?"

"Twenty-three, actually, and I can do this job."

He sat his satchel on the counter, and logged into the desk's control panels. "Well, we'll see. If you pass the entrance test, you can go on down for your shift. If you fail, you can retest in a year, if there's an opening."

He held out a scanner. "Clock in here. Even if you don't pass, you'll be paid for your time."

"Thank you," Mira said, holding out her wrist. A blue light flashed, clocking her in.

The man toggled through icons on his desk, before pinching a bar of hovering light, and dropping it in front of her. Her wrist sucked in the light-bar, and a paper-sized hologram materialized in her hand.

"You have forty-five minutes to complete as much as you can." He pointed to a row of chairs along the wall. "Just work until time runs out."

Mira took a seat, and a count-down timer lit up in the corner of her test. The questions started out very basic, increasing in difficulty with each one. By the time she got to the thirtieth question she was solving hypothetical questions rather than fill-in-the-blank on parts and general maintenance.

The clock was already down to its last three minutes, when she reached a question that made her pause. *What would you do if you came upon a release valve lever that was stuck, and needed to be shut off immediately due to building pressure?* Mira tapped in her answer, biting her lip, realizing that this question was probably added to the test within the last few days. She hit 'enter,' to finalize her answer, readying herself for the next set of questions, but none came.

Five seconds later, an alarm sounded. Time was up. She returned to the counter and pinched the sheet-sized display of light, causing it to collapse into a weightless bar again, and dropped it onto the proffered scanner.

It all came down to this. Had she studied enough? Her chest tightened.

The man read the results, lines of unreadable words reflecting in his eyes. He looked up at her, shaking his head.

Her heart seized.

"Well, I guess you're qualified. As far as I can tell, you got a perfect score."

"Seriously?" Mira said, letting out her breath and her whole body relaxed, "So, what now? Just head down and find the supervisor?" Her relief was replaced by trepidation as she realized she'd have to face that monster again.

"Yes. You'll be working with Jim today." He scooped up some light and dropped it onto her wrist, "that's your elevator access. Jim should be waiting for you on sublevel twenty-three."

"Got it. Thanks," Mira said, thanking whatever bit of luck had gotten her out of working with Mr. Griffith.

She left the office and got onto the elevator, patting her chest to try to get her accelerated pulse under control. It was one thing to pass the test, and quite another to perform the job.

Before she knew it she was once again standing in the dark underbelly of the city, holding onto the hand-rail as the catwalk swayed.

"Now what?" She mumbled, regaining her feet and focusing on the walkway directly in front of her. A burst of steam escaped from a nearby valve making her jump, and her heart hammered, thinking of the last time she was here.

"Hello?"

"Hello," came a not-too-distant reply.

She squinted and saw someone coming down the walkway.

"I hope you haven't been waiting long, I just..." The man stopped speaking as he reached her and blinked in surprise, "...sorry, you're, uh, smaller than I expected."

"You're the second person to say that today." She straightened her back, "I'm not that small."

He pulled on his thick mustache, looking her over, "Well, this isn't easy work down here. You've got to have a bit of muscle and grit." He shook his head, "But, we've been shorthanded for days and my wife would love to see me home at a decent hour. So, I'm willing to give you a chance. Don't mess it up, hear?"

"Yes, sir," Mira said quickly.

He led her down a long corridor, passing row after row of intersecting walkways and platforms.

"How come there aren't any horizontal transporters down here? It'd make getting places a lot faster," Mira said.

Jim glanced over his shoulder at her, "Are you tired, then?"

"No. It just seems like a waste of time. We've been walking for almost ten minutes now."

"There are a few transport systems on other levels, but this level is periodically flooded to cool the engines for cleaning, check for leaks, put out fires and test the emergency pump systems. Most of the equipment on this level is manually operated and maintained. That's why we're here."

"Wait. Water reaches up this high? We're still a couple stories above the bottom of the city. That's a lot of water, couldn't that sink the ship?"

Jim stopped walking and turned around, "It doesn't reach this high, and partitions are raised, so only a small section at a time is submerged."

"Oh."

He squinted at her, "Who hired you? I thought you were a mechanic."

She cleared her throat, "I am...kind of."

He rolled his eyes and threw up his hands, "What? We asked for someone with experience."

"Well, I'm studying to be one." It was sort of true, she had been studying to pass herself off as one, "And I passed that test of yours. I'm a fast learner too. Just give me that chance you promised." She stood tall, trying to stare him down.

"Fine. We're almost there anyway," he said turning to continue on, mumbling under his breath as if having a double-sided conversation just loud enough for her to hear, "This one is really too old, and a bit forgetful. What should we do with him? *Oh, no problem, send him to Jim.* This one is unstable. Probably shouldn't be working with people. *Just, send him to Jim.* This one isn't really a mechanic, but wants to be. Where should we send 'em? *I know! Jim.*"

Jim stopped. In front of them loomed a wall covered in pipes, valves, levers, cranks and geared apparatuses. "Alright, this is where we're working today. Do a good job and you can come back tomorrow. If not...you won't. I'll have to shadow you today, to make sure you know what you're doing."

Mira swallowed, as a dry lump settled in her throat. She'd have to work harder to prove herself now.

Jim caught her attention again, "Okay, our main job today is to check pipes for leaks. Record the leaks, if there are any, and fix them. Got it?"

Jim said, talking slowly as if Mira wouldn't be able to follow along.

"Got it. Do we bleed the lines, or just open and shut off each valve? Do we also check the main gates, or do those remain closed at all times unless we're using them?"

He raised a brow, appraising her, "We *do* need to bleed the secondary lines, but not the main lines. And yes, the gates will need to be opened and resealed. It's the best way to check for gaskets that are wearing down. We'll do the gates first. And afterward, maybe we'll go our separate ways so that we can get done faster…if it looks like you can handle it."

Mira nodded, "Got it."

She performed task after task seamlessly that day, surprising Jim by her competence. Before too long, he was letting her do things on her own and only came to check on her occasionally.

Finally, he approached her and patted her on the back. "You did good today. Meet me at the elevators tomorrow, nine am sharp."

"Yes, sir," she said, and made her way out of the sub-levels with a little more spring in her step than when she entered.

Chapter 6

Over the next few days, Jim and Mira worked several sections of the sub-levels together. She was getting in the groove of this juggling act between work and school. She rarely saw anyone other than Jim during the day. Mr. Griffith did show up to talk with Jim once in a while, sometimes looming over Mira while she worked, but never stayed long. Thankfully.

"Ready to open this puppy up?" Jim said as he walked over to a large furnace door.

"Sure," she said, getting up from the pile of dried seaweed bricks she'd been sitting on.

He stepped up to the furnace and grabbed one side of a giant wheel. "Once we open her up, we have to clean her out, and check for corrosion..." He pulled on the wheel in quick hand over hand motions. The door popped open, singing a high note as it swung out.

"Climb on in," Jim said, his voice echoing inside the cavernous chamber.

Inside, a slick gray film covered every surface, thicker in some areas than others. After an hour of scrubbing, Mira's arms felt like lead weights had been tied to them, and her shoulders were threatening to go on strike, but she pushed on.

Eventually, Jim threw his rag onto the growing pile by the door. "Nicely done. Easy enough, right? Just two more to go," he said, his voice echoing inside the empty chamber.

Mira groaned, not sure if her joints could handle scrubbing two more furnaces. But she didn't complain aloud, afraid to show she couldn't handle this job.

Luckily, the other furnaces were much smaller, and they spent most of their time repairing worn vents.

"Alright, on to the last job for today. We'll be checking valves, just like the first day. Think you can do it without me breathing down your neck?" Jim asked.

Mira stretched her sore shoulder muscles and smiled, "yeah, I can handle that."

"Alright, just go that way, until you reach sector E. I'll go this way…it's got more complex valves," he pointed the opposite direction, "when we're all done, we'll meet back here. Record any unusual readings on the pressure gages as you go. If any of them are in the red-zone, contact me immediately." He tapped his wrist a couple of times, and held it over her wrist until it flashed. "Just tap it three times and it should connect you directly to me."

"Got it," she said.

"Oh, I almost forgot…" he held up a finger, "…if a pipe is painted red, do *not* touch it without gloves. If you forget that, you'll really wish you hadn't. Here." He handed her a pair of old leather gloves, then turned and left.

The work went quickly, and after what felt like only minutes Mira realized she had traversed nearly two hundred yards down the sector. A line hissed as she released steam from a valve and hot water dribbled onto the floor. No leaks so far, no worn gaskets or problems. With how often these were checked, it wasn't surprising.

The rhythm of the engine closest to her was like a lullaby and she had to fight to keep her eyes open. Working and studying so much was catching up to her. She hoped she could make it through her internship while working this job—if she passed the exam next week. She blinked away fatigue and stretched, releasing a yawn; glad the day was almost over.

From the corner of her eye she thought she saw movement, and the metal flooring several yards away creaked. She turned to get a better look, but saw nothing other than hundreds of yards of open catwalk and pipes.

"Hello? Jim, is that you?" She said, calling out to whoever might be there. There was no reply. Her tired brain was making her paranoid. The only sounds were that of water flowing through pipes, engines turning and the unnerving subtle groaning of the metal hull moving through the water.

She rolled her eyes at her childishly-active imagination, and continued toward sector E. She was nearly done.

A few minutes later she reached the end of the sector, and started to turn back, but saw one solitary light on halfway down the catwalk in sector E. Strange.

"You done?" a voice asked through her wrist device, startling her.

She tapped it and responded, "Yep. Just got done. I'm going to go turn off a lantern that's been left on in sector E, then head back."

"No. Just leave it. Your job is done for the day. Let's go home."

"You sure? It'll only take a minute."

"Yeah, just come on back."

Mira shrugged, "Okay, boss," then jogged back to the junction where Jim was waiting.

"Any problems?"

"Nope. Everything looks good."

"Great. Let's go home." His mustache twisted up into a smile, "you're doing good here, kid."

Mira beamed at the compliment, ignoring the 'kid' part, "thanks."

As made their way to the elevator she reached for her digi-reader, to study as they walked. It was gone.

"Jim?"

"Yeah?"

"I dropped my digi-reader. I've gotta go back for it."

"We can get it tomorrow. I'm not paying you to get your digi-whats-it."

Her stomach twisted at the thought of leaving it behind, "I really need it tonight. I've got a big test that I'm studying for. Just clock me out when you get up top. You can do that, right? I'll be right behind you. I swear."

Jim tapped his wrist, noting the time and sighed, "Okay. I'll clock you out. Just hurry. This sector is supposed to be cleared in an hour for submersion. They like everyone to be out of the lower levels at least half an hour prior, so they'll be shutting down the elevators about then."

"Don't worry. It's not going to take me that long," she said as she ran back the other direction, scanning the catwalk as she went.

By the time she made it to the end of sector F, she was losing hope that she'd actually find the digi-reader, wondering if it'd dropped down to the lower levels or got left behind in one of the furnaces.

Turning to head back she saw it peeking out from behind a pipe, near the wall.

"Oh, thank goodness," she breathed, clipping it securely to her belt.

Looking over, she saw the lone green glow in sector E again. Jim hadn't wanted her to bother with it before because he was eager to get home, but she had no reason not to go turn it off now. It'd take less than a minute.

Upon reaching the light, she stopped mid-stride. There was a curtain hanging over the doorway of make-shift room that had been hidden by pipes before.

Curiosity pushed her forward over a narrow plank that straddled the gap between the catwalk and the strange room. She lifted the curtain, revealing a large chamber. Along the back wall were rows and rows of books. Actual, real books.

Furniture took up a majority of the moderately-sized room. Someone was living here.

In the middle of a small table was a potted bush. Roses? She'd never seen a real rose before. The blossoms were yellow, slowly fading into orange with dark pink tips. Like a sunset captured in a flower. Where did this come from? She stepped into the room to get a closer look, bending down to touch one of the silky petals. As she did so a single yellowed leaf fell, dropping onto the table.

"What are you doing here?" someone roared, shattering the silence. Mira clapped her hands over her ears and turned to see Mr. Griffith entering the room.

Chapter 7

Mr. Griffith pushed her out of the way, as he yelled, "What do you think you are doing here? Get out. Get out now!"

Mira stumbled backwards, too stunned to defend herself.

"Out!" he roared again.

She scrambled to the door, skirting around him, yanking the curtain so hard it fell in a heap behind her as she darted through the gap.

It felt like her feet weren't even touching the metal as she ran. After a few minutes her lungs burned. She chanced a look over her shoulder and thought she saw something following her, but couldn't be sure.

She forced herself to keep running. Tears filled her eyes and she wanted to scream in frustration. How could she be so stupid? Even if she passed the nursing test on Friday, she'd need a good paying job to get her through the internship phase. She'd be fired for sure after this.

Just as Mira rounded the corner to meet up with the main catwalk, a horn blared. She shrieked, lost her footing, and tumbled to the floor rolling with too much momentum on the shaky walkway. She groped for something to stop her and grabbed a pipe. A red pipe. Searing pain shot through her hand and she lurched away. That final movement propelled her body under the railing and off the side of the catwalk.

She slapped her hand on the ledge, but released it before she could stop herself; the pain from the fresh burn pouring down her body in a wave. Her heart jumped into her throat and every muscle tightened as she dropped.

She slammed into a group of wires. They whipped her as she broke through them, and flung her face first into a pipe. The hollow gong of the impact echoed around her and she fought through the pain and fuzz, grabbing at anything that might slow her.

She twisted around just in time to land flat on her back on top of a pile of wooden crates. It snatched her breath away and her stiff body tumbled down the wooden mountain, landing hard on the floor of the city ship, while boxes toppled and crashed around her.

Too stunned to move, she lay still, taking in what had just happened. There wasn't a single part of her body that didn't hurt. Warm blood tickled her skin, rolling from her nose toward her ear. She brushed the hair out of her face and wiped her nose, cringing as she touched it.

Her nurse's training kicked in and she tried to calm herself so that she could assess her injuries while lying there. Her entire palm was burned, along with the bottom half of all of her fingers. She shook as she examined it more closely. Some of the skin was peeling away to reveal shiny pinkness underneath. Swollen blisters took up the other spaces. The burns were likely only superficial, despite how bad they hurt. She touched her ribs gingerly, definitely bruised, but not broken. There was a large knot on the back of her head and of course, her nose was broken, making it hard to breathe.

She could still move her arms, and head—but not her legs. Something was wrong. She sat up, noticing for the first time that her legs were pinned under a large crate.

"Well, this is just great."

Distantly, Mira thought she could hear water. Like someone had turned on the sink in a bathroom far away. Her eyes went wide. They'd begun immersing the sector.

"No. No. No. No," she said, pushing on the crate with her good hand.

"Help!" she screamed. "Somebody help me!"

She tapped frantically at her wrist device, "Jim!" No response.

She pulled up her contact list, selecting every single person, "Help me! I'm stuck on the bottom of the ship and it's about to be covered in water. I can't get out." She looked around for some sort of reference, "When I fell, I was leaving sector F, only a hundred meters or so from the elevator. Please hurry," she said, trying to keep the panic out of her voice.

A thin rivulet of icy water coursed across the floor. Mira gasped as it wrapped around her. She pulled desperately at her legs, hoping the crate would float when the water level rose higher. But it didn't. She snatched a slat from one of the broken crates and used it as a lever to lift the other crate. It started to lift, then with a crack, the wooden slat snapped.

The cold water climbed up past her navel. Her breath caught and her body trembled. "Help! Somebody, please! Help!" She screamed, knowing it was futile. As the water reached chest level, she remembered Mr. Griffith. He was down here. He could save her.

"Mr Griffith! Help! Please, I'm trapped! Please!"

Before long the water level was at her shoulders, and she couldn't hold it together any longer. Huge, hot tears rolled down her face. She lifted her arm out of the water, checking her device. No one had responded yet. Not even her father. She tapped the line, "I love you, for always, papa," and ended the simple message as the water licked her neck.

Her chin trembled and she screwed up her face, fighting against the panic to let out a final, throat-numbing scream.

The seawater crept up to her jaw and she tipped her head back, sucking in deep breaths until her mouth went under the rising tide.

Within seconds her entire body was submerged. She pulled at her legs again, and the giant object shifted. Yes! She tugged harder, pushing against the heavy crate with both hands. The effort was draining. She released huge air bubbles, pushing with everything she had left, and it shifted again, but settled back down. She was still pinned.

Her lungs hurt. The pain in the rest of her body was all but forgotten. She wanted to breathe in to relieve the burning. She fought to keep her mouth closed, but it opened against her will, swallowing water, breathing it in. Her lungs spasmed and sucked in more water. Every muscle in her body seized and her vision began to darken.

Just before everything went black, she thought she heard something. It was too late.

Chapter 8

Mira came to, dragging in a halting breath. Someone was talking to her, but she couldn't comprehend the words. Her stomach muscles tensed and she turned onto her side, heaving. The vomit burned like lava as it came out through her mouth and nose. Pain returned full force. Everything hurt.

For what seemed like several minutes, she lay there, gasping and coughing before the spasms died down, replaced by uncontrollable shivers.

"You're going to be okay." A deep, soothing voice assured her.

She looked up to see a shirtless man kneeling over her. Water dripped off his hair and beard, running down over his chest. Slits fanned out on his neck. Were those gills? She blinked, her eyes were playing tricks on her. Was she dreaming? No, this pain was too real.

"Mr. Griffith?" She asked in a slightly nasal voice. "You saved me?"

"Looks like it," He said, relief evident on his face as he reached around and gently lifted her to a sitting position, "What happened?"

She cleared her throat and coughed a few more times, wincing at the feeling of broken glass rattling in her lungs, "Well, I was kind of freaked out by *someone*, and managed to slip and fall while running away." She wiped a drop of blood from her nose and gasped at the rush of pain.

"Careful, it looks like you broke your nose," he said, leaning in to look at her hand, "What happened there?"

"Red pipe." She pointed to the offending piece of metal behind him, "I grabbed it just before I fell." She felt uncomfortable beneath the gaze of his gray-blue eyes and found herself looking away, staring at the slits on his neck again. She opened her mouth to ask if they were gills when he seemed to notice her stare.

He turned away from her and put his trench coat back on, popping up the collar, "We need to get you someplace more comfortable until the elevators come back on line. It'll be awhile. Can you walk?"

"I think so." She grabbed a rail with her good hand and pulled herself up. A wave of dizziness hit her and she leaned into the railing for support. "Maybe give me a minute," she said, sitting back down.

He shook his head, "I don't know why I asked. You're in no condition." He slid his arms beneath her and lifted her up, cradling her against his chest.

Her pulse slowed and she relaxed, settling against him, "Mr. Griffith?" She said.

"Call me Damon," he said.

She swallowed and tilted her head to look at him, "Damon, I'm sorry I invaded your privacy earlier. I didn't think—"

"No," he interrupted, "I'm sorry. I planned on apologizing to *you* tomorrow. I'm used to being left alone. I didn't expect anyone to be there...I overreacted. Seems to be a flaw of mine."

"No, I'm sorry—"

"Stop," he adjusted his grip to hold her more securely. "I don't deserve your kindness after the awful way I've behaved around you."

She wasn't sure what to say. He had behaved horribly, but he sounded truly sorry for it. She thought about how curiosity had driven her to invade his privacy, when she went to shut off that light. "We all have our flaws."

"Right. You came down here to find your father, I acted like a crazy person and you actually came back here to take his place."

"I had to. I needed this job."

"Exactly. You did what you had to do, even when you didn't want to. I'm not half that brave. Plus, Jim has nothing but praise for you. You're brave, smart and beautiful. Not flawed."

She laughed uncomfortably, "Oh, I have plenty of flaws. You just don't know me well enough."

"Well then, challenge accepted. I'll just have to get to know you better."

Although he probably meant nothing by it, she became keenly aware of his body heat penetrating her wet clothes and his hand on her thigh.

She squirmed a bit so that he loosened his grip and tried to change the subject, "so, Damon, I've never seen a rose in real life. Is that what that flower is called?"

He nodded, "They were a gift from my mother; the last thing I got from her before she died. They're meant to look like the sunrise, to remind me of the mornings we spent together when I was small. But, they haven't been doing very well lately, and I guess I'm a bit protective." There was pain in his voice as he spoke.

"For what it's worth, I'd be a bit protective of them too."

He grunted some sort of assent and for several minutes, neither of them spoke.

A groan followed by a high-pitched whine echoed across the expanse of the ship. Mira jumped and pulled herself closer to Damon.

He laughed, "Don't worry, it's just the pumps kicking on." He pointed up ahead with his chin, "...and we're here."

He carried her inside his apartment and set her on the couch. "You'll need to get out of your wet clothes."

She shrunk, noticing that his home was just the one large room. There were no separate chambers for privacy.

He rummaged through a dresser, and brought out an old uniform, "These coveralls will be huge on you, but it's better than nothing."

She felt heat rising through her, definitely better than nothing. There was a blanket draped over the arm of the couch and she reached to pick it up, hoping to use it as a shield.

"Don't. You'll want a dry blanket. I only have the one. I'll step outside. Just holler when you're done," he said, disappearing through the doorway.

Changing was difficult. She was only able to use one hand to remove the wet clothes clinging to her body, and every movement made her more aware of her bruises and scrapes. Her tight shoulders didn't want to bend as she hooked them into the sleeves. But she got them through, zipped the ugly thing up, and sat back on the couch, relieved.

"I'm done." She called out, sniffling back blood that had started to drip from her nose again.

Damon returned and put a kettle of water on the stove, then grabbed the blanket from the small twin bed and arranged it across her lap. He seemed to be on auto-pilot as he pulled out a beat-up first aid kit, took her hand and smeared burn cream on it.

She stifled a scream as the cream brought the pain in her hand to life again, stinging and growing hot, before finally cooling and blissfully numbing everything it touched.

Damon wrapped it gently with gauze; then applied bandages to the other visible cuts and scrapes on her face and arms. Her heart skipped around erratically and she wasn't sure if it was from her injuries or from Damon's gentle attentiveness as he cared for her.

She felt like some sort of damsel in distress being ensnared by the charms of her rescuer, and it annoyed her. She wadded up a piece of gauze and gingerly pushed it into her nose. He was being kind, and she was grateful. Nothing more.

"Thanks," she said, with a more pronounced nasally voice, running her fingers over the bandages with her good hand, "You did a really good job. If I didn't know better I'd think you were in nursing school too," she said, cocking an eyebrow.

He smirked, "Nope. All my schooling comes from those books." He thumbed over his shoulder at the shelf overflowing with paperbacks of all shapes and sizes. There had to be hundreds there.

"How *did* you get all of these?"

"Guilt payments from my father, mostly," he said, pinching his lips together in a tight line. "But some were gifts from my mother."

Mira nodded, then hissed, bringing her hand to her head as pain exploded behind her eyes.

Damon's brows knit in concern, "I don't have access to pain medicine..." he moved to the stove and poured a steamy cup of tea from the kettle, and brought it back to her, "...But I've got this. It should help."

She sipped the steamy brew and sank back into the couch, savoring the warmth spreading through her body. Without even meaning to, she started to drift off to sleep. She vaguely felt the tea cup being removed from her hand and being lowered onto the couch before the sweet bliss of dreamland swallowed her whole.

***

Hours later, Mira woke to a pungent smell and a soft tapping sound. She was momentarily disoriented as her eyes struggled to focus. Moving to sit up, she had to force her stiff legs to obey her commands.

"Ow!" she said, along with her entire body as it screamed in protest.

Damon looked up from the stove, where he was stirring something, "Good morning. Ready for breakfast?"

She wrinkled her nose, surprised that the smell could penetrate the gauze she had stuffed up there, "sure."

He plopped lumpy yellow mush onto a plate and brought it to her.

It was some sort of egg substitute, hopefully it tasted better than it smelled. Definitely not what she was used to, but it'd feel good to get something in her stomach.

He went to get his own plate, and sat down across from her. "Sleep well?"

"Yeah, I think so," she said, rubbing her neck.

"I was worried you had a concussion when you fell asleep so fast. When you started snoring, I knew you were fine."

"I don't snore," she said, through a mouthful of egg.

"Well, if you don't snore, the language you talk in your sleep is awfully guttural."

She gaped. "It's because of my nose...and this cotton. I don't normally snore."

"Uh, huh," he raised his brows, "I think I found your flaw."

She laughed, grabbing her ribs, "Ouch!" and tossed a pillow at him, "don't make me laugh. It hurts."

He batted it to the ground with a chuckle. "How bad is it? Need more tea?"

"No." She put her hands up to ward off the question along with the tea that had knocked her out the night before, "I'm sore, and it hurts if I move too fast, but other than that, better than I expected."

He looked her over, and nodded, "you're one tough biscuit. Sorry I don't have any real pain medication."

"I'm fine," she said, though she secretly wished he did have something other than the tea.

What must it be like to live down here, away from everyone else, without access to the little things she took for granted? "But, why don't you have access to regular medicine?" She asked before she could stop herself.

He ruffled his hair, and it gave him the appearance of a mad man, "Well, you don't think it's normal for someone to be living down here, do you?"

She almost laughed as she took in his manic appearance, but she bit her lip and shook her head.

He shrugged, "According to the ship system, I don't exist. If you don't exist, you can't buy certain goods."

"How does that work? You have a job. You're a supervisor for goodness sake."

He looked away, "I'm an anomaly. I was never supposed to be born. I was never implanted with a fancy tracking device in my wrist, because according to doctor's records, I died at birth." He moved his hands to the collar of his coat, hesitated; then took it off, revealing the slits again. "I was my mother's first child. They knew by the second trimester that something was different. You're a nursing student, so maybe you've heard of pharyngeal arches?"

"It sounds familiar, but I don't remember what they are," she said.

Damon grabbed a tattered book from the floor by the couch and flipped to a well-worn page, "Well, fetuses go through a stage in early development where it looks like they have gills, right?"

She nodded, leaning forward to see the sketch on the page.

"Those are the arches," he said, closing the book. "Mine actually did develop into gills, and they told my mother that she needed to *stop me from maturing.* But she refused. Her husband loved her enough to agree to hide me. I lived with them, and my little brother—officially their only child—in secret until I was ten. That's when mother died, and father moved me down here. I guess he didn't kill me, out of love for her, but he didn't want the risk of having me around either. I got books and rations for years, then, one day all of that stopped." He shrugged, "So, I just started working, and everyone looked the other way. I found an old ration-card, and was able to get it activated. My pay is deposited on that. I worked my way up to supervisor through the years...and that's the short version."

"Wow," Mira said, pulling the blanket up under her chin. She wanted to ask more about his life down here, but found herself asking instead, "How was your mother able to stop them from taking you all those years ago?" tears stung the corner of her eyes and she blinked them away, "my mother was forced to abort my older sister because she would've been born with chromosomal abnormalities."

He looked down at his hands, "I'm sorry about your sister. That should've been my fate, too. My father used his government connections to stop it, I'm sure."

"Who's your father?" She asked, trying to recall any officials with the last name Griffith.

"Nobody," he said, "I'd rather not talk about *him.*"

Noting his tone, her eyes moved to the roses, then to the plate now devoid of egg substitute. She had fresh eggs at home, thanks to her mother. It was a luxury that most in their station could only dream of. "I have a chicken," she said.

"What?" he said, looking at her as if she'd grown a third eye.

Mira laughed, "I mean, I have something special from my mother too. It's a chicken. Mother saved for years to buy Gloria. She brought her home only a few months before she passed away."

"Why a chicken?"

"She grew up on a farming barge, outside the city. She became orphaned as a young teen and survived by rummaging through the trash to find scraps for her pet chickens, then eating the eggs. I guess she got Gloria to remind me of who she was, and where she came from. She was tougher than I'll ever be."

"I doubt that," Damon said, gathering the dishes off the table and walking them back over to the sink.

"I worry about what it will do to Papa when that chicken dies. He's already lost two daughters—my older sister Sabrina died when she was eight—then losing the one before she was even born, and my mom two years ago. They had me when they were a lot older, and I'm all he has left. He's all I have too."

"He's lucky to have you, Mira." Damon said.

His sincere smile and intense eyes sent a thrill though her, and she had to look away, "thanks. I'm the lucky one though. He's always supported me, through everything." Suddenly, her eyes popped open wide. "Oh no. He probably thinks I'm dead!" She tapped on her wrist, displaying her messages. One was flashing in her in-box. But it wasn't from her father. It was from the North-Point Hospital.

Chapter 9

Mira tapped the flashing message, *"Sebastian Ricci, has been admitted to North-Point General for multiple injuries requiring surgery. You may present this letter at the front desk to gain admittance to his room. Regards-Dr Levitt."*

"Is everything okay?" Damon asked, trying to crane his neck to see the message.

"My father's in the hospital." She tapped out a quick letter to her father, hoping he'd read it before viewing the messages she'd sent yesterday.

"When will the elevators be back up?" Mira asked.

He stood and looked out the door, "shouldn't be too long. Maybe thirty minutes? It's mostly drained."

Mira raised herself up, grimacing as her muscles objected to the motion. "I need to be at the elevators as soon as they are running again."

Damon moved in front of the door. "You can't just leave."

She started, taking in his size for the first time since her rescue. "But, my father needs me," she said, glancing around the room for other escape options.

"Of course," he laughed, amused by her reaction. "I meant, you can't leave by yourself. You're in no condition. Plus, you probably want to get back into your old clothes." He popped up the collar of his trench coat again, running his fingers through his hair, flattening it down, "Your clothes are over there." He pointed to the clothes-line next to the stove where they were hanging. "I'll wait for you outside."

"You're going with me to the hospital?" she asked.

"No. I'll ride up to the main level with you though. We'll find someone to escort you the rest of the way there."

"Oh." she said, realizing she really did want him to be with her. She could use someone to lean on right now, and not just physically.

He seemed to notice her dejection. "I'm an anomaly, remember? It's too risky for me to go with you, especially to a hospital."

She nodded, understanding.

As soon as he was out of sight, she painstakingly changed clothes again, and met him outside. "Alright, let's go then."

Before too long they were turning the corner toward the elevators. Mira stared at the spot where she'd rolled off. The water was low enough that she could see the wreckage below. She shivered, rubbing the goose-bumps that popped up on her arms.

Damon put his hands on her arms, guiding her around the corner, skirting the slats where she'd thrown up.

As they approached the elevator, she sat against the wall. The red light above the door was lit, indicating that it was still offline.

"You can go back. I'm sure I can make it from here," she said.

Damon sat down next to her, "I'll stay. I said I'd take you up to the main level, didn't I?"

"True. And I kinda like your company," she said with a smile, patting Damon's knee with her bandaged hand.

"Mira?"

"Yes?"

"Thanks, for not rejecting me—for not being freaked out by me when you found out I was an anomaly."

"Well, I snore," she said, nudging him.

He laughed, "that's true," and settled his hand softly on top of hers, not holding it, just resting it there.

Her stomach fluttered. His touch was so reassuring. Without thinking, she leaned in, rested her head on his shoulder and sighed, enjoying how comfortably familiar it felt to be near him.

"So, why nursing?" he asked after a few minutes of silence, shifting to get more comfortable.

"It's a stepping stone. I couldn't afford to go directly into med school. One day I'll be able to get my doctorate, and then be part of a research team for Porter-Alan's disease or Alzheimer's."

"That's ambitious. I sense a story behind those specific diseases."

Mira nodded, "my mother died of Porter-Alan's, and Alzheimer's runs on my father's side." She cleared her throat unsure if it was still raw from the trauma yesterday or if she was getting choked up thinking about her father, "I'm beginning to see the first signs of it in him...it scares me. I—"

A loud buzzing noise interrupted her and she looked up to see the light change from red to green.

"Oh! It's online again, right?" Mira said, using Damon's shoulder to push herself into a standing position.

"Yep. Let's go."

Within minutes they were both in the break room relating their tale to Jim.

"Well, you look terrible," Jim said.

"Uh, thanks," Mira said, touching her face self-consciously.

"If you wanted to get out of the de-salination cleaning, you could have called in with the flu, or scurvy, or something. You didn't need to go through all that," he said, shaking his head in mock disapproval.

"I'll keep that in mind for next time," she said, smiling.

"So, you need an escort to the hospital?" he stood and straightened out his pants. "I've got an hour before I have to clock in. This paperwork can wait."

She started to say that she'd be fine, but Damon shot her a look, "Yes, that'd be great."

"Hey, I hear that they have someone who's agreed to sign up under that new protocol thingy. He'll be the first. The Governor is going to be at the hospital today to witness the signing," Jim said.

Mira felt sick. Why did this new protocol feel like a personal attack? She thought it was supposed to be a few months before it went into effect too. She turned to look at Damon, hoping he could read her expression. She wanted him to go with her.

He shook his head slightly, seeming to understand her silent plea. "Jim, make sure someone at the hospital looks her over. She's been through a lot more than she's letting on," he said, before turning to leave.

***

A TV in the hospital lobby was playing propaganda commercials about the citizens' duty to sacrifice for the greater good, obviously leading in to the main event to be held there later. Mira cringed at the blatant brain washing.

After checking in, she made her way through the halls with Jim on her tail, finally reaching the wing with her father's room. Two military officers flanked the door. She rushed forward and was pushed back by one of them.

"I'm sorry. You can't go in there," the taller officer said.

"That's my father's room. I was sent a summons by the hospital." She tapped on her wrist device, pulling up the message, and turning so that the officers could see the image. Her ears grew hot and she tried to ignore the anxiety building inside.

The smaller officer nodded, "Alright, you can go in. But you…" he pointed to Jim, "…have to stay out here."

Jim put up his hands, warding off trouble, "Sure, sure." He looked to Mira. "You good? I should probably get back, anyway." He tapped his nose and pointed to hers, "Have someone check out your injuries while you're here too..."

"Thanks, I will." She waved to him and pushed the door open.

Her father was sitting up in bed, reading some papers on a clipboard. A nurse was fussing with some tubing dangling from an IV bag. Other people were in the back of the room, setting up camera equipment.

"—now this is just ceremonial, of course. We'll have all the official stuff written up later," a man standing near her father said. It was Governor Wilhelm.

The room seemed to expand and all the voices sounded miles away. Mira felt light headed. She hurried to her father's side, sitting down before she fell. "Papa? What's going on?"

"Mira?" he said in surprise, reaching out to pull her closer to him while scanning her face. "Are you okay?"

"I'm fine, just a little work accident. Are *you* okay?"

Her father sighed, "I went out for a walk yesterday morning, and fell. I broke my shoulder and bruised up my hip pretty good."

She slid the clipboard off his lap, and held it out of his reach while she read the words in bold black ink. There were blank signature lines at the bottom. "What..." She whispered, looking around the room, "...is this?" She was drowning all over again, air refused to enter her lungs.

"History in the making. That's what," the Governor said. "Your father has agreed to be the first to sign."

"What?" She said again, eyes wide with shock. This was a nightmare.

Without pausing to consider her state at all, Wilhelm pointed to the papers in her hand and said, "To go along with the new protocol issued; those with terminal diseases are also given the option to terminate early, in exchange for a lump-sum payment to be transferred to their family."

"I thought the whole idea behind this was to save resources. How does paying people make sense?" Mira said, somehow speaking through the fog in her head.

A man standing behind Wilhelm pointed to a colorful poster with graphs leaning against the wall, apparently made for some sort of presentation. "It does save resources. It saves on medication that would have been administered. In most cases, that medication hardly helps anyhow, wasting it. It'd also save on housing, hospital care, hospice, and food costs. We've done the math. A lump sum payment is by far the lesser of the costs, but leaves the individual a way to contribute to their family before they leave. It's best for everybody."

"No! No, it's not best for everybody," Mira said, unable to keep the anger out of her voice. "I guarantee that none of you will be subjected to this 'voluntary termination.' You won't ever be in the position to need to choose. This is genocide! How can you not see that!" Hot tears spilled from her eyes as she spoke. "He's not signing!" She threw the clipboard, sending it skittering across the floor.

"Mirabella," her father pleaded.

She could see the resignation in his eyes. The peace.

"No, papa. No," she laid her head on him, sobbing.

"Sweet, Mirabella. Listen to me. I'm dying. During the surgery they found a tumor. It's inoperable. And my liver's failing. I have a year at the most to live. If I do this, I can leave knowing your schooling has been taken care of. You wouldn't be left with mountains of debt. I want to do what is best for you, while I still can."

Mira's jaw hung open and she moved away from her father. Unable to contain the frantic energy inside of her, she kicked an empty chair, sending it crashing to the floor, "This isn't what's best for me!" she screamed, turning back to her father. "Listen. I don't care if I have to work overtime for the rest of my life. It would all be worth it knowing I had a little more time with you, even if it was just one more day." She returned to him and held his hands, blinking back tears, "...even if it was just one more day," she repeated.

Her father dropped his head, looking at her hands in his own, "I just wanted to do something for you. I don't want to be a burden."

"You're not a burden. You're family. I need you."

Governor Wilhelm cleared his throat, interrupting them. "He's already agreed to the deal. Unless you can come up with a way to pay off these hospital expenses, with this new diagnosis he will automatically be put in the societal burden category." He held up the clipboard, with its papers neatly gathered back and secured, "This is a way he can leave on his own terms, and help you before he goes."

Every head turned as the door to the room slammed open.

"Brad?" Mira said.

"Mirabella?" He looked her over, taking in her swollen nose and disheveled appearance. "What happened?"

"Just a work accident. I'll be fine," she said, looking away. Why did he have to be here?

Brad strode to Mira, taking her hand, "I heard what was going on and came to see if you were okay."

She couldn't look at him.

"Father, I will take on this family's burden, as my own," he said.

"I can't let you do that. The burden will be too great. You have a future family to worry about," Wilhelm said, in a rehearsed manner.

"This could be my future family," Brad said, turning to Mira, "if you'll marry me."

Realization hit, and puzzle pieces fell into place. Was he actually using this new protocol to trap her? She pulled her hand out of his and looked down at her father. She'd have to agree. She had no choice.

"Just a second," she said, standing and walking to the back of the room, forcing herself to breathe, and think.

"Well?" Brad prodded.

Mira turned back to face him, every muscle in her body tensed. She looked at her father, lying in bed, with the clipboard back on his lap.

"Okay," she said.

Brad smiled victoriously.

"Stop!" The door banged open for the second time.

Mira did a double take, looking back and forth between the man in the doorway and the man standing by her father. Two Brads?

No. His eyes were gray-blue, not sky-blue, and he was bigger. Their features were almost identical, but their style was not. Brad wouldn't be caught dead in a trench-coat.

"Damon?" she asked, shocked.

His beard was shaved and his hair was trimmed short, but it was him.

"Damon?" Both Brad and Governor Wilhelm said together, one in astonishment, the other in anger.

"What are you doing here!" the Governor demanded.

"I've come to stop this," Damon said, looking to Mira. Every other eye in the room was on Damon. His eyes flicked to the camera that was poised for the interview, and he gave a subtle 'go ahead' nod to her.

She understood what he wanted and pushed the red button on the camera, nudging it with her shoulder to point at him.

"You know this is wrong," Damon said.

The man who had pointed to the charts earlier stood, "We are simply trying to save humanity by conserving resources and—"

"Trying to save humanity?" Damon said, interrupting him. "Like you do by getting rid of all the anomalies?"

He removed his trench coat. The slits on his neck stood out in contrast to his pale skin.

"How? How did you? Who?" the man stammered.

Damon grabbed Brad's arm and pulled him to his side, "Who? I'm Damon Griffith Wilhelm, eldest son of Governor Wilhelm, the hypocrite."

Wilhelm pointed a finger at Damon, "You aren't supposed to come up here! I can't protect you from what they'll do. I've warned you."

"You mean you've scared me. You told me that people would be afraid of me; that they'd shun me and try to kill me. But no one I've ever met has treated me as poorly as you."

Mira moved forward, gently turning Damon to face the camera, "This man saved my life yesterday. Yes, he is an anomaly, but without this difference," She reached up and brushed her hands near his gills, "I would've died. No one else could've rescued me. Please, listen. Our differences make us better, not worse. We are stronger, because we all have different strengths, not because we can all fit into the same mold. We should be encouraging variety within our species. We should be embracing our older generations; learning from them and sharing in the kind of wisdom that can only come with age. That is what will ensure our survival. What we look like doesn't matter. It's what we *do* that makes us what we are."

Governor Wilhelm jumped up from his seat, faster than a man of that size should have been able and pointed a fat finger at Mira, "I do what needs to be done—what others don't have the stomach for. My job isn't always pretty, but someone has to do it."

"Why are you the one that gets to decide what has to be done?" Mira said, then looked at the camera again, "Our Governor and his supporters want to cull our population. How can they expect this of us, when they don't even follow the rules themselves?" Her face was flushed with color and she swallowed back the congestion caused by the tears she was trying so hard not to release.

Wilhelm lunged at Mira, and Damon blocked him, knocking him unceremoniously to the floor.

"Your nice speech isn't going to fix the problem." Wilhelm said, rolling to a sitting position. "We've still got resource problems that are only going to get worse."

"No, you're right," her mind raced, knowing she needed to say something or she'd lose this debate, and the stakes were too high. A thought formed in her mind and she ran with it, "Well, we could start by not making chickens so expensive. That's never made sense to me. They are natural recyclers, taking our scraps and turning them into food. Every household should have several, not just the elite."

The chart man spoke up, "not a bad suggestion, but it won't solve everything."

"Maybe that's just it. The solution is more than one answer. We have a ship full of smart people who are capable of thinking of solutions that don't involve genocide."

"Turn that camera off!" Wilhelm yelled, crawling like a mad-man toward it.

Brad awoke from his stunned stupor and quickly crossed the distance, shutting it off.

The guards outside could be heard arguing with people. Seconds later, the door was forced open and an army of people poured in.

A middle-aged-woman pushed her way to the front of the crowd, "Mr. Wilhelm, as president of the Free Citizens Committee, we can't let you sign anyone to this new protocol. You've gone too far. No more slaughter in the name of preservation. Your time as governor is over."

Wilhelm hauled himself off the floor with enormous effort, "You have no power here," he said, panting.

"Actually, we do, because you've gone against the rule of law. Come with us peacefully to the courthouse to resign. We're not waiting another day," the woman said.

"I want all your names," he said, adjusting his suit over his plump body. "Brad, call my lawyers; have them meet me at the courthouse. This isn't over."

Someone grabbed his arm and he jerked it away.

"Don't touch me. I'm coming peacefully."

The crowd filed out, and the camera crew followed, leaving Mira, her father, Damon and Brad alone in the room.

"I've got some phone calls to make," Brad said, turning to leave.

When he reached the door, Mira called out, "Brad..." He turned to look at her, "...I'm sorry."

And she was sorry for the position he was in, but nothing else.

Brad looked away from her, glared at Damon, and stormed through the door.

Damon wilted into a chair by the bed, "I can't believe I did that."

Mira rested her hand on his shoulder, "I'm just glad I wasn't misunderstanding your signals back there," she laughed, feeling an ache in her shoulders as she finally relaxed, "Are you going to be okay?"

He grabbed her hand and pulled her down to sit on the arm of the chair. "I should have done it long ago. I just never had enough courage. Maybe you're rubbing off on me," he said with a half-cocked grin.

"Ahem." Her father cleared his throat.

"I didn't forget you, Papa," she said, moving over to the bed, hugging him gently.

"You know, not to brag, but my birthday wish may be coming true. I wished for you to find someone who could truly love you. Being alone is a beastly burden. I can see that Damon is a good man."

"Papa!" Mira said, shocked. "This isn't a fairy-tale. I barely know Damon."

"Ouch." Damon said, clutching at his chest, "you save a girl twice and she says she barely knows you."

"I meant that his wish *isn't* coming true. I mean, not yet...I mean, I don't know what to say about that." She poked her father, "don't do that!"

He laughed looking at Damon, "Thank you for saving her. I owe you everything."

"Anyone would have done the same thing, Mr. Ricci."

"Not anyone. You risked a lot coming up here."

Damon shrugged, "I didn't think anyone would accept me if they knew what I was, but she did, without a second thought."

"Leave it to my Mirabella to see the beauty in others and then help others to see it too. You know that is what your name means, right? To see beauty."

Mira smiled, rolling her eyes, "So I've been told."

***

A few days later Mira tiptoed through her apartment, readying herself for the day as quietly as possible. She didn't want to wake her father. He needed his sleep.

Her nerves were surprisingly calm, considering that today was the day of the big test. After all that had happened over the last few days, the nursing test seemed pretty insignificant, but her dream hadn't changed.

She slipped on her jacket and opened the door, then paused. There on the doormat was a single sunset colored rose resting on a card.

She opened the card and read, *'You've got this. Go change the world. -Damon.'*

Mira grinned, pressing the card and flower to her chest. Her world had already changed forever.

THREE MEN IN A SUBMARINE – TO SAY NOTHING OF THE VAMPIRE

BY LYNNE LUMSDEN GREEN

"The Strategic Advantages of Submersibles
1. *'Tis private: a man may thus go to any coast in the world invisibly, without discovery or prevented in his journey.*
2. *'Tis safe, from the uncertainty of Tides, and the violence of Tempests, which do never move the sea above five or six paces deep. From Pirates and Robbers which do so infest other voyages; from ice and great frost, which do so much endanger the passages towards the Poles.*
3. *It may be of great advantages against a Navy of enemies, who by this may be undermined in the water and blown up.*
4. *It may be of special use for the relief of any place besieged by water, to convey unto them invisible supplies; and so likewise for the surprisal of any place that is accessible by water.*
5. *It may be of unspeakable benefit for submarine experiments."*

John Wilkes, 1648
One of the founders and a lifelong member of
The Royal Society of London for Improving
Natural Knowledge

Somewhere in London, on the docks, 1814

The workshop was busy, even at this time of night, choked with steam, noisy, and blazing with heat, with at least a dozen men hard at work on various projects. The smithy tolled like a great bell, while a fountain of sparks sizzled as they rained down from the hammering that accompanied the welding. The room was surprising well lit, thanks to a profusion of Faraday electric lamps, but the flashes from the welding created strange shadows on the roof and walls. Everything stank of the death of metal: coal, hot iron, burning tin, and singed copper; of course, something had to suffer and die in the creation of a new invention.

The man-powered submarine dominated the centre of the room, for it was nearly 13 yards long and 10 feet across the beam. It was highly polished and gleamed like fish scales – the only piscine attribute it appeared to display. To Sir Joseph Banks' eyes, it looked like someone had taken the hulls of two boats and glued them together to form an enclosed space, and then clad them in copper plate, brass beams, and rivets. It looked lumpy and graceless; unlike a fish of any description. He had been expecting something less clumsy, with the sleek lines of a pike or a shark.

"I can't imagine anything that looks less like a predator," said Sir Joseph, president of the Royal Society. He felt angry, rather than disheartened. He banged the armrest with his fist to emphasise his remark. "This is a monstrosity. It looks like it will sink like a stone."

Mr George Caley, botanical collector (retired) and currently Sir Joseph's assistant, was pushing his employer's wickerwork chair and twitched to see his employer so excited. "Remember your health, sir," said Caley, retaining his faint Yorkshire accent even after so many years abroad in the antipodes and further years spent living in London, "or your good wife will be having my guts for garters."

Sir Joseph rolled his eyes, but ceased his protests. He was an old man; exposure to the chill night air made his bones ache and tended to make him grumpy. At least it was warm in the workshop and his pains were fading into twinges. Sir Joseph

Banks was, as a favour to the Crown, supervising any scientific research relating to the war effort. He might have declined the honour if he had known it would mean sneaking off to covert, late-night meetings.

It wasn't in his nature to be secretive. He was a firm believer in Science being separate and above political differences, and encouraged communication between scientists no matter what nationality they were, even the French. Proper science was meant to take place during daylight hours with lots of witnesses, not the other way around.

It never occurred to Sir Joseph that he could have delegated any late night meetings to one of his colleagues in the Royal Society or that he could have sent Mr Caley in his stead. It wasn't that he didn't trust others – certainly, Mr Caley had proved himself to be dependable and able to work without supervision for years – but Sir Joseph had always taken the motto of the Royal Society to heart: '*Nullius in verba*', which Sir Joseph took to mean 'take nobody's word for it'. He'd found that nobody could replace the knowledge gained by firsthand observation and experience. Being confined to his wheelchair by gout was *not* going to prevent him from doing his duty.

The recently made Duke of Wellington, Field Marshal Arthur Wellesley, patted Sir Joseph on the shoulder with his fine-boned hand. His long face might have looked severe with his high cheekbones and thin mouth, except his features were generally lit by a merry smile, and the expression in his eyes was always kind (Sir Joseph privately thought the Duke looked too good natured to be a proper soldier). When he spoke, his voice hinted of his childhood spent in Ireland, though the lilt was being eroded as he cultivated a plummier accent. "I know it doesn't look like much. It is a work in progress. But Napoleon has encouraged great strides in science, and we can't be left behind."

Sir Joseph shook his head and said, "Napoleon's scientists abandoned this design. And Fulton had already tried to get our government interested in his man-powered submersibles before going home and forgetting about the project entirely. I believe he is now working on designing steam-powered ocean-going ships, and good luck to him. So why did we build another vessel based on Fulton's designs? Why not copy the design of one of the other submersibles?"

"To be sure, the British research on Fulton's design stopped because our victory at the battle of Trafalgar took away our main motivation to continue. Our London office still had copies of Fulton's designs," said the Duke. "However, I feel the man-powered submarine could be very useful in gathering information."

"Spying, in other words," said Sir Joseph. "All that secret poking about leaves a bad taste in my mouth, I'm afraid."

"I don't see it as spying. I see it as gaining information that might save the lives of my men. And maybe the lives of some of the French navy as well."

"Isn't it a tad underhanded using Napoleon's own submarine design against him?"

"Not at all," said the Duke. "Isn't it the stated goal of the scientific community to have a free exchange of ideas and information over and above the mere shackles of politics?"

"Fiddlesticks!" exclaimed Sir Joseph. "You are parroting one of my speeches. Don't throw my own words back at me."

The Duke gestured to some of the other inventions around the workshop, cannons and guns and such. "Isn't it better to see science used for spying rather than making weapons?"

Sir Joseph was about to make a sharp retort…

Mr Caley cleared his throat in a respectful manner. "Milord," was all he said, but the reproach in his voice was the leash for Sir Joseph's temper.

At this point, one of the welders appeared to finish his task, for he set his tools to one side. He climbed down a stepladder and started making his way over to the visitors.

Sir Joseph noted with approval the welder's goggles and leather cap, heavy leather gloves, even heavier leather apron, and extremely robust leather boots. He trusted a man who took his work seriously and dressed appropriately.

The apron was gently smouldering from the constant flow of sparks, and the welder removed it before approaching the visitors. Under the apron he wore sensible green overalls, and this revealed a surprisingly slim, almost boyish physical frame. Then he took off his gloves and cap and goggles, revealing a cheery grin with far too many sharp teeth and a luxuriant flow of red curls. The welder was a female! And a vampire!

"Who is this?" spluttered Sir Joseph. "I don't recall any vampires in the employ of the government."

There was a softly muttered curse from behind him. Sir Joseph subsided. He hadn't used to be so curmudgeonly, but being confined to a chair soured his temper, when he forgot his body was no longer as active as his mind.

Mistress Liùsaidh Lesley – known as Lucy to her friends – smiled at the Duke of Wellington. With her red hair, white skin and green overall, she resembled a Christmas decoration or a peppermint candy cane, most appropriate for the coming winter season. She turned to the Duke.

"Good evening, your Grace. I'm assuming you didn't warn them?" she said. Her voice was a warm contralto, also accented, this time with a Scottish brogue from the Borderlands. Sir Joseph guessed she originated from Berwickshire or somewhere close to it.

Am I the only native to London here? he thought privately. *Ah well, all the brightest and best in the Empire end up in the capital eventually.*

The Duke smiled back at the young-looking mechanic. "No. I didn't have a chance. Sir Joseph insisted on accompanying me to this test dive. He was most persistent." He turned to the elderly man in the wicker chair and said, "Sir Joseph, may I present Miss Lucy Lesley, our chief mechanic and engineer. Mistress Lesley, this is Sir Joseph Banks, president of the Royal Society and his assistant, Mister Caley."

Miss Lesley bobbed, in what approximated a curtsey in her overalls. "I am honoured," she said.

"It is a pleasure to meet you," said Sir Joseph, bowing his heavy, leonine head in return. Miss Lesley looked about twenty, but to be an engineer she had to be much, much older. Sir Joseph wondered how she had become interested in the science of machines and engines, and how long she had been working for the British government. He turned to the Duke and asked, "Arty, how did you come to make Miss Lesley the head of this project?"

"Miss Lesley comes from a tradition of Scottish engineers. She is a master craftsman in the field," said the Duke. "The Crown was approached by a group of British vampires who offered their skills in return for a promise of recognition as citizens; the vampires want to have the same rights as the living."

Miss Lesley nodded. "Being declared dead can be an awful bore. I've had a dreadful time retaining my ancestral home, because my cousins keep taking me to court, just because they believe they should inherit the place since I am 'dead'."

The Duke continued on "The Crown could see an opportunity to benefit the war effort and it was decided to give them a chance to prove themselves. Miss Lesley had some very clever suggestions and so she was given charge of building and operating the *Nautilus II*. And, due to her nature, she is very good at keeping secrets."

"I heard what you said about her looking clumsy," said Miss Lesley. "A swan looks very clumsy on the land, too. The *Nautilus II* will prove her worth once we get her wet."

"My dear, any engineer worth their salt is never going to say their project isn't workable," said Sir Joseph, but he smiled to take the sting out of his remark. "It might need more time, more money, more research, more equipment and more manpower, but an engineer will get it to work in the end or die trying."

"That's where I'm ahead of the game," said Miss Lesley.

Sir Joseph coloured up. "Please forgive my rudeness. That was an inexcusable thing to say."

Miss Lesley shook her head making her curls bounce in a lively jig. "No need to apologise. I could see it wasn't meant in a nasty way, which makes for a refreshing change." She turned to face the submarine, and her expression softened into maternal pride. "I do believe, gentlemen, that you are here to accompany me while I take my treasure out for a short excursion. Then you can decide if she has any grace or not."

"Will all of us fit?" asked Sir Joseph. Even though the *Nautilus II* dominated the workshop, it didn't look like it would be spacious on the inside.

The Duke rubbed his hands, anticipating his comrade's reaction. "It isn't as comfortable as a clubroom, but I think you are going to be pleasantly surprised."

There was a certain amount of fuss to get the portly Sir Joseph into the submarine, since he was no longer trim or limber. At first, he suggested that he could climb the ladder up to the conning tower, where the hatch was. After all, he had once scooted up trees and clambered over cliff faces in search of rare plants.

Gritting his teeth with determination, Sir Joseph stood up, with the faithful Caley hovering at his side. Sir Joseph shook off his assistant with a gruff, "I'll be fine."

Stop treating me like an invalid, he fumed silently.

He gripped the ladder for support, ignoring the pain in his feet. He went to pull himself up to the next step. The pressure of the step on the joint of his big toe felt like some creature was savaging his foot. Humiliated and betrayed by his own infirmity, his arms couldn't support his weight. He felt himself slipping.

Mr Caley jumped forward – followed closely by Miss Lesley – and grabbed him before he fell. "Thank you," he said, gruff nearly to the point of rudeness.

In the end, Miss Lesley and Mr Caley had to carry him up the ladder and then lower him through the hatch in the conning tower. He came embarrassingly close to not fitting through the hatch.

"It looks like his coat is catching on the edges," said Miss Lesley. "It might be best if you take it off, Sir Joseph."

Mr Caley was very red in the face as he helped Sir Joseph out of his coat. He was a rangy fellow with a surprising amount of strength, but Sir Joseph was not a small man.

"I'm regretting all those puddings," said Sir Joseph, as way of an apology.

"Not as much as I am, milord," muttered Mr Caley.

Sir Joseph allowed Mr Caley the impertinent remark, since his assistant was trained as a botanical collector and not as a nursemaid. Mr Caley duties were meant to be more those of a secretary and research assistant. Neither Sir Joseph nor Mr Caley had ever imagined that Mr Caley would have to try and carry Sir Joseph into a tin fish, and certainly not with the able help of a lady vampire.

Overall, entering the submarine was not an experience that Sir Joseph enjoyed; it was so undignified to be slung around by someone who resembled a slight, pretty girl, even if she was much, much stronger than any man. It galled him that the entire episode was being witnessed by the Duke of Wellington. At least he knew the man wasn't a gossip.

Once inside, he was settled into a comfortable chair in the main cabin. The chair was upholstered in leather, and it was fastened to the floor by a screw so that the chair could be swung to face in any direction, and then there was a lever that could fix the chair in place when you didn't want it to swing. Sir Joseph took the opportunity to catch his breath and inspect his surroundings.

His chair was one of five in the cabin. The cabin itself was small but as luxuriously appointed as the chair, panelled in oak with polished brass fittings and elegant scrollwork decorations, so that it looked more like an office than a craft of war. It smelt very strongly of beeswax and oil. The submarine had only a few tiny portholes, so heavily glazed that he only caught a dim, obscured view of workroom. Behind him was another hatch which led through a bulkhead into the propulsion room.

This hatch was open, and Sir Joseph caught glimpses of several people busily working with pedals and gears.

The Duke took the chair beside him, and Caley sat closer to the bulkhead. The chair closest to the front of the cabin, and closest to a desk set with switches, dials, levers, wheels, and gauges, was taken by Miss Lesley, after she had sealed the main hatch.

"Where is the captain?" asked Sir Joseph.

"That would be me for this jaunt," replied Miss Lesley in a severe manner that brooked no argument, as she toggled switches and pumped a lever.

"May I ask you a question, Miss Lesley?"

"Of course, milord," said Miss Lesley, and she tapped a glass-covered dial. "Ask as many as you like. I can't promise that I'll know the answers to all of them, but I'll do my best."

"I've actually seen a copy of the plans for this vessel. Isn't there a false sail supposed to be attached behind the conning tower, to make the submarine resemble a sailing boat?"

"Ah! I know this one. That false sail created more problems that it solved. The *Nautilus II* isn't meant to dive very deep, but it is still meant to be able to dive under the keels of ships. The original *Nautilus* did manage to dive to below ten fathoms.

We can't dive with the sail up, and getting out to lower and unstep the sail negates any attempt at secrecy."

"Oh yes. That seems obvious now," said Sir Joseph.

"May I add to Miss Lesley's answer?" asked the Duke.

"Of course!" said Sir Joseph. "After all, this is your project. Fulton's plans would have been forgotten, languished, if you hadn't pushed to see this submarine built."

"I am pleased you see it that way," said the Duke. He gestured to the ceiling and the walls surrounding them. "Originally, these man-powered submarines were meant to have a bomb or two on board. The sailing ship disguise was to obscure the submarine's function and let it get close enough to an enemy vessel to blow a hole in its hull. Miss Lesley adapted the design to make a silent and hidden vessel that could make sorties into enemy waters and spy out the lie of the land and the location of troops and camps."

"I see. Very clever," said Sir Joseph. "It reduces the risks taken to obtain information." As much as Sir Joseph disliked spying and sneaking, he preferred spies to bombs.

Miss Lesley turned to the Duke and said, "Your Grace, we are ready to launch. Do you want to do the honours?"

The Duke shook his head. "The *Nautilus II* is yours to command."

Miss Lesley rewarded him with a charming smile. She shouted into a large shell shape hanging from the ceiling. "Chocks away!"

There was a clanging noise and a bump. The submarine started to tilt nose down. Then there was the sensation of movement, of falling. When Sir Joseph glanced at one of the portholes, he could see blurry objects moving past the glass. The vessel tilted further and gained speed. Then there was a tinny splash, foam and dark water danced past the portholes, and the *Nautilus II* slid into the water.

We must be on rails like a steam locomotive, thought Sir Joseph. *But I don't remember noticing rollers or wheels.*

Since it was nighttime, once they were submerged it was like diving into an ink bottle. The lights inside the submarine could only illuminate the water for a couple of yards. All Sir Joseph could see were anchors and chains looming out of the dark for a moment before they disappeared back into the murk behind them.

"I would advise everyone to hang on to something," announced Miss Lesley.

There was series of clanks and clicks, as catches released their hold on the *Nautilus II.* Then the submarine jerked as it bobbed away from its moorings. Sir Joseph – gripping his armrests for all he was worth – was grateful for the warning, as he might have been propelled from his seat otherwise. The hull beside his head hummed a deep note, sounding like a gigantic tuning fork; soon the humming was replaced by rather alarming creaks and groans as the hull adjusted to the pressure of the water.

The point of the man-powered submarine was to make the craft as silent as possible, for the sound of an engine could be heard for long distances in the water. As well, an engine has exhaust fumes, smelly and hard to eliminate. Sir Joseph wondered if the *Nautilus II* was that much quieter, with the whirring and clanking that was being emitted by the propulsion room. He looked around at his fellow submariners, who were stirring in the seats.

"Might I suggest some sort of safety harnesses for the chairs," said the Duke of Wellington. "Just as a precaution."

"An excellent idea, your Grace," said Miss Lesley. "I tend to forget mortals are easily bruised or broken."

In the soft light of the cabin, the vampire looked ... more sinister. More alert. Sir Joseph noticed her canines seemed sharper and more prominent.

Miss Lesley noticed his expression. "You need not fear me, my lord," she said. "I would never harm anyone under my protection. But I must let my more monstrous nature assert itself while we are under the water, so that my senses are much more acute and my reflexes are faster."

"Well, that is just using good sense then," remarked Sir Joseph. "I had heard some rumours to that effect."

"Indeed. These days, we tend to use vampires for all our risky tests," said the Duke.

Miss Lesley nodded and said, "Of course I would never endanger you or his Grace, the Duke of Wellington. This isn't the first time the *Nautilus II* has been fully submerged. Those first tests are like the dress rehearsal of a play; this is when any design flaws will turn up. Most of the problems have been fixed."

"This is only meant to be an inspection, isn't it?" asked Sir Joseph. He looked nervously at the walls, almost expecting to see them leaking. Then it occurred to him that his assistant was being very quiet – much too quiet for the garrulous George. He swung his chair around to check on Mr Caley.

Mr Caley's skin was nearly as pale as Miss Lesley's complexion, his eyes were squeezed tightly shut and he was shaking, slumped in his chair like a sack of grain.

Sir Joseph's temper evaporated. "Good lord, man. Whatever is the matter, Mister Caley?"

Mr Caley opened his eyes with reluctance. He gulped and rolled his eyes, and said, "Well, your lordship, I was never a good sailor at the best of times. And I'm not overly fond of tiny, enclosed places, since I've spent most of my time out-of-doors under a big sky. I'm sure my nausea will pass."

"Fiddlesticks! I never took you for a pansy, Mister Caley, for all your botanical skills. Buck up! Show some backbone."

"Yes, milord," said Mr Caley. He sat up in his chair, but he gripped the armrests with desperate strength.

"Don't be too hard on Mr Caley," said the Duke. "Bravery comes in many forms. I wouldn't have liked to trot off into the wilderness of New South Wales to look for plant specimens, with nothing but a backpack and hat, with that entire great unknown before me."

"Hah! I'll bet you've never had a fearful moment in your life!" said Sir Joseph.

The Duke looked thoughtful. "Once my blood gets up, I am like that boy in one of Mr Anderson's fairy tales, I lose all fear. If I'm afraid in battle, it is not for my own safety, but for my soul. I'm afraid of becoming a butcher and killing men unnecessarily."

Sir Joseph thought for a moment before he spoke. "That seems unlikely. Your interest in creating a success of the *Nautilus II* would indicate it isn't in your nature to seek unnecessary death." He looked at poor Mr Caley, as white as a baker's best flour. "This excursion can't be too long, anyway. We need to keep the *Nautilus II* a secret. So we have to have her back at the dock well before sunrise."

"Can we trust the men manning the pedals?" asked Sir Joseph.

"Yes. Sir Joseph," said Miss Lesley. "For the same reason you can trust me. They are all vampires and used to keeping secrets. But, if that isn't secure enough for you, the crew are all vampires that I have personally converted. They cannot speak, because I have ordered them to not to.”

“I beg your pardon,” said Sir Joseph. “Did I hear you correctly? Is that the specific reason why you chose them for crew? Because they can keep a secret? They are not specially-trained submariners or scientists?”

Miss Lesley smiled, and then stopped when she realised her expression wasn’t particularly reassuring. “Well, in a battle, a submarine is very likely to be damaged. Vampires can see very well in the dark, and it gets dark a few fathoms under the water even on the sunniest days. All vampires have extraordinary strength and reflexes, so they can keep pedalling the ship for a lot longer than mortal men. They don’t really need to breathe, and they can’t be killed by drowning or pressure.”

“Goodness. Then why aren’t all our troops vampires?” asked Sir Joseph.

Miss Lesley stopped smiling and shifted in her seat as it has suddenly grown too small for her, but she answered honestly all the same. “Well, in a battle, vampires can die just as easily as anyone else, from untipped arrows, wooden pikes, or having our heads cut off by swords. We can't fight during the daytime, of course; this is why all the portholes in the *Nautilus II* are made from a special safety glass that filters out the dangerous elements in the sun's rays. And then, there is a lot of blood in a battlefield. It would send most vampires into a frenzy and make them rather useless as soldiers, to be honest. They might end up killing men from their own side."

"Ah. I see," said Sir Joseph. "Certainly, I can see the advantage of an entire crew of vampires in submarines. But what about food?"

"These man-powered … vampire-powered submarines are just for short voyages. Sabotage. Spying," said the Duke. "That is why I pushed for the government to fund the building of the *Nautilus II*. I know that the French abandoned the project, but the French didn't have the genius of Miss Lesley to call upon."

If Miss Lesley could have blush, she would have. "You're too kind, your Grace. But I've given some thought about the food option, if the government were to make a decision to attempt a longer journey. In the deep ocean, it is very cold and food keeps better chilled. So, for a long journey, I am certain I could rig up something."

Sir Joseph decided not to ask where or how they would obtain those provisions. Instead, he said, "Well, Miss Lesley, I see that you have plans to become a mermaid. You will make a particularly beautiful one."

"Thank you, Sir Joseph, for the compliment, but can I point out that mermaids traditionally lured sailors to their deaths by singing beautiful songs. I'm afraid singing is not among my accomplishments," said Miss Leslie. "However, we four could always have a go at a barbershop quartet."

"I'm not certain Mr Caley is up to singing," said Sir Joseph. "However, if he gets his sea legs-"

It was then, by sheer bad luck, that an anchor from an unseen ship was released on top of the submarine. Everyone in the cabin heard the splash and rattle, and then suddenly the whole vessel rang like a bell as the metal anchor struck them. Because the *Nautilus II* was moving at a fair clip, the anchor dragged its way over the top of the hull, scraping over the copper plates and catching at the ribs and rivets. It then became entangled in the structure around the rudders.

The Nautilus II began to bob and jerk like a fish snared on a hook, as the ship and anchor began to drag it along. Mr Caley turned a sickly green.

Sir Joseph knew a bit about the history of submersibles; he knew that the Spanish *Ictineo I* had been scuttled in an accident with a cargo vessel. The German *Brandtaucher,* another prototype submersible that had been powered by human beings rather than an engine, had sunk during diving trails. It looked as if the *Nautilus II* was going to suffer a similar fate.

"Bloody hell," exclaimed Miss Lesley and swung her chair back to face her panel of instruments. Her hands were frantically busy as she tried to stabilise her vessel.

Sir Joseph tried to brace himself in his chair, so that he wouldn't be tossed around the cabin like a ball. However, he could feel his hands and legs weakening.

Bloody gout! thought Sir Joseph.

Mr Caley was starting to moan and looked as if he might throw up. The Duke was firmly gripping his armrests, but his expression was rather cheery (to Sir Joseph's surprise).

Near the ceiling hatch, a damp patch appeared. It grew rapidly, and water started running down the walls and dripping from the ceiling. It took only a minute for the floor to be awash with half-an-inch of water and it was rising rapidly. It sloshed around everyone's boots and smelt strongly of rotting fish, sewerage and the ocean.

I guess this is my time to die, thought Sir Joseph. *Well, I never did want to die quietly in my bed.*

He was surprised at how calm he felt. He supposed it was due to the full life he had led, and his constant battle to bring the light of rationality to the world. He liked to think of himself as the candle maker, helping others to shine against the darkness of ignorance. When a man has done his best all his life, he had few regrets at the end of it; well, maybe he had just the one ... that his wife had no children or grandchildren to comfort her after he was gone. He gave himself a mental shake for such grim thoughts.

But what about the Duke? he asked himself, glancing over to his colleague. *Arty is an essential part of our war machine. And poor George came back to England, thinking he would die safely in bed between clean, white sheets.*

A quick glance at Mr Caley showed him to be manfully containing his nausea. Sir Joseph wished he could take back his hard words about Mr Caley's fortitude. With all the tossing about, even Sir Joseph was feeling ill.

Against all common sense, the Duke was looking happier as events advanced. By now, He was grinning like a maniac as the submarine bounced him around, enjoying the experience just like a small boy on a carousel. Sir Joseph supposed that a soldier would enjoy the danger inherent in the situation; you didn't become a professional soldier because you liked things safe and cosy. However, someone had to take charge of the situation. Miss Lesley was too busy fighting with the controls to think.

Dash it all, thought Sir Joseph. *I might be old but I'm not dead yet. Time I put my much-vaunted intellect to work. We need not die here.*

"Lucy! Take her up! Blast any pretence at secrecy. We must save the Duke at all costs!" ordered Sir Joseph over the din.

"Aye, milord," said Miss Lesley. She shouted into the shell again. "Emergency breech! All hands prepare for an emergency breech." She turned back to her passengers. "I know you're all already hanging on. Be ready for an almighty bump!"

Lucy dragged at a lever and the *Nautilus II* rolled and yawed and spun. There was a sudden blast of bubbles past the portholes as the submarine sprang to the surface like a frolicking dolphin. Sir Joseph was pushed back into his chair by the force of their rapid ascent and felt his ears pop.

Everyone was jolted out of their seats as the *Nautilus II* rebounded from her leap into the air. Sir Joseph was flung into the ceiling and then the side of the cabin, to land in an untidy heap with the Duke and Mr Caley on top of him. For a moment, no one stirred, waiting for more gymnastics, until Sir Joseph groaned. The other two men hastily crawled off him.

"Milord! Are you unhurt?" asked Mr Caley. "Mrs Sir Joseph Banks will strangle me if you are injured while you are in my care."

Sir Joseph took a cautious look around. The submarine was still dancing a lively jig, but the action was smoother and water was no longer seeping through the ceiling. Most of the lights had been doused during the accident, but two lamps were still flickering. He felt a sore patch on his bottom lip, where his teeth had cut him while he was being tossed around. He put his hand to his mouth and came away with blood on his fingertips.

He looked up Miss Lesley, who had kept her seat. Their eyes met, and they both looked down to his fingertips. The vampire woman's eyes gleamed very red, nearly as red as her glossy hair, and her teeth visibly lengthened as he watched. He felt his fingers tremble.

Miss Lesley – Lucy – jumped out of her chair and onto the ladder to the conning tower hatch. Her fingernails elongated into talons, as she grimly unscrewed the door fastenings. As soon as the hatch opened, there was a sudden gust of chilly fresh air into the cabin; Sir Joseph hadn't noticed how stuffy the air had become. Then Lucy climbed out into the night faster than the eye could follow.

Sir Joseph nearly collapsed with relief.

It was but a moment later that the men heard the crunch and groan of metal being rendered. And the *Nautilus II* ceased its frantic dance.

Sir Joseph looked to Mr Caley. Poor George was muttering curses or prayers under his breath, but he no longer appeared to be close to vomiting.

He bent over Sir Joseph and helped his employer to his feet.

Pulling himself back onto his chair, the Duke looked rather disappointed the wild ride was over. When Arty saw Sir Joseph looking at him, he grinned.

"I think we can say the excursion was successful," said the Duke. "No one has died."

The sounds of complicated destruction were still coming from the region of the rudders.

The Duke added, "And I do believe Miss Lesley is doing some on-the-spot structural modifications."

"As one does," said Sir Joseph. He wondered if it was appropriate to send flowers to a woman for not eating you. Maybe a nice cameo bracelet? He would have to ask Lady Banks ... then again, thinking of his wife's face as he tried to explain the circumstances, maybe not.

Mr Caley settled Sir Joseph back into his seat and cleared his throat. "May I ask a question, milord?"

"Certainly," said Sir Joseph. "At this moment, I believe you can ask me anything." Sir Joseph prepared himself for a request of termination of employment. And he couldn't really blame George. He rather felt like resigning his position with the government himself.

"This is meant to be a weapon for use against the French?" asked Mr Caley. His expression was earnest, serious.

"Yes? Your point being?" asked Sir Joseph, bewildered.

"Well, sir, I can see that it will be a very effective way of demoralising their troops," said Mr Caley. "But how are we going to convince them all into taking a ride?"

The Duke of Wellington roared with laughter...

NO GOLD WILL SLOW ME
BY JONATHAN FICKE

Thick clouds rushed past Lanta's windshield as she kept the nose of her screamer on the tail of the craft in front of her. She muscled the stick between her legs to pull out of the deep dive and threaded her screamer through a ring floating in Titan's heavy atmosphere. She gritted her teeth against the g-force and rolled to the right, lining up the bright red nose of her screamer at the next ring.

"They're coming up on the final leg!" A voice crackled in her ear, distorted slightly by the hard plastic helmet and the sound of her breath reverberating in her mask. "Will Marcus be the one to finally unseat the champion?"

"Not a chance," she muttered, adjusting her line and burying the throttle.

Her screamer shook as the electro-ion engine redlined. Instruments spun on the panel, unable to cope with the stresses she put on the craft while she cut through the methane skies of the moon. She resisted the urge to pitch up; the final approach drew them directly toward the golden ringrise overhead, and the natural inclination to increase altitude toward the sight had ruined less experienced pilots.

Off her three o'clock side, she inched even and then in front of Marcus' screamer. He looked over at her from his cockpit, and though his face was covered by his own mask, she smiled as she imagined his look of disgust.

With alarm klaxons blaring in her ear, she tore through the final ring.

"What a finish! Ladies and gentlemen, boys and girls, intelligences of all kinds! What a finish! Lanta prevails!"

Lanta backed off her throttle, and banked softly toward the gleaming steel island on the horizon dotted in gold and blue navigation beacons—the hangar attached to the Titanocarbon Corp. mining installation. She glanced down at her console and confirmed that the landing computer had picked up her flight path. Next to the blinking confirmation monitor hung an image of the bright blue skies and emerald waters of Earth.

"Getting closer," she breathed as she nudged the throttle forward slightly.

Lanta was in a hurry to get the screamer down. She had winnings to collect.

#

Riker, the owner of the hangar and all of Titan's racing circuits, wore his mask inside. Lanta didn't know how he did it. When she was on-platform, she relished being unencumbered by life support systems. He reached out to hand her a disc of Titanocarbon Corp. Credits, the payoff for her win. She scanned the disc and bit back a curse. Where were all of her winnings?

"What the hell is this?" Lanta demanded. "Where's the rest of it?"

Lanta imagined Riker sneering behind his mask. "Costs more and more to keep the docks running every day. I'm not running a charity."

"This isn't enough to live on," she hissed.

"And it's a loan. Your screamer was dry as a bone. You owe me money, so you better get in the sky again and keep winning.

Lanta clenched her fist and tucked it into the pocket of her gray flight suit, unwilling to trust that she wouldn't reach out and yank an oxygen hose from Riker's mask if she didn't physically restrain herself. She opened her mouth to protest, but thought better of it and settled for storming off into the main concourse of the airport.

"Quite a win today," a man called out and walked calmly across the concourse. He was tall with ebon skin and dark gray hair. His eyes were a complicated brown eyes that burned so bright as to nearly be orange. He wore a tight dark jacket over a simple gray shirt and pants, and carried himself with an air that made it clear he was no Titanocarbon Corp. laborer. "What is it that drives you into the air with such a reckless abandon?"

"Do I know you?" Lanta asked. She'd had unwanted attention in the past, and was in no mood to tolerate a man with an upjumped sense of self.

"Evidently not," he smiled and extended a hand. "Apologies. Mel Jager."

Lanta let his hand hang in the air between them, unclasped.

"What do you want, Mel Jager?" She asked.

"Don't get much news from the inners out here, do you?"

She started walking and Mel dogged her heels. "We get some. Most of us are busy and don't like having our time wasted."

"I'm here because I grew bored with the Venusian circuit." He jogged in front of her and held out a palm-sized holopad that projected an interplanetary freighter. "Come race for me."

Lanta stopped in her tracks, eyes following the boxy contours of Mel's freighter. "I only race for myself," she said, weighing the promise of a ride to the inners against the restriction of being beholden to whatever angle Mel was playing. "Besides, why would I race for you?

"Race for me, and I'll get you into Earth atmo. You'll be leaving fools in your draft faster than you can blink."

Earth. It was too good to be true. And if it wasn't, Lanta forced herself to maintain her composure, to not betray how her heart raced at the prospect of getting off Titan.

"Nobody can beat me on Titan. Why would I leave?"

"Was the same for me on Venus," he said. "Don't you get tired of having nothing left to prove here? Of having everything your heart could desire on this frozen ball of carbon?"

Mel had no idea she was in debt. He actually thought she was successful here. The concept baffled her. "How do I know you're not blowing smoke?"

He clicked his holopad and a sharp-lined screamer replaced the freighter. "Race me, and I'll prove it to you."

He was asking her to trade Riker as an overlord for Mel. Was the change of scenery worth it?

"I'll race you," she said, the wheels spinning in her mind. It was time to do some bluffing. "But there has to be a wager. Let's talk stakes."

#

Lanta's console lit green as the systems of her screamer came online in turn. Oxygen flowed through her mask, twin hoses connected to her suit and the life support systems she wore. She waited patiently while the pre-race countdown ran and only spared a single glance at Mel's screamer on its launch pad to her left.

"What a treat," the announcer blared. "The undisputed champion of the Venusian Sky City Circuit—Mel Jager!"

"Let's get on with it."

She focused on the digital clock hovering between her launch pad and Mel's as it ticked to zero. When it did, she jammed her throttle forward and pitched up, easily drawing lift through Titan's thick methane atmosphere.

Outside of her cockpit the air was lethal cold, in the eighties Kelvin, but beneath her mask she breathed hot. Mel's screamer cut in front of hers on a direct line for the first ring, and she cursed having to fly from behind off the pad.

Lanta pushed her screamer to its red lines, cutting through turbulence and trusting the screamer to hold together while she pulled every risk to draw every inch of advantage from the course.

"There is no harm in losing," Mel's voice crackled in her ear. "It's not like I'm a child. I'll give you the chance to win your money back."

Lanta didn't answer, save to push her screamer into the dive that began the final ring sequence on the course. When she pulled out of the dive and rolled onto the final trajectory, she was nose to nose with Mel. Everything in her cockpit screamed at her to ease back on the throttle, but she pushed it further, harder.

A faint aroma of ozone filled her mask. Some system taxed beyond its capacity was starting to fail and those failures were starting to compound, but she maintained her pace and kept her nose at the final ring.

To her side, Mel's screamer drifted up toward the golden arc of rings in the sky ahead. She couldn't refrain from smiling as Mel's wasted energy was the only opening she needed. Lanta physically forced the throttle as far forward as she could, as if she could reach the blue skies of Earth if she could only push the throttle far enough. With a primal scream Lanta beat Mel to the final ring, and finished her career on Titan undefeated.

"Don't worry," she said. "There is no shame in losing. Besides, I'm sure there's enough room on my new freighter to let you tag along to the inners. We've got races to win on Earth."

EVORIA OF FANDOLANIA
BY LINDA MCMULLEN

Between an uncomfortable high tea under the white parley flag and the winter sunset, Father offered Paramir's envoy our unconditional surrender.

The envoy was Vice-Foreign Minister Palachani – a picture of bland dignity in an imperial cape – no doubt sent to reassure us that our new overlords could be merciful. *Could.* Milovoria – a world of sea and iron in our sister-system – had fallen to Paramir a decade earlier. They resisted, for a time; now our experts say three of their five continents will not be habitable for another century. They sent their mechanical armies to strip Milovoria of its iron and gems...

And then – Paramir came for us.

Paramir – a rising power, revitalized after the internal collapse of their mortal enemy, Quallo…

Paramir's brawling Trade Minister arrived uninvited, and demanded that my father, the king, cede the contents of our mines. When he refused, they sent their ships. 'Ships' fails to describe their fleet – dragons of legend forged in steel and titanium, battleships that ripped the sky. Auguries of our blighted future.

Paramir's initial attacks were surgical: vaporizing a hamlet adjacent to the pit head, but leaving the road and bridge untouched. Obliterating a temple here, a library there. Father pleaded with our Zartan allies for aid, for succor…and he and his ministers wrangled long into the night: what could we possibly mobilize to combat this technological horror? Our tiny fleet had been all but destroyed in the fighting with Milovoria a decade before. We had been rebuilding. Not quickly enough.

Our ministers shouted; one general scrambled; he ordered his men to take what we had, to repair de-commissioned fighters and raid the museums if necessary. Many of our brave pilots lost their lives driving their rickety crafts into the fuselages of those star-bound beasts in an attempt to buy us a little more time.

We learned the Zartans too were under attack.

"Father," I ventured, "I...ultimately, they seek the fruits of the mines.

Father said, "Let the men worry about such things." His eyes were shadowed after unslept days.

"But Father – they *must* land troops, and soon. We must know how we are to meet them – we must call up the troops and –"

"Evoria. The *men* will manage."

Our army was still assembling when they landed, our men blinking the sleep out of their eyes after scrambling toward the capital. Unaccustomed fingers curled around the hafts of weapons – calloused fingers accustomed to plows, or scythes. The general led within the belly of a top-of-the-line mechanical elephant, purchased from the Zartans.

We anticipated Paramir's mechanical beasts, the beams of light that could eradicate a village, their legions of chrome-helmeted troops...

We never anticipated the lone men, the stragglers, who could almost have been some of our own. Some of the 'ungifted,' as Mother called them, charitably. They landed behind our lines, ran among the people with wild eyes, and breathed in their stunned faces.

For two days, the fighting raged, and smoke hovered over the fields just below the palace.

On the third day, in the capital the sores erupted, on faces and hands and feet, on backs and bellies and arms and legs, swellings, bleeding...

...the afflicted begging for death...

...days passing...

Our best physicians, helpless...

One chrome-helmeted, armor-encased soldier took up a small girl on the brink of death and injected her with an orange serum. Within the hour the child's skin had begun to clear...

But for the others...

Burials.

Funeral rites.

And the battle raged on.

Father emerged from his meetings only to clasp our hands, wordlessly. "Father," I began, but he merely shuffled into his chambers.

Vigils at the palace gate. Pleadings. Then torches.

"Father," I cried, brimming with suggestions about requesting the sunny orange vaccines for, at least, the children, about – but he merely put up his hand. Heeding neither my mother's pleas nor the shouts of the populace, he said, "Good night, my family," and withdrew.

The following day, the envoy landed, and requested tea.

My mother, brother, and I all pleaded to be part of the discussions, but in vain. Mother spent the afternoon in tears, or at prayer; my brother, watchful, leonine, paced up and down the corridor. I tried to imagine what we might say to our people, to strike that careful balance among acknowledgement, preparation for the worst, and...resolve...

Even in the face of certain death.

Paramir would never leave us alive.

Father emerged, with a look of ovine embarrassment.

"Mura," he began, clasping my mother's hands, "they have been good enough to leave us our lives."

To my astonishment, she rounded on him, fiercely. "What *exactly* does that mean?"

"We...have tonight. To get our things. I shall abdicate, and we will go into exile."

"At least we'll be together," she said, with an effort.

Father's feeble smile failed. "Bisoro will succeed me."

My brother's face lit up, before he remembered himself – and well before my mother's glare blazed.

"He will henceforth be known as the First Proconsul of Paramiri Empire in Fandolania." Our whole world – now a tributary state. I resisted the urge to bury my face in my hands. "His son may inherit...if all goes well..."

"And our people?" I asked, quickly.

"Subjects of the empire. As long as they pay their taxes –"

"What about Evoria?" my mother demanded, throwing her arm around my shoulders.

The envoy came in, then; through his interpreter, he smirked, "I hope I'm not interrupting."

"No," said my father, his lips collapsing against his teeth.

He turned toward me, and mustered all of his diplomatic finesse. I am, on the best of days, 'presentable'. "I suppose the girl will do."

"Do what?" I asked, before I could stop the words. My father took my hand.

"You will help seal the peace."

"Father –"

"Evoria," he said, heavily. "We're all depending on you."

I finally understood, that I was being given in marriage to the emperor's son.

My mother cried out, and embraced me, but hissed in my ear, "At least the offer is a *marriage*. Remember that."

The next day, the Paramiris began distributing the curative vaccines – beginning with children and miners.

Vice Foreign Minister Palachani informed me that I was permitted to bring one trunk, one attendant, and one android, of my choosing. My ladies-in-waiting – my friends and companions – sobbed at the prospect of leaving our home; Orinta was on the point of a love-union; Zela worried about her ailing mother; Phanira was terrified of travel. I embraced them, and I said I understood, though my heart trembled. My mother offered her newest maidservant, Narista, who had just come to work for her before the troubles began: "She is a likely creature – very clever, you know."

I agreed; it could only be helpful to have someone from home. I did not like to refuse my mother's offer. And...admittedly, I did not wish to lose face before the Paramiris: a deposed princess with no attendant would look like a beggar, not an exile.

When I spoke with her, Narista said, "I have nothing to keep me here."

"Evoria," murmured my mother, pressing her handkerchief into my hand. "Your father –" Her look said more than her words could. She straightened. "I can give you nothing but my heart's blood and my blessing, child. I pray that you will find some happiness and –"

Her voice caught, and we embraced.

"It is time, Princess Evoria." My android, Falada – another purchase from Zarta – rolled toward me. Androgynous and faceless, yet with a somehow equine expression, Falada nevertheless had a knack for sparing my tears. I bade my family farewell, took a final glimpse of the palace on its promontory and the sun gleaming over the fields and the sweep of home – then Narista, Falada, and I followed the envoy aboard the Paramiri cruiser.

The ship was a blur of chrome and gleaming red lights, or perhaps I had something in my eyes.

The ship was at least a full technical generation ahead of ours, perhaps two. My cabin included a bed – cool to the touch – a window – and built in furniture; it was ultra-modern, spartan, evoking both luxury and a correctional facility. Narista was next door to me, and Falada recharged in a cabinet between our rooms. The ship's technology could produce food and entertainment, and its communications system understood our tongue. We wanted for nothing.

The envoy invited (charged?) me to dine with him; I went, head high, back straight. His questions were darts about our military collapse and our human and material resources now available for Paramir's exploitation, only modestly blunted by the interpreter's tact. Falada waited on us; the envoy watched him through window-slit eyes.

I changed the subject. "I know very little of your language, sir. Do you have any books or programs that might help me acquire it?"

His eyebrows drifted northward. Narista passed before he could answer, summer in the sway of her step; she glanced at Vice-Minister Palachani beneath lowered lashes. "Why…er…that is…yes – it's available in your room. Just tell the computer, 'Paramiri language'."

"Thank you." I excused myself, and stopped at Narista's room to remind her of our obligation to maintain a dignified distance.

"Of course," she replied; her voice silk and satin.

I turned to go, then glanced back at her – her face remained blank as a doll's.

How could I impress upon her that grace and dignity were all we had left?

I spent my days repeating the undulating vowels of the Paramiri language, absorbing the words for hello and good morning and good evening. Politeness counts, I thought – and I knew it would be months before I could forge more complex thoughts, such as, *I feel some trepidation in joining your family as a spoil of war.*

I enjoined Narista to join me, but she complained that using the computer felt too artificial.

"Indeed?" I returned. "What do you suggest?"

She said, "Vice Foreign Minister Palachani–"

"I'm certain he has other duties to attend to, rather than teaching either of us." Indeed, he was frequently in communication with his capital, though, at this distance, responses still took five to six hours.

Falada materialized in the room, ready to turn down my bed. Narista helped me undress. When they had gone, I sat on the edge of the bed, breathing deeply into my mother's handkerchief.

I thought I heard Narista's voice addressing Minister Palachani in the hall, but I must have imagined it, because the noise ceased immediately, and I drifted off.

Several days passed in uneasy dinners and decreasingly gentle reminders to Narista to be polite, and no more. We sailed through space below a white flag, the vanquished remnants of a once-proud –

"Oh, shut up," snapped Narista. I turned back toward her (she was undoing the buttons of my dress) when I felt something cold kiss my spine.

"What –" I began.

"Take off your dress," she said.

"I –"

She jabbed the blunt-nosed flasher further into my back, and I'm not sure if she's put it on 'stun' – or a higher setting. "I said, take off your dress."

I dropped the gown – then whirled around, grabbing her wrist, and twisting it until she dropped the flasher...

...but she was crafty; she brought her pointed heel down on hard on my instep. I let out an undignified howl and sank to my knees, at which point she retrieved the flasher – Paramiri-made and definitely stolen – and my dress. She draped my gown around her neck, and held the flasher so close to my right eye that the point doubled.

"You're now Narista. The maid. You will sleep in the shoebox I've been calling home. You will wait on me, and do my bidding. I am now Princess Evoria."

My scan for madness in her eyes registered; she slapped me.

"I am taking your name and your position. Since you have made such poor use of them." Her eyes narrowed. "You don't deserve your honors, you know. Your Father let the enemy destroy my village, and murder thousands upon thousands – and you did *nothing* to stop them."

I winced. Then I took a breath, my mind whirling; I should decline to argue the point, and focus on the practical.

"You can't possibly imagine this will work. The Vice Foreign Minister –"

" – will be only too delighted to have *someone willing to listen to his ideas* whispering in the prince's ear."

At this point, we turned, having heard a metallic *click*; Falada's mechanical eyes dilated.

"Get out!" shrieked Narista. "Get *out*, or so help me I'll shoot, and stop this wench's heart."

Falada gave what he clearly hoped was a reassuring half-bow. Narista instead turned to him, and pulled the trigger; his central processor lit up in fireworks, and he rolled backward, groaning, into the hall.

"I'm going to marry the prince. If you say a word – to anyone – I will kill you. And I will do everything in my power to have the Paramiris finish off your parents and your weakling brother. Do you understand me? Do you swear to never say a word?"

"Yes," I breathed.

In a trice, Vice-Minister Palachani appeared, with a power cord in hand. "Falada is currently emitting smoke – but I understand from him that there was…some disturbance?"

"Yes," said Narista, recovering herself first, her flasher tickling my lashes. "My maid here has gotten quite uppity, but I have dealt with her satisfactorily."

Palachani looked from her to me and back again; I glanced toward him, collectedly I hope, urging him with my eyes to do the right thing…

"I am very glad to hear it," he announced, smiling – and he handed Narista Falada's power cord.

Then he was gone.

Narista – now calling herself Evoria – gained my room, my things – my place. Even my mother's handkerchief. She had me wait on her – fetching and carrying whatever trifle she wanted – with a simpering smile. I required all of my better angels to stop me from slapping her face. Each night she dined with Vice Foreign Minister Palachani and ensured that I ate scraps. Any form of humiliation she could visit upon me, she explored, except one: she never asked me to help her undress, as that would have required her to turn her back.

Mother, I thought. *If you knew, your heart would break.*

One evening, weeks later, Vice Foreign Minister Palachani announced that we were nearing

We landed in Paramir, and for a moment I forgot my misery, my exile, even my drab and scratchy clothes, as I gazed at Azamontis – the capital of the Paramiri Empire. The city center rose in breathtaking spires, a mesmerizing ballet in stone and steel – easily a century beyond our technology.

The Vice Foreign Minister's shuttle awaited us – a plush, miniaturized version of the cruiser we had just exited. Narista (still calling herself Evoria) and I followed the Vice Foreign Minister aboard; his staff materialized and took our things aboard, including toting the blank-faced and deactivated Falada aboard. My eyes failed to take in the whole of this megalopolis, which swamped the horizon. Tiny individual flying pods – *airbirds* – and larger shared craft, nicknamed *buzzards,* circle in the complex helices of Paramiri air traffic.

Narista-Evoria snaps, "Get away from the window, and help me with my earrings."

My earrings; my mother's gift to me, on my last name-day.

We arrived at the palace; the royal family had graciously agreed to receive us immediately. The palace's grandeur eclipsed the city's; Azamontis was a pale moon compared to the sun-gleam glory of Paziral Palace.

Burden and alcohol had added twenty years to the Emperor's face; he was barely five years older than my own parents, but looked as though he could be *their* father. The Empress – a famous beauty, plucked from obscurity by virtue of golden hair and a cupid's-bow mouth – demonstrated only languid interest in us. The heir – my intended – the man I *was* destined to marry – appeared to be a young demigod with a sardonic smile: Pazolor. His eyes devoured Narista, and appeared to be well satisfied with the meal.

I could not credit his first words to her, the woman he *thought* should be his bride...

My face glowed scarlet, and Narista turned to me, demanding a translation. "*You've* been buried in those stupid language programs for weeks. What did he *say*?"

I offered a slightly edited version. "He said, 'I'm just grateful you aren't a toad.'"

The official interpreter arrived, tousle-haired and out of breath, and presented the younger son, Ryamor. Less handsome than his brother, certainly, but he bid us welcome and hoped aloud that we would be happy in Paramir.

Narista and I curtsied.

"Have you any requests?" he asked.

"Yes, thank you," replied Narista, with a regal gesture. "I wish to adapt to my new home as soon as possible, so I would like to have a new maid, to teach me the ways of this land."

Appreciative looks all around; only Ryamor arched an eyebrow.

"Would you be so kind," she added, turning to me with acid sweetness, "as to find some employment for my old maid?" I could hardly conceal my disbelief – or outrage. "Our religion teaches us that we should be courteous and modest, but I fear that presumption and arrogance have hardened her heart. I would be glad to see her grow in holiness," she added, patting my hand with cherubic concern. I feared my mouth hardening into surly, corroborating lines.

"Of course," said Pazolor, with a meaningful glance at his brother, who quieted. He offered Narista his arm and offered to take her on a tour of the gardens. One of the servitors timidly touched her sleeve, and asked about the android.

"Oh, that old thing. You can melt him down for scrap," she said; the peals of her merry laughter trailed after her.

The cook turned up her nose at me; she had no use for a foreign wench in her majestic kitchens; the housekeeper too felt my inferior hands would spoil the pristine imperial linen, and preferred her shining android fleet. I, like Falada, had become a relic in this brave new world.

"Let her tend the geese," announced Pazolor, and Narista glowingly agreed.

The geese had been the present emperor's mother's pet project, and she had insisted that her birds preferred a human touch. Even after her passing, they remained on the grounds, in her memory. I looked after not only the geese, but the full range of domestic and exotic fowls who roamed the grounds and gardens, as the assistant of a lively and slightly lame young man called Conralo. But before I could so much as introduce myself –

"Break them up!" he hollered; two geese were clashing viciously, and the smaller bird's left wing was already streaming red. I found a stick, and managed to swat them apart.

"Idiot! You could have hurt them. Durn! I'd rather have an android than you."

"It's nice to meet you, too," I returned, pointedly.

To my astonishment – and relief – he laughed.

I'm doing my duty, Mama.

Learning to tend the birds was not difficult; with study and Conralo's tutelage, I grasped the rules of avian interaction – and later intuited the birds' particular friendships and cliques. I had, therefore, ample time on my hands to pursue other interests – asking the names of every flower and tree that grew and every dish I ate and everything else I ran across. My vocabulary grew by bounds with every hour. In spite of myself, I began to feel...perhaps not 'at home,' but, at least, unperturbed at waking up every day in a foreign capital, light-years from home...

Conralo and I developed a guarded friendship; he explained the nuances of Paramiri palace culture, the shades of recognition accorded successively higher levels of the aristocracy at the palace, the taboos, the scandals of note. I went so far as to ask a question about a seemingly abandoned building in a far corner of the palace grounds.

"What's that?"

"Prince Ryamor's shed."

"His *shed*?"

"Yeah, he's got piles of junk from every corner of the galaxy. He ought to have been born a tinker, not a prince. His rotten luck, I suppose."

The geese, up to their old tricks, were determined to both end this interesting conversation and to make life difficult for the chickens. One male terrorized a small flock of females; I shooed them apart, ushering the chickens into the shared roost. Conralo nodded his approval.

I bit my lip, but my face felt like it was glowing. "Conralo, I have an idea."

I explained. He said, "Make it so."

I directed the worker-androids in simple Paramiri, my vision becoming manifest...then I sensed a presence nearby. I turned – then flushed, and curtsied. "I beg your pardon, your highness...I did not see you."

He waved off my apology, cheerfully, and asked, "What new world are you creating?"

I said (well, what I conveyed, in my poor Paramiri, was, "The geese sometimes menace the smaller birds...we're constructing little retreats that only they can access. And we've tried to have them blend in..."

Indeed, each roost had been built to resemble a traditional dwelling from each part of the empire...the first coop was, of course, a painstaking replica of my own home, designed by the androids from the images I had compiled.

"Ingenious," he said, and I could detect no sarcasm in his tone.

"Thank you, your highness."

To my astonishment, he remained: we spoke about the birds in Paramir and he asked me about the birds at home; then gardens in general; then crops; then food crops; and an hour passed undetected. Then we discussed our favorite foods, and the best meals we'd ever eaten, and I recalled the food at the banquet at which we welcomed the Milovorians after a diplomatic dust-up of some sort, and only then realized what I'd said.

"That is...the royal family allowed the servants to...sample some of the dishes afterward."

He arched an eyebrow, but before either of us could say more, his royal brother approached, and that ended the conversation.

My avian palaces were soon complete. Conralo declared them "a triumph" and the birds were quite clearly flourishing – and yet I could not settle, caught myself perpetually turning toward something not there. I had never attended to my hair before and I still cared nothing for it now – particularly since it was to remain covered – but I could not stop myself from removing my hat and fidgeting with it. I ...and I could not, for the life of me, see why. Conralo gave me a knowing look.

"What?" I demanded.

He just smirked. I programmed one of the androids to steal his hat daily so I could indulge my agitation privately. Just as I began to rebraid it for the third time, I received another visitor to my castles, this one much less welcome. Narista slipped away from her 'intended' for a moment to pretend to admire my handiwork. "I see you've recreated Fandolania Palace."

"The androids did it."

"Mmm," she said, pointedly dubious. "I heard you engaged Prince Ryamor at some length. I just came to remind you to *mind your place*."

My eyes narrowed dangerously. "I *did*."

She slapped me across the face. "Remember: I have the ear of the second most powerful man in the empire. If you can't mind your place, at least mind your mouth. For your family's sake." And then she was gone.

Mama, Mama, Mama, I cried, in my mind. *I am trying to do my duty, as I ought...but...*

My face had grown strangely hot. I kept away from Conralo for the remainder of the afternoon, and tidied up after the birds. The sun had just kissed the distant rooftops and my eyes were strangely wet; I heard a voice say, "The birds look wonderfully well."

The corners of my lips stole upward, somehow. "Thank you, your highness."

"Are you – quite all right?" he asked, catching sight of my face – and he offered me his handkerchief.

"Yes, I –" I stopped. "You are very kind, your highness."

He gazed at me for a long moment. "This must be very different from your home."

I thought of the ships darkening our sky, the smug expression of the vice foreign minister after his humiliating meeting with my father, the people dying for want of the orange serum, and my face must have changed because he added, "Coming here cannot have been easy for you."

All my words seemed to have fled. "You are very kind," I repeated. Then I remembered. "But a prince need not concern himself with the foolish behavior of a mere goose girl."

"My brother will become emperor after our father, but I will serve as his advisor. And so it is crucial that I should understand the many peoples of the empire." His eyes were a green-grey I'd never seen before, the color of the summer grass in the twilight. "Especially –"

Our eyes met.

"It is...not my place, your highness," I whispered.

"I'm asking for your help," he replied.

Something crackled beneath my ribs.

"Come with me," he said, and for a moment he forgot himself and half-extended his hand...and I nearly reached for it. We recovered ourselves, however, and I followed him as I was bid. He took me to the far corner of the grounds, to the "shed" that Conralo had spoken of so dismissively...

"Come inside."

It was not a shed.

The outside appeared to be a sort of complex hovel, masking the meticulously organized museum that lay inside. I caught glimpses of the vestiges of dozens of civilizations living under the Paramiri empire, painstakingly organized, lovingly described...shelves full of books in an assortment of languages...surprise, interest, delight, appreciation, all registered; still more, I was impressed – that he, a second son of one of the world's most powerful empires, should have taken the time to *try* to understand...

"It's –"

There was no word for what I felt in my native language, either; fortunately my face told all. He beamed.

"Please look around, and touch anything you'd like. Several of the artifacts in here are replicas; I've got the real antiquities more carefully preserved."

I did look at the 'museum' – and, too, at his less immaculately organized workroom. It contained shelves and pegboards and tables piled with delicate brushes and gloves, glues and fabrics, a potter's wheel, a welder's mask, wires and batteries and labels and elements I could not even name...

I stood amazed.

He described his recent projects in some detail until we noticed that the failing light no longer illuminated the other's features, and we hastily, and separately, made our way back to the palace.

Conralo pulled me aside, afterward. "Be careful there, goose girl."

I could regulate my behavior; my interior was another matter. In spite of another altercation with Narista (when I most unfortunately and certainly unintentionally trespassed upon a lovers' tête-à-tête in the garden, as she and Pazolor whispered hideous nothings to one another) my days were sunshine. Prince Ryamor seemed very fond of the gardens and I not infrequently ran across him in the course of my work. And, in one shining moment, he whispered:

"I care for you."

"I care for you too, your highness."

"No 'your highness'. Not if you mean it…"

"I care for you…Ryamor."

My heart, though half-consumed with thoughts of home, swelled just a little.

And then came many days in which I did not see him; the wedding frenzy which had consumed the rest of the palace had finally reached even Conralo and myself; his master instructed him (and, by extension, me) to redouble efforts to make certain that the birds were looking their best, and to catch some doves for the festivities. The actual trapping failed to achieve the levels of romance that their release might, and I ended the day sweating, dirty, and sore. I had not even a moment to wonder why I had not seen Ryamor, or to fuss with my hair.

And, naturally, that was when he came. "I must speak with you."

"Your highness, I'm not fit –"

His face was unusually solemn. "I try not to exercise royal prerogative, but this is the moment."

He escorted me back to his museum, threw open the door, and turned on the lights.

"Falada!" I cried. And...he did not move, or speak, but his sensor flashed at the sound of my voice... "You...found him! You got him to work again!"

Ryamor seemed to choose his words. "Yes...after my brother's fiancée suggested confining him to the scrap heap, I recovered him. And – it's not very modest to say so, but with some inventiveness and cunning I've gotten him to work again. Not everything…but the voice and recording functions are now available." He frowned. "Do you have anything you'd like to tell me?"

"I…can't," I replied.

"I've already got proof," he said. "I just want to hear it from you."

"I swore an oath," I replied, miserably.

"I'm very sorry to hear that – *Evoria*," he replied, and then, picking up the remnants of my former android, he stormed out.

There was nothing I could say.

Princess Evoria of Fandolania wed the Emperor's son, Prince Pazolor, in a dazzling royal ceremony unmarred by my stunned and heartbroken presence. The former maid Narista glowed in unparalleled beauty except for a five-minute span immediately before the ceremony, when she launched a certain android from her window. Her first order as princess was that his head should be detached from his body and nailed over the city gate, and his metal body destroyed by the populace. Vice Foreign Minister Palachani saw to it personally.

Her second order was that I should be banished from the palace.

Her bewildered but indulgent bridegroom, I learned later, agreed that I should not remain to irritate her royal presence any longer. The guards came for me shortly after the ceremony, as I hid in the shade of a willow, watching the geese at the far edge of the grounds. I would have preferred to walk, but they insisted that their orders were to drag me out. "I don't want to be any trouble," I said, so I made no protest as they hefted me under my arms and hauled me toward the front gates, demonstrating to every human servant, android, and passing aristocrat that I was a disgraced servant being cast out for her wicked ways...

"Stop!" cried Prince Ryamor. The guards stopped. "Let her go."

They dropped me without first setting me on my feet; I tumbled into the dust. Prince Ryamor himself helped me up. "Escort us to the throne room," he proclaimed, with a rare hint of imperiousness that would have been irritating on any other occasion. But at that moment, all I could feel was relief, and confusion.

We strode through the palace, past the stunned onlookers, until we reached his royal parents on the dais.

He bowed; I took my cue, and curtsied.

"What are you playing at?" demanded Pazolor, who – with Narista – was bidding his parents farewell before their honeymoon. "Why are you here with the goose girl?"

Someone – I believe the emperor himself – had the good sense to empty the room of everyone except the parties concerned.

When only the six of us remained, Ryamor said, "I have been silent too long, and I am sorry, brother, for the pain this will cause you. But mother, father – my brother has *not* married Princess Evoria. His bride is an imposter, a scheming and ambitious maid, and this –" Here he pulled me forward by the wrist – "is the real princess."

The room was ominously silent.

"That is preposterous," declared the emperor. "One has only to look at this beautiful girl –" He gestured to Narista – "to know *she* is the true princess. This goose girl is..." His mouth twisted, and he cut the rest of his sentence mercifully short. Physical perfection was never my gift, and, having spent much of the day experiencing varied and painful forms of distress, my appearance was well short of an already low standard.

"I can prove it," said Ryamor. "I have video evidence, taken from the android Falada –"

"He's been destroyed," sneered Narista. "Pazolor, I won't listen to these conspiracies another minute –"

"She's right," admitted Ryamor. "The originals are gone forever."

He turned to me, and grinned.

"But I made copies."

The shouts of an irate and confounded maid ringing off the stone walls were some of the sweetest music I had yet heard.

The prosecutor rested his case, and the dragon was slain, about an hour later.

Then things began to move very quickly:

Pazolor begged his parents to ignore the evidence of their eyes, and ears; he adored his wife; she had confided the truth to him before their wedding and he didn't care, he didn't care, he didn't care, he loved her...

His father, the suddenly empurpled emperor, raged at him for failing to tell his father and sovereign the truth, for knowingly concluding a compact with a *maid*, and for wantonly dispossessing the *rightful* princess...

"You will not want, my son. I will send you away with enough funds that you and your wife might live comfortably forevermore – but –"

Ryamor anticipated his father's words, and said, "Reflect, father, please, I did not intend –"

"I know you didn't," the emperor said, tiredly, "but I *have* reflected, and it is right. Pazolor, I immediately, and irrevocably, terminate your right of succession. Ryamor, you are now my heir. Guards!" he called. They came, and they

made it so. Narista spat after me as she left, and Pazolor hissed, *"Haven't you done enough for one day?"*
And then they were gone.

Before I could comprehend what had befallen me, Ryamor begged his father's ear; he whispered something, and the emperor nodded, regally. He returned to me, and knelt, with the smile I had grown to treasure:

"Evoria, my princess, my goose girl, my love, will you marry me?"

I said yes, with all my heart.

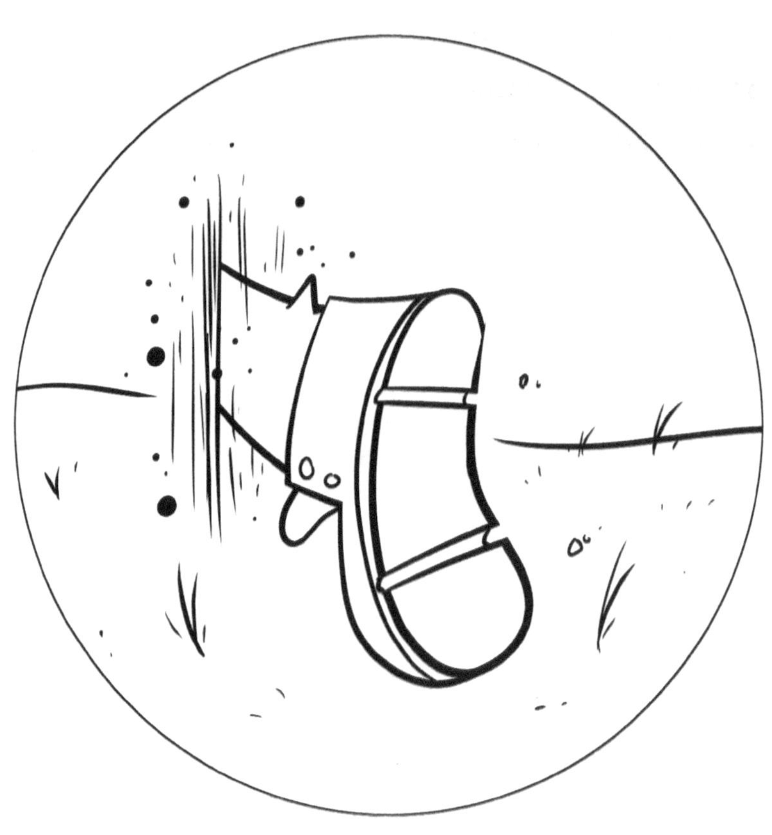

JACK AND I
BY SHANNON MCDERMOTT

I never understood Jack.

I tried to, you know; I thought it was my duty. But he was an odd one. I remember afternoons when I would sit at my desk, my books piled in front of me and the sunlight stretching out over them. The window was right there, up against the side of the desk. The tatty gingham curtain kept the sun out of my eyes, but I left it open enough that I could see out. I thought, from the way Jack acted, that people couldn't see in.

He would come tumbling into the back yard, sticky with the choco-honey wafers that we couldn't afford and that Mother bought for him anyway. (His book-bag would be dumped by the front door, his homework poking out. After dinner, when we put on the night-cast, Mother would ask him about it. He would smile and promise to do it, later. He wouldn't. Was he a liar, or just that thoughtless? I never knew.)

And I sat there, my homework all out before me, and watched Jack. The walnut tree was always dropping dead, knobbly branches. Jack would grab one—usually one almost as long as he was—and chase figments of his imagination across the yard, swinging and stabbing. Eventually he'd plop down onto the ragged grass. And he would lay there, staring up at the sky—for hours, sometimes.

I said it was strange. Mother said he was a dreamer. Much good it will do him, I said, when he doesn't do anything—not his schoolwork or his chores or even comb his hair, and you don't make him. (I didn't say this again, because that night she locked herself into her room for a crying jag, and she had had one only the week before. But I thought it often.)

By the time Jack hit thirteen, I had given up on understanding him. But on the last day of August that year, I made another of those useless efforts my conscience sometimes tripped me into. I had my suitcase in one hand; I was on my way to the bus stop, to the little university seventy miles away that had rewarded my diligence with a scholarship. I saw Jack as I walked by the living room, and I felt soft toward him because I was leaving. I also remembered particularly that our father was gone, leaving broken memories in my mind and nothing in Jack's.

So I stopped. I told him that he was the man of the house now that I was going; I told him to listen to his mother and mind his grades and do his chores—all the things I had always done, and he never had. And I left, knowing he wouldn't do a thing I said.

He had more fun than I did. But I knew that my life would be better than his, sometime after the education and the work, someday when the reward came. I felt tolerant, sometimes even sorry for him. It would be hard, I thought, when he could no longer skate by on our mother's lenity. I knew I would help him then, if he could be helped. For his part, he never took more than a passing moment's notice of me. That was his way, even with Mother: bursts of attention, maybe even affection, and then the long periods of indifference when he was out of reach in his own head.

It was my last year of college when things changed, though I didn't notice it at the time. Mother called me at the university, frantic because she'd let Jack go out with the car the night before and he hadn't come back.

Well, what did you expect, I thought. I said that she should wait, that Jack would be back soon enough. That he went off on flights—she knew it—and it was longer and farther now because he could do it with a car.

This did not comfort her.

When my classes finished that day, I made the long bus ride back to help her look for him. The next day I skipped my classes. When night rolled around again and we still had no sight or word of Jack, I was finally alarmed. We sat together at the kitchen table, trying to think of the next thing. I felt guilty—like it was my fault, like Jack was my responsibility.

And he walked in on us. He walked in through the back door, dirty and cheerful and looking insufferably pleased with himself.

Mother hugged and cried and fussed, and it was a few minutes before I could get in the obvious question: What about the car?

He had sold it. He gave Mother a wad of cash—old, dirty paper, the sort used in slum shops—and his most charming smile.

I exploded. But Mother shushed me. She scurried to the stove, Jack sat at the table to wait for his meal.

I left. I slammed the door behind me and got on a bus and spent the night creeping through seventy miles of stops. I spent the next three days in a red haze of anger.

Jack always had money after that. Mother thought he was clever. I waited for him to be arrested. Years went by just the same—two, three—and I was impressed at the reprieve.

Then Jack announced his first invention. I was drowning in a huge city, cold and so far away but a place where they were still hiring. I heard it over the news—it was on all the waves—the young genius from the bad side of town who had cracked the mystery of clean heat...

A coworker came up to me the next day while I stared at the headlines. Funny, she said—the same last name as you.

Funny.

Three or four years later he did it again. I was still in the cold city, trying to claw up to opportunity. The news didn't sting so much this time, but I carried it like a weight on my shoulders for weeks. A year later, Jack did something truly alarming: He moved to the city.

I could not, in decency, ignore him forever. I dashed off a quick note, telling him to look me up when he was settled in. I knew he would forget, but I had reached out and it was enough to shut my conscience up for a good long while.

But he did look me up. We started talking again; it couldn't be avoided, especially when Jack bought Mother a nice place downtown and she insisted on hosting dinners. It wasn't so bad. I sometimes went from those evenings with Jack to broody nights spent measuring the past and the future and our rewards. But I had my consolations. In those years I began to crawl up the rungs of the ladder—nothing compared to what Jack had, but something for me.

And so we came to this year. Jack had a barbecue one hot June day, told Mother and me he was leaving on business the next day and would be out of reach until he came back. She showered him with maternal warnings; I went back for seconds.

The next day, I realized I had forgotten my wallet at Jack's house. By the time I escaped work and made my way to where Jack lived on easy street, sunset was fading away into night.

I rang the doorbell. I did it as a kind of moral rite before implementing my real plan, which was to break in. Jack had never been careful, had rarely even been conscientious. Surely he had left one door or window unlocked; his mansion had so many.

The back gate was ajar. I took it as a good sign and crept around to the back of the house—crept, because it is impossible to strike a free and upright walk when you know you intend to commit illegal entry.

I rounded the corner of the house and started at the sight of a man kneeling down on the well-groomed lawn. I had been preempted, I thought. Another burglar was already loose on the property. But if a burglar, what was he doing out on the lawn?

Perhaps the manly thing would have been to tackle the trespasser and demand an explanation. But I didn't have that sort of motivation when only property was at stake; at least, only Jack's property. I pressed into the shadows against the house.

The man rose. He lifted his head to look at the sky, and the dying orange light caught on his face.

Jack.

He burrowed his hands in his pockets, bowed his head. And he stared at his lawn.

I stared at him. I did not understand what he was doing, but I had never understood him. As a child, he had stared at the sky. Now he stared at the ground, and why not?

Light sliced through the air in front of Jack. I blinked. It had come out of nowhere, gone into nothing—surely I had imagined it.

No. I had seen it. But surely...

Jack stepped forward and disappeared.

My whole body jerked. Then I contemplated whether I was really in my bed or maybe the hospital, about to wake up any minute now.

I didn't. So, after a little more contemplation, I cautiously approached the point where Jack had vanished. A narrow beam of green light shot up from the grass. It cut off half a foot above the lawn, without tapering or dimming.

It cut off like something had gotten in front of it and blocked it, but I didn't see anything.

I knelt down. I eyed the light, reached out a hand to where I didn't see anything.

A tunnel winked into existence in front of me.

My heart surged up against my ribs. I yanked back my hand.

The tunnel vanished. But when I put out my hand again, it was there again. Was this where Jack had gone? But he didn't so much as get down on his knees. He couldn't have crawled away into a tunnel.

I stretched out my hand. It hovered there in the opening of the tunnel, shaking a little. I stared at the tunnel, at my hand, at the blackness deeper in. I thought of Jack.

I thought.

Then I crawled into the tunnel. It felt like steel beneath my hands and knees, hard and smooth and very cold. But I was glad of that. The discomfort had the sting of reality.

On I crawled. I couldn't imagine where the tunnel would end, and so I wasn't afraid. I felt suspended, waiting for a cue to know how I should feel.

Light up ahead. I slid my hands into it, scrabbled at nothing, and tumbled onto the ground. I blinked up at a grooved, gunmetal ceiling and felt no pain.

I sat up. A room—a large room, actually—spread out around me. It was blank, without furniture or any other object, and gray all through. The floor—which looked a little like linoleum and felt a little like rubber—was gray. The walls—oddly textured, like someone had painted bed sheets over them—were gray.

After a moment of observation, I stood up. A door and a window stood by each other in one wall, both oversized. The door must have been thirteen feet high; the window began at a height about level with my chest but made up for it by cutting as high into the wall as the door. It was half-open, and noises rumbled in from outside. I walked over and looked out.

A black road—wider than any highway I had ever seen—rolled out in front of me. I couldn't see the other side, just huge metal contraptions lumbering down the middle of the road while people swarmed at the margins.

The people. My eyesight almost blurred with the explosion of strangeness—a rainbow of colors punctured with the dingiest browns and deepest blacks, shapes tall and stunted and creeping and bulking and gawky and willowy.

I planted my hands on the window sill—it was wide as a ledge—and hoisted myself up for a clearer view. I think I would have stared and leaned forward until I pitched headfirst out the window—but I saw Jack.

Jack stood at the edge of the swarm, throwing a green scarf around his neck with a jaunty motion. Then he strode away down the black road.

I rushed to the door. But I couldn't even try to open it, couldn't find anything that looked like a handle or a knob or a button or a panel.

I rushed back to the window. I clambered up onto the sill, dropped to the ground, and took off after Jack. I could barely see him, a shrinking figure down the road, and I pushed to follow him.

Literally pushed. The crowd was even stranger up close, and whatever was driving down the road looked like nothing so much as tin blimps the size of houses. But this was a city, and I understood the city. I shouldered and elbowed my way after Jack. I think I would have lost him if not for that green scarf flapping over his shoulder.I stayed on his tail and I gained on him.

Oddness flickered in the corners of my eyes—gray-white skin, slitted green eyes, a sturdy figure that barely reached my elbow and a pale, spindly figure whose elbow I barely reached. But my attention was tunneled in on Jack. I didn't see much of the people I shoved past, and I didn't think about what I did see.

Jack pushed past a couple people to the wall—this was when I noticed there was a wall— and slipped through a large, empty entryway.

I followed. I stumbled out of the swarm, through the entryway, and into grass up to my shins. Thick, coarse, and blue-green—but grass. A house stood in the middle of the weird lawn, three times as big as Jack's mansion.

Jack stood in front of a black door twice his height. His back was to me, but his hands were hooked casually in his pockets.

I ran to him as much as I could run through grass like that. He turned around, and all the casualness went out of him.

I scrambled up the wide front steps and grabbed his shoulder. "Jack!"

He pushed me away. "How did you get here? Go back to the beanstalk."

The end of this command was gibberish, but I got the main point and it made me angry. I shoved him, but no harder than I had shoved all those strangers while following him. "You think I'm going away?"

"You think you're staying?" He squared off, like we were about to brawl right on the doorstep of that alien house.

I squared off, too. Maybe we were.

Then the door opened. A giant stood there, at least ten feet tall—a woman, and that was the worst part.

I recoiled a step or two. Jack stepped forward, making gestures that mimed eating. The giant woman smiled at both of us, and it was all I could do not to shudder. Then she moved aside and pointed the way indoors.

Jack looked at me, wanting me to turn around and leave—thinking, maybe, that I would now that I had seen the giant. So I barreled past him into the house.

The giantess pointed down a dark hall, branching off in a corner of the foyer. I obeyed. Jack caught up with me in the hall, nearly treading on my heels, and hissed, "Don't eat. You hear?"

I did hear. I hadn't decided to listen.

I walked out of the dark hallway into a bright kitchen. It was recognizably a kitchen, and that was comforting; the table and chairs and oven were monstrously oversized, the sink studded with odd mechanisms, and the shelves stocked with unidentifiable foodstuffs—but a kitchen it was.

The giantess directed us to the table and fetched a couple plates of food. I studied what had to be meat, encircled by bluish root vegetables. There were no utensils.

The giantess grabbed a tray with tall, opaque glasses and hustled out. I waited a moment in case her hearing was unusually good and then asked, "Do they eat with their hands, or do they think we do?"

"Don't eat. I don't want to have to carry you out of here." Jack jumped down from the chair. "Stay. I'll be back." He dashed away, to the stairs in the back corner of the kitchen, and scuttled up them with more silence than I would have guessed possible.

I stayed at the table and thought about many things.

Noise erupted in the house, somewhere above me. That, I thought, is it, and I slid off the chair and looked around for an escape route.

The stairs in the corner began to shake and echo with pounding. I settled for a hiding place and, racing across the kitchen, I climbed into a barrel next to the well-stocked shelves. By a stroke of grace, it had space. I settled down on a pile of scaly vegetables that filled my nose with a pungent odor.

Footsteps pounded into the kitchen. I heard Jack shouting, but he sounded like a child against the bass voice that answered him, rumbling like thunder.

The sound of a large object being dragged across the kitchen—a click like a door opening—violent shuffling that ended with an emphatic slam. More footsteps, slower this time, and the bass voice grumbling.

Silence.

I released all the breath I had been holding in my lungs. I noticed, added to the pungency of the vegetables, the stink of my own sweat.

I knew what to do, but I gave it a few minutes. When all stayed quiet, I climbed out of the barrel and scanned the room. I thought the giant had shoved Jack into a closet, but I saw no closet door. Doors were, in fact, unusually scarce in that kitchen—no pantry, no closet, no cabinet. Only...

I scurried to the oven. After a horrible moment of fumbling, I sprang the latch and the door popped open. I ducked to look inside.

Jack blinked up at me, the side of his face bruised but the scarf still tied around his neck.

I gestured. "Get out!"

He hissed back, "Get in."

"Are you n—"

Then the stairs creaked, and I practically dove into the oven. Jack pulled the door shut, or nearly shut; his fingertips stayed against it, and light cracked through the top.

Footsteps scuffled in the kitchen, slow but heavy. Then the ring of glass and a splash of liquid. A gusty sigh. The footsteps scuffled out.

"We'll wait till the light goes out," Jack murmured. "That means they've gone to bed. We'll get out then."

"How do you know they don't have any plans for you before that?" I asked this because it was sensible, and also because I was irritated.

"Because I know their eating habits. They like their meat as fresh as they can get it."

My stomach twisted. "Why did you come here?"

"To steal the giant's singing insect. And I had it in my hands up there. How was I to know it would call for help?"

If I could have seen Jack in the dark, I would have smacked him upside the head. "Maybe because it's a *singing* insect, you moron."

"I've done this before." He sounded confident, not at all the emotion I would have thought appropriate to the situation. "You don't know how many times."

I remembered the contraptions he had presented to the world as his own inventions, and the universe shifted and made sense again. "Two," I said.

"Three." He sounded triumphant now.

Of course. The money.

Then the bizarreness of the fact that my brother had been stealing from giants in some other world crashed down on me. "But how—how did you do it? How did you get here?"

"I sold the car for some magic beans."

"Oh, please do expand." My sarcasm reached such a level it nearly burned my mouth.

But Jack laughed. "You remember me selling Mother's car. I was a stupid kid, out sniffing for adventure, and an itinerant traded me a handful of beans for the car. Told me to plant them, one at a time, and they'd make me rich."

"That is almost the stupidest thing I've ever heard."

"Yes," he agreed. "But did you notice? It did make me rich."

I pondered that, another startling fact in a long line.

"Look." He shifted, then a small green light glowed out of the darkness. It rose from Jack's palm, from…

From what looked, by its shape and size, like a bean.

"Take it," he ordered.

I did. I rubbed it between my fingers, marveling.

"I plant it at twilight," Jack said. "The beanstalk grows like a ladder straight up to the sky. But you know; you've climbed it."

"I never climbed a beanstalk."

I felt him freeze. "Then how did you get here? I thought you followed me."

"I did follow you. But I didn't climb a beanstalk." I would have been impatient—would have thought all this talk about a beanstalk up to the sky was nonsense—if I hadn't held a glowing bean in my palm.

"Then—"

I closed my hand around the bean to stop it from distracting me. "I saw you out on the grass, and I saw you disappear. I didn't see you climb up a beanstalk. You were just gone, all at once. And when I went over to the spot, and put my hand out, I saw a dark tunnel. I crawled through it and—well, here I am."

"A tunnel?" Then: "A tunnel! You would see a tunnel."

The words cut through me because I saw at once that they were true. Jack saw a ladder to climb, I saw a dark tunnel to crawl through and hope—because that was the shape of our minds, that was what life was to us.

Jack lowered his voice. "We're going to run back to the beanstalk and hightail it home. You have to realize—these giants aren't the bosses of the place. But they are the bullies of it. They take what they want and everyone's afraid to stop them. No one is going to help the giant catch us after we run. But no one will stop him, either."

"Why are you messing with the giant?" I was angry again but I whispered, probably because he did. "Doesn't anyone else in this place have stuff that you can steal?"

"Of course. But the giant takes all the best stuff, so he has all the best. And no one is as dangerous as he is."

So he regarded the giant's penchant for eating intruders as a reason to steal from him. I never understood Jack.

The light disappeared from the crack in the oven door. I hastily stuffed the glowing bean into my pocket; Jack gently pushed the door open. We crawled out into the kitchen.

As I got to my feet, my knees cracking, Jack said, "Go on back to the beanstalk. I'll meet you there."

"And what are you going to be doing?"

"I am going to get that singing insect."

There was enough light in the kitchen to make out the shapes of things, so I hit him. "I'm coming," I said.

He stood there for a moment. But neither of us could force the other to stay or go, so he slunk off to the corner of the kitchen and I followed.

We crept up the stairs, and it was slow going. They were higher and deeper than human stairs by a good shot, and I hit my foot against a couple of steps. After that I got a clue, but it wasn't natural work, silently navigating those gigantic steps.

At the top, I found myself in a wide-open space. There were glowing rocks scattered around—lights that looked like decorations or decorations that looked like lights, I didn't know. They gave a dim sort of illumination to the room. Items were plopped and piled up all across the floor, forming sloppy shapes in the near-darkness. Maybe if I could have really seen the items instead of just their shapes, I would have been impressed. But I thought they junked up the place.

Jack stole off toward a darker portion of the room. I kept after him. I realized, as we got closer, that we were heading toward the giant, sprawled out on a mass of cushions and blankets. My heart sank down to my feet, but we kept walking.

An enormous insect—fully as large as my hand—nestled near the giant's head. It looked something like a cricket with moth wings, and every bit of it was gold.

I stopped. It was time just to watch.

Jack sneaked up to the giant's bed and crawled over it. When he was close enough to touch the giant, he reached out very slowly and then, in one fast motion, he nabbed the gold insect.

The wings fluttered, I knew it was about to squawk, and amid a rush of despair, I thought very bad things about Jack.

Jack's hand shot up, his fingers twisted the head. And the gold wings froze mid-motion, and it didn't so much as chirp.

He crawled back over the giant's bed. I'm not sure my heart beat until he finally stood on the floor again.

Jack darted over to me. He gestured me to follow—somehow conceiving that I might possibly need the signal—and we scurried back to the stairs and down to the kitchen.

I could feel my heart beating again, hammering on my ribcage. I grabbed the corner of the table and breathed.

Jack squeezed my shoulder, though I wasn't sure what he meant by it. Then we hurried on, the need to be quiet putting on us the terrible need to be slower.

Back down the hallway, black now that the house was dark, and finally to the door. Jack scrabbled against the doorframe.

The huge front door creaked a few inches open. Jack dug his fingers into the narrow space and heaved open the door. I felt almost that I was living again.

A roar shook the house, just human enough to carry the tone of murderous rage. We fled.

Down the steps in a flash, then beating over the tall grass. We spilled out the entryway into the road.

The tin blimps still lurched across it, light flashing from them to the walkers on the margins.

The swarm had thinned, but it was still thick enough to prevent an all-out race. We threw ourselves into the crowd and gave it our best shot.

Another roar thundered above our heads. People began scattering all around us. They were getting out of the giant's way, and by accident they got out of ours. Then we could really run.

And for everything that was in us, we did. My blood rushed through my body—hotter, faster than it had ever been before.

Footsteps thundered behind us, crashing down with awful weight. Jack's head began to swivel.

"Don't look back!" I yelled. I'm not sure why; it just seemed like the thing to say under the circumstances. But he listened, and we ran.

The crash of the giant's pursuit grew closer.

Jack swerved. He dashed to a lumpy gray building and climbed through its tall, half-opened window.

I raced after him and clambered through the window with considerably less agility. By the time I jumped onto the floor, Jack was already across the room. I knew he had found the portal because his arm, stretched toward the wall, was gone halfway up his elbow.

He was watching me. I hollered, "Go!"

Jack nodded, turned away from me, and was swallowed up out of sight.

I sprinted to the wall. When I thrust out my hand, the tunnel appeared. I stooped toward it and then, for no good reason, I looked back.

The giant filled up the window, swinging a metal club.

I saw the glass shatter. One second of time froze for me, and I saw the window splinter along a hundred white, jagged lines. Then the pieces broke apart, flying outward.

I dove into the tunnel. I felt a hard impact on my shoulder, a fiery slicing. But I had even less time for pain than I had for fear. I crawled down the tunnel.

A shout, too large to be human, rang out behind me. I felt a massive hand close around my ankle.

But if it was big, it was also clumsy. I yanked my foot out of the giant's grip and lunged forward.

I landed on a green lawn, in broad daylight, and bowled over Jack. He fell, sprawling on top of me. I shoved him, yelling, "It's coming!"

Jack sprang to his feet and darted away. I sat up, but I felt very strange, distant and dizzy. I fumbled through my pockets as though I might find a gun there.

I found the magic bean. I pulled it out and stared at it and an idea flashed in my mind like lightning. I surged up to my feet, stumbled a yard or two, and went down to my knees. Good enough, I thought, and dug my fingernails into the soil. Then I pressed the magic bean into the shallow groove.

And I waited, my breaths shallow and rapid. After an eternal minute, light flashed up from the bean.

"It won't work!"

I looked up at the shout. Jack loomed over me, holding an ax up with both hands like he was about to let loose. "It won't work," he repeated. "The giant won't climb up a beanstalk."

No. He wouldn't crawl into a tunnel, either. But he wouldn't see a tunnel and he wouldn't see a beanstalk. He would see something that was like his life, the way he had always seen it—wide open and his for the taking.

"Jack," I said, "trust me."

He stared at me. Had I ever asked him for anything? What right did I have to ask him for that now?

None, maybe, but I needed it. "Trust me," I repeated.

He opened his mouth but didn't manage to get anything out.

The giant crashed into the world, still holding his metal club. He lunged at us.

I threw myself to the ground. Jack dodged to the side, turned back, and extended the ax close over the earth.

The giant's foot tangled on it, wrenching it from Jack's hand. The giant didn't fall. He only stumbled.

And that was enough. The giant stumbled through the portal, disappeared from our sight.

Jack grabbed the ax and slammed it down on the bean. He did it again, again, again—a frenzy of violent blows.

Sparks exploded up from the bean, accompanied by a tremendous flash of light that left my vision spotted.

That was it, I thought, blinking and breathing in. It was over.

Jack dropped the ax. "You're bleeding," he said, with a tone as though he were informing me of the fact. "Take off your shirt."

I did. Jack, kneeling down beside me, used my shirt to stop the bleeding. "There," he said after a few silent minutes. "Hold it. I'm going to call the med-techs."

He got up and went into the house. I pressed my bloody shirt against my bloody shoulder and considered the light in the sky. Full day, but still morning. I was going to have to call out from work. What was I going to tell them?

Jack came out again and stood above me. "They will be here soon. Do you want me to help you into the house?"

"And bleed all over your nice carpet? I couldn't afford the cleaning bill." I only sort of meant it as a joke, and it only sort of sounded like one.

A pause. Then Jack sat down by me. "Sure you can. At least after I sell this." He undid his jacket and took out the golden insect.

I eyed it. "It's—"

"It's mechanical. Worth a fortune and we each get half."

That had always been the good part of Jack, that impulsive generosity. I had not even thought of making a claim.

Jack twisted the thing's head, and it turned on. Its eye blinked, and its wings fluttered like it was getting ready to sing, or fly. Jack switched it off. "I'll figure it out in my work room," he said. "You'll like being rich. It's loads of fun."

And it wouldn't really matter what I told my boss when I called in. That was nice.

"That"—Jack's tone was suddenly morose—"was my last bean. The one you planted and I smashed. They only work once, you know—one trip, there and back. Once you make the return journey, the beanstalk goes away."

The portal closes, I thought. That's the better way of putting it. I said, "At least they made you rich before they ran out."

"But where can I go now to get chased by enraged giants who want to eat me?"

He really meant it, and my first thought was to smack him. My second was to inform him that nobody needed that in their lives. My third... "Maybe that itinerant will find you again."

"I hope so. But I was never sure why he found me the first time. Maybe I was just the one stupid enough to believe the truth. But I always felt that I never really lived up to how big the gift was."

"True, I'm sure." If he said something like that to me and expected disagreement, he deserved what he got instead. "You did some good with those contraptions. Not a whole lot. But"—a happier thought came to me—"you didn't do any bad. No giants loose on Earth or anything." I shifted, gingerly adjusting the wadded-up shirt over my shoulder. When I looked up, Jack was staring at me.

"I know you're my brother," he said. "But I think that maybe we could be friends."

"We can try, anyway." I had tried long ago when he was little, and he never showed any interest in what I offered. But maybe he had been trying these last couple years, and I had been too occupied with myself to see.

The med-techs found us after a couple minutes—me and Jack, with my blood-soaked shirt pressed against my shoulder and the ax on the ground.

Jack hid the singing insect under his jacket as soon as we heard the med-techs at the back gate.

*　　*　　*

That day I resisted the encouragement of a doctor, a counselor, and a police officer to tell the truth. The next day I went back to work. I still had a living to make until Jack made the sale, and I was still deciding how to best use a sudden fortune for productivity and fulfillment.

But though I stayed planted at my desk, I kept wandering away mentally. I daydreamed of that flight down the wide black road, of those strange vehicles and strange people, of tricking and tripping the giant out of our world. When Jack and I got together and he talked about finding that itinerant, I told him—I couldn't help being rational—that it was more or less impossible. But I also told him that there were people coming through, and not just us; the itinerant proved that. There had to be other itinerants, and other magic beans. Other ways to make portals. That other world was there, and the barrier could be broken through. We knew that. It was the most important thing to know.

Before I knew it I was a dreamer too. I had gotten a taste of that strange other world and now I wanted the whole meal.

I understand Jack.

ABOUT THE AUTHORS

W.O. Hemsath has a B.A. in Screenwriting, four lively sons, and will do just about anything for a good back scratch. In addition to short stories, she writes novels about aliens addicted to classical music, inspirational non-fiction books, and her favorite guilty pleasure—song parodies. On the weekends, she can be found neglecting laundry and dishes in favor of binge-watching Netflix with her husband. You can learn more about her writing at whitneyhemsath.wordpress.com.

Savannah Grace has been published in Splickety Magazine, Havok Magazine, and in the book Project Canvas, among other places.

E.B. Dawson was born out of time. Raised in the remote regions of a developing nation, traveling to America was as good as traveling thirty years into the future. So, it's really no wonder that she writes science fiction and fantasy. Her stories acknowledge darkness, but empower and encourage people to keep on fighting, no matter how difficult their circumstances may be. And as an avid philosopher, she infuses her work with Socratic questions. When not writing, she tries to make a difference in the world by showing love and compassion to those most broken.

M.R. DeLuca has short stories published in "Shadows in Salem," "After the Happily Ever After," "O Horrid Night," and "Strangely Funny V." In addition to the beauty of words, M.R. enjoys numbers, speleothems, and homemade whoopie pies.

Art Lasky's work has appeared in: "Drunken Boat," "Third Flat Iron Anthologies," "The Lane of Unusual Traders," "Fall Into Fantasy," "The Rabbit Hole," "Crypt-Gnats," and "Home Planet News Online."

Susan W. Lyons is a longtime fan of marvelous old creation and wisdom stories found in the literature of folk and fairy tales. The opportunity to make them new again in "Once Upon a Future Time" is irresistible. Susan's first novel, Time's Oldest Daughter (Aqueduct Press, 2017), brings together several creation stories using 21st century metaphysics. "Just Like That," which appears in this anthology, transports the Seven Dwarves to an asteroid where they mine precious metals for the Corporate Homeland. Susan, her husband Tom, and Goldy the Cat live in Portland, Maine.

Deanna Young was born and raised in Aztec, New Mexico but now lives beneath a different set of desert mountains in Erda, Utah. She loves to collect random facts, eat cherry cheesecake, and cook with green chili; though she usually avoids doing all three things at once. When she's not reading, writing, or spinning in circles, she's trying to convince her garden that Erda isn't a desert and her four kids that it is. Flooded basements are only fun in stories.

Lynne Lumsden Green has twin bachelor degrees in both Science and the Arts, giving her the balance between rationality and creativity. She spent fifteen years as the Science Queen for HarperCollins Voyager Online and has written science articles for other online magazines. Currently, she captains the Writing Race for the Australian Writers Marketplace on Facebook and is an assistant editor for the Queensland Writers Centre magazine, Writing Queensland. She has had flash fiction stories included in Flashspec, edited by Neil Cladingboel, and another in Flashspec Two. A short fantasy story was published in the EnVision anthology, sf-envision.com, another fantasy short story in The Phantom Queen Awakes by Morrigan Books, and in the 2016 Oscillate Wildly Press Monsters Among Us anthology, the short horror story "Beyond the Walls of Sleep." Two stories were included in 2017's Return anthology, one a straight fantasy and the other a steampunk narrative. Her latest short story is in Fairytale Riot, volume 4 of "The Clarion Call."

Jonathan Ficke lives outside of Milwaukee, Wisconsin with his beautiful wife. He graduated from Marquette University with a degree in public relations, which (in a manner of speaking) is another form of speculative storytelling. His older brother introduced him to Tolkien at a young age, and, despite his book shelf's persistent pleas for mercy, he's voraciously consumed the genre ever since. For as long as he can remember, he dreamed of being an author, and the thought of holding a book containing his words in his hands is a dream come true. His work has appeared in "Writers of the Future, Vol. 34" and "Tales of Ruma." When he's not reading or writing, he is turning lumber into sawdust and, when all goes according to plan, furniture. You can find him on twitter @jonficke, where he mostly muses about woodworking, basketball, and writing.

Linda McMullen has been previously published in Chaleur, Burningword, Typishly, Panoply, Open: Journal of Arts and Letters, Allegory, Enzo Publications, The Write Launch, Palaver, Curating Alexandria, SunLit, Five:2:One, and Every Day Fiction; other pieces are forthcoming in The Remembered Arts Journal, Coffin Bell Journal, Raw Art Review, Weasel Press, Dragon Poet Review, The Poet's Haven, Scribble, and The Anti-Languorous Project.

Shannon McDermott is the author of The Valley of Decision, as well as the Sons of Tryas series. She is a staff writer with Lorehaven Magazine and a contributor at SpeculativeFaith.com. To learn more about her and her work, visit www.shannonmcdermott.com.